It has been sixteen months since Princess Esofi arrived in Ieflaria, and eight since her marriage to Crown Princess Adale. The princesses have a peaceful life together, preparing to become co-regents and raising their baby dragon, Carinth.

Their peace is shattered when Esofi's mother, Queen Gaelle of Rhodia, arrives in Birsgen. She has heard about Carinth and believes that she deserves custody of him due to her greater devotion to Talcia, Goddess of Magic.

Adale and Esofi have no intention of giving up their son, but Gaelle is impossible to reason with—and there's no telling what lengths she'll go to in order to get what she wants.

THE QUEEN OF
RHODIA

Tales of Inthya, Book Three

Effie Calvin

A NineStar Press Publication

Published by NineStar Press
P.O. Box 91792,
Albuquerque, New Mexico, 87199 USA.
www.ninestarpress.com

The Queen of Rhodia

Printed in the USA
First Edition
May, 2019

Print ISBN: 978-1-950412-79-2

Also available in eBook, ISBN: 978-1-950412-78-5

Warning: This book contains mention of past child abuse.

For Freya, a cat who makes faces

Cilva
Sterentand
SIABAELD
Veravin
THIYRA
Eskas
Rhodia
Dossau
Etrea
THE WINTER STRAIT
Silver Isles
IOSHORA
Iftaria
Ixbaia
The Xytan Empire
TO ELVEN LANDS
Visolda
THE SUMMER STRAIT
AQUIIM
Masim
Coplar

Prologue

GAELLE

Queen Gaelle of Rhodia—Great Mother of the Silence of the Moon, rightful owner of half of her country's marble quarries, and wife of King Alain—regretted that she was not a dragon.

It was not just for the obvious reasons: the terrifying size, the ivory teeth, the breath of fire, and the gift of flight—though that certainly would have been reason enough. What Gaelle really envied was the dragons' abilities to lay eggs. What she would not give to be able to eject a child from her body and go about her business while it lay in a fireplace for a year!

But it was not meant to be. And so, grudgingly, Gaelle had her children in the ordinary way. Her only comfort was the fact that she could hand them off to the nursemaids until they were old enough to hold an intelligent conversation.

Her eldest son was Gael, crown prince and heir...and the only one of her six children whose name she could recall at any given moment. Gaelle disliked children greatly, but as Gael grew into manhood, his temperament pleased her. He was strong and solemn, as unshakable as a mountain. Like his father, he was blessed by Iolar, with a knack for detecting trickery, and had discovered every hidden passageway in the palace by the time he was ten years old. He would make an acceptable king someday.

Next was Eloisa, firstborn daughter. She had Talcia's magic, as any princess of Rhodia should. Like her brother and her father, she was even in temperament, with none of the shrieking rage that Gaelle was sometimes known for, though that was not to say she was not capable of vengeance. When it came to her blessing, her self-control was excellent and her magic a sparkling shade of ruby. If, Talcia forbid, something should happen to Gael, she would be a suitable replacement. If not, she could be married to another member of the Rhodian nobility for the sake of strengthening alliances.

Eloisa had been followed by Matheo, second-born son. Gaelle could see no reason that her other children should not be regents. They could spread her power across Thiyra, and perhaps further still. When Matheo was only a year, she signed an agreement that he would wed the three-year-old princess of Dossau when the two came of age. Matheo was educated in the ways of Dossau as well as Rhodia to prepare him for the foreign throne he would ascend someday.

Next came Esolene, similarly promised to the prince of Eskas and educated appropriately. Her blessing, the color of a sunset, was not as powerful as Eloisa's, and so Gaelle would not be sad to send her off. Esolene was thin and fragile, with little outward passion. Gaelle had been disappointed at first, but then out of the corner of her eyes, she noticed things that piqued her interest—a tongue like a driver's whip, little fingers that pinched and twisted, a foot that occasionally stuck out at just the right angle to send sisters or servants sprawling—and all this hidden behind a watery smile.

The following year brought Esofi. Gaelle sent ambassadors to Xytae, to ask the Empress Irianthe if she would agree to a betrothal between Esofi and her son, Ionnes. But the Empress rejected the proposal, citing that the age difference between their children was irreconcilable. So instead Esofi was betrothed to Albion, Crown Prince of Ieflaria. Esofi had a placidity that bordered on laziness, but her mastery of magic came to her as easily as breathing, and she could perform maneuvers that the older princesses could not, even with a half-eaten biscuit clutched in one chubby hand. She killed her first wyvern at age eight, her first elf at fourteen.

And last of all was Esybele. All babies were the same in Gaelle's eyes, shrieking and squalling, but this one seemed to do more of that than most. If not for the nursemaids, Gaelle might have put a pillow over the girl's face and let Adranus sort her out. When Esybele learned to speak, she had a carefully chosen insult for everyone who crossed her path. Furthermore, Esybele was not above throwing herself on the ground and beating her fists if she felt she had been wronged, screams ringing through the marble halls.

Gaelle frequently thought of the Empress of Anora, across the sea. It was said she not only had two husbands, but also three wives. That, Gaelle supposed, must have made the production of heirs terribly convenient. She could not imagine how many alliances she could secure with that many offspring! But the Temple of Pemele in Rhodia forbade such practices. To Gaelle, this was an injustice. For why should Pemele's laws be different in Anora than they were in Rhodia? She had never received a satisfying answer to that question and suspected the priestesses did not know.

Thiyra was a small continent, a stony beacon in the midst of grey seas. It could take months, even years, for news of other lands to reach it. So the tale of what had happened in Ieflaria did not reach her until Duchess Tiphanie's daughter arrived back home.

On that evening, Gaelle stood before a fireplace with a glass of red wine, wishing she was out with the mages hunting elves who strayed too far from their own shores instead of trapped in her own palace with reports to review.

When Tiphanie knocked at the door, Gaelle could not even bring herself to pretend to be irritated by the distraction. She watched as the duchess entered the room, followed by a younger woman.

"My Queen," said Tiphanie with a curtsy. "Forgive the intrusion at this hour, but my daughter has just returned with...shocking news."

Gaelle turned her gaze to the girl, who was still dressed in her travelling clothes, and found she could recall nothing about her.

"Lexandrie accompanied Princess Esofi to Ieflaria," said Tiphanie helpfully.

"Ah, her," said Gaelle, only partially enlightened. "Yes."

Tiphanie touched a hand to Lexandrie's shoulder. "Go on," she said. "Tell her majesty exactly what you told me."

Lexandrie met Gaelle's eyes. "Princess Esofi has a son."

Gaelle pursed her lips, somewhat disappointed. After an introduction like that, she had been anticipating something interesting. "Is that all?"

"No," said Tiphanie. "Perhaps...perhaps my queen ought to sit down."

"Be silent," commanded Gaelle. Then she looked at Lexandrie. "Continue."

"He is not a child," Lexandrie glanced at her mother anxiously, who only gave a nod of encouragement. "That is...Esofi's son...he is a dragon."

The wineglass fell out of Gaelle's hand and shattered on the floor.

Chapter One

ADALE

Generally speaking, Ieflarian hair wasn't very good at holding a curl. But that wasn't stopping the ladies of Birsgen from trying. And it was not just the nobles or merchants. In the last month alone, at least three different servant girls had cut off their long braids and attempted to sear their hair into careful ringlets, the sort Princess Esofi wore.

Crown Princess Adale regarded the trend with a mixture of derision and pride. She had thought it would die down after the wedding, but now the alchemists were even selling some sort of potion that would turn dark Ieflarian hair blonde. Lady Brigit had nearly killed herself with one just a week ago, thinking she was meant to drink it instead of pouring it onto her hair.

Esofi, for her part, wasn't reacting to her many imitators. These days, she spent most of her time seeing to the construction of the university or caring for Carinth, the baby dragon that she had been given to raise a year and a half ago.

Carinth had done a great deal of growing since then. He stood just below Adale's knee when he was on all fours. If he balanced on his hind legs and stretched his neck out, he could almost reach her waist. His wings, when unfurled, were twice as wide as the length of his body, though he had made no real attempts to fly yet. Despite his length, he was rather thin, and not nearly as heavy as one might expect. Adale and Esofi supposed that this was because he would some day be able to fly.

He knew his own name and the meaning of "no," though he sometimes liked to pretend that he did not. He ate meat, raw or cooked, as well as sweets and pastries from the kitchens. He refused all vegetables and most fruits but would also go after moths, crickets, and frogs if they caught his eye. He had his own room, fully furnished (though Adale wasn't sure what he was meant to do with a writing desk) but preferred to sleep on a single blanket near the fireplace. Adale had learned to shake her boots out before putting them on every morning, because there was a good chance one of them would contain a silver fork or a jeweled necklace.

Adale's primary fear had been that the Ieflarian people would reject Carinth. After all, he was a member of the species that, until very recently, made it their goal to rid the world of Men. But she had not seen anyone react badly to him. In fact, he seemed to be quite popular. He was not at all afraid to accompany the royal huntsman on his rides, or help the maids with their washing, or join Knight-Commanders Glace and Livius in their morning meditation in the chapel. When he went missing, he was usually found hovering around the feet of the kitchen staff, waiting for something good to fall from the tables above.

The only real problem was that most people regarded Carinth as a very interesting dog, rather than an intelligent creature that would someday be able to speak.

Adale and Esofi's wedding had been eight months ago, in early spring, so early that traces of snow melted in weak sunlight and acolytes from the Temple of Eyvindr were hired to make the flowers bloom. All her life, Adale had always assumed that marrying would mean a loss of her own identity, somehow. She wasn't sure where or how she'd developed this notion, but she'd been expecting marriage to transform her into someone she did not recognize. And some things were different now, certainly. She was living with Esofi in the rooms traditionally reserved for the heir and their spouse, rooms she'd spent her entire life thinking would someday be Albion's. Alongside that, she was raising a baby dragon as her own son.

But at her core Adale was still *herself*.

Now it was autumn. The harvest was long past, and there was a chill in the air, though it was still a few months to midwinter and Esofi's nineteenth birthday. That day, she found Esofi and Carinth out in the garden, sitting in a patch of weak sunlight. They were accompanied by Mireille, one of Esofi's two remaining waiting ladies.

Esofi held a primer designed for very young children and was reading to Carinth in an authoritative voice. Carinth rested in her lap and gazed up at her with bright golden eyes. Esofi wore an Ieflarian dress today, for Carinth had a bad habit of pulling the jewels out of the bodices of Esofi's beautiful Rhodian gowns, as well as shredding the petal-soft silk with his claws as he climbed up onto her shoulders in the same way that a cat might. Still, Adale could see the tiny pockmarks all over the fabric. They were the same marks that now marred Adale's own dresses, and the clothing of many members of the castle staff.

Esofi smiled as Adale approached. Carinth lifted his head and ran over to greet her, standing up on his hind legs to check if she had anything interesting in her pockets.

"How are we?" asked Adale, rubbing her hand over the tiny nubs that would someday be curling horns on Carinth's head.

"He swallowed a lizard," sighed Esofi, setting the primer down. "That's practically cannibalism. Sometimes I swear he only does it to hear me scream."

Adale and Esofi had only a rough idea of what normal dragon development was like, informed by old, half-forgotten books kept by the Temple of Talcia. They knew it would be a while before Carinth learned to breathe fire, but they had no idea when to expect speech from him or if he was the correct size for his age. Their books had also said that he wouldn't begin attempting to fly until he was about a year old, but his first birthday had passed, and he was still showing no real signs of trying, no matter how often Adale tossed him up into the air.

Esofi worried about this constantly, and she wasn't reassured by Adale's claim that Talcia, Goddess of Magic and creator of all dragonkind, would probably let them know if something was seriously wrong. Talcia was the one who had given Carinth to them in the first place, so Adale did not think such a thing was unreasonable to expect. Fortunately, Esofi also had the new university to distract herself. And Carinth was unquestionably happy.

"My parents have summoned us," reported Adale. "Apparently there's important news they want to discuss."

Esofi stood and brushed off her skirts. "Do you know what it's about?"

"I have no idea. They only said they wanted both of us there."

Esofi nodded. "Mireille, can you take Carinth while I see to this?"

"Of course!" Mireille crouched down so he could easily climb on to her shoulders. "Oh, when did you get so heavy?" she asked, struggling to right herself. As she walked away, Adale heard her informing Carinth that she expected him to give her rides in return once he was large enough.

"You really don't know what this is about, then?" asked Esofi, once they were out of Mireille's hearing range.

"No, they wouldn't say."

"Did they seem angry?" Esofi looked a little worried, and Adale felt herself smile at the absurd notion that her parents might ever find fault with anything Esofi did.

"I don't think so. Why? Have you done something scandalous lately?" teased Adale. "Something I ought to know about?"

Esofi smiled faintly. "No, nothing like that. I just hate to think I've disappointed them somehow."

"I'd find that unsettling as well," said Adale. "Disappointing my parents is my responsibility. I'd thank you not to steal it from me."

Esofi's weak smile turned into a soft laugh. Nevertheless, she said, "Must you always speak so harshly about yourself?"

"I'm only saying what everyone else is thinking."

"That is *not* true."

Adale would never believe that, but it warmed her to know that Esofi thought so highly of her. So many members of the court could not see Adale as anything other than the wild young woman she had been for the first eighteen years of her life. She expected they never would.

When Adale and Esofi arrived at King Dietrich's study, they found both of Adale's parents waiting for them, as well as both of the Order of the Sun's resident knight-commanders: Commander Glace, who led the Ieflarian paladins, and the exiled Commander Livius who had done the same in Xytae until Emperor Ionnes expelled the entire Order several years ago. Standing just beside Knight-Commander Livius was another paladin, a young woman in chainmail that Adale did not recognize.

Paladins, with their rigid adherence to law and order, were never Adale's favorite people, but they had been instrumental in helping defend Ieflaria from the dragon attacks before Esofi's arrival. There had been no further attacks since the Emperor's death, but everyone knew that could change at any moment, and so Adale was grateful for their continued presence.

"What has happened?" asked Esofi. Adale found herself equally taken aback by the size of the gathering.

"Today I have received a letter from Princess Ioanna of Xytae," explained Livius. "It is...unexpected, to say the least."

"Princess Ioanna?" Adale frowned. "Isn't she...what, four years old?"

"Seven, actually," said Livius. "She will be eight this coming winter."

"What does she want?" asked Esofi.

"You may see for yourself." Livius passed the letter over to her. Adale and Esofi both leaned in to read it. The handwriting was a little awkward but still legible.

Knight-Commander Livius,

I do not know if you remember me, but my name is Ioanna Isinthi. My father is Ionnes of Xytae. I have been wanting to write to you for a long time but did not know how to find you.

I will probably not become Empress for a very long time, but when it happens, I want to bring the Order of the Sun back to Xytae. I also want to end my father's war with Masim. We do not have any right to their lands. But the Temple of Reygmadra is already telling my father that my sister would make a better Empress.

I think something bad is going to happen. If it does, I hope that the Order of the Sun will help me. I am not asking for a promise from you right now because I know it is too early for that. But I want the same things for Xytae that you do. We will be stronger together than we are alone.

I am sorry this letter is not longer, but I am in the middle of being rescued from a cult.

Respectfully,

Ioanna Enessa Isinthi

"What's this about a cult?" asked Adale.

"Never mind that part," said Livius. "That matter has been handled."

"She is trying to secure a political alliance with the Order, then?" asked Esofi. "I have to admit...at her age, I would not expect such a thing."

Adale was inclined to agree. At seven years old, her only concern had been stealing extra desserts from the kitchens. She wasn't even sure if she'd been literate yet, let alone coherent enough to ask a stranger for help securing her place in the succession.

"The Xytan court is significantly more cutthroat than the court at Birsgen," said Queen Saski. "I would be more surprised if she was not seeking allies. She may very well reach out to Ieflaria next."

"I'm inclined to call this a ruse," said Esofi. "Ionnes may be searching for an excuse to attack Ieflaria. If it looks like we are harboring paladins who would oppose his reign..."

"But Ioanna is his rightful heir," pointed out Adale. "He should be happy to have paladins supporting her, even if he doesn't care much for them personally."

Knight-Commander Livius crossed his arms and glanced over at the lady paladin, who still had not uttered a word. "Perhaps," he said slowly. "But then, perhaps not. The situation is...unique."

"How so?" asked Dietrich.

"Your majesty," said Livius, "you know it is not in my nature to gossip idly. But I met Princess Ioanna on several occasions before my exile. And it is my suspicion that, if she were examined by the Justices, she would be declared a truthsayer."

"What?" demanded Adale's parents in unison.

"You have never mentioned this before, Livius," said Saski.

"I am not authorized to make a formal assessment of Ioanna's blessing. And for a time, I doubted myself. But Dame Orsina—" He gestured to the young woman. "—has come to the same conclusion. She encountered Princess Ioanna several months ago and states that her blessing is what has alienated her from much of the Xytan court."

Everyone turned to stare at the paladin. She clasped her hands behind her back and shifted uncomfortably.

"Is this true?" demanded Dietrich.

"Dame Orsina does not speak the Ieflarian language, Your Majesty. She has come to us from southern Vesolda," explained Livius. "But I have no reason to doubt her word."

"Will you respond to Ioanna's letter?" asked Adale.

"I fear it may be dangerous to do so," said Livius. "If it is intercepted, the consequences could be disastrous. Nevertheless, I expect this is not the last we will hear from Princess Ioanna. And I think everyone in this room has an interest in seeing her take the throne."

"But that may not happen for decades," said Adale.

"That is why you and Esofi are here today, Adale," said Saski. "If a civil war breaks out in Xytae upon Ionnes's death, you may be the ones to decide whether or not Ieflaria will support Ioanna."

"We can't take a risk like that," said Esofi immediately. "Our army is no match for the Xytan legion. If Ioanna is deposed, her replacement will immediately seek to punish those who allied with her."

Adale wasn't surprised to hear this. Esofi usually erred on the side of caution, especially when it came to political machinations. Personally, though, she thought supporting Ioanna might be a risk worth taking if it meant having a reasonable ruler on the Xytan throne.

But Adale was much newer to meetings of politics and strategy, and she lived in constant fear of saying something foolish and discrediting herself. She decided that she'd raise the point with Esofi later, when they were alone. Esofi's judgment would be much softer than her parents'.

But Ionnes was young and healthy. He might live for another fifty years. And in that case, Adale and Esofi would not need to decide on the matter until they were old women. The thought was a little cheering. Surely fifty years would be long enough for Adale to accumulate the wisdom to make the correct choice?

Or maybe Ionnes would be shot in the forehead by a Masimi bowman tomorrow and the choice would be her parents'. That would be even better.

"There is no need to make a decision today," said Saski. "We only wish for you two to be aware of the situation as it unfolds. Do not discuss this matter with anyone except each other. We must be discreet until we know more."

The meeting came to an end, and everyone was dismissed. Adale sighed in relief, knowing they'd been lucky today. Meetings such as this could go on for hours, if the situation was urgent or if people felt like bickering over details.

"Was Ioanna at our wedding?" asked Adale as she and Esofi began the walk back to their room. "I think I remember a girl around her age. Hovering around the cake."

"No, none of the Isinthi family was in attendance. You are thinking of Princess Vitaliya of Vesolda. She was at our betrothal celebration as well. The one you missed."

"I heard you left early anyway," teased Adale.

"Only because I was so dreadfully bored." Esofi pressed a fleeting kiss to Adale's cheek. "Or something like that. I'm sure I had a good reason."

Esofi wasn't very demonstrative in public, but apparently this was typical of Rhodian people. She frequently hid her kisses behind fans or parasols, which Adale found adorable and silly in equal measure. She also jumped when someone grabbed her hands or hugged her too quickly, but the Ieflarians at Birsgen were learning not to do that.

Adale tried her best to respect Esofi's preferences by letting her initiate contact when she was comfortable with it. She did not want Esofi to dread going out in public with her, nor did she want to embarrass her more than she already did.

Unfortunately, this had prompted well-meaning priestesses of Dayluue to start approaching Adale with questions. How was her relationship with Esofi? Were they happy? Were they communicating? Was there anything the temple could do to help?

Adale found herself repeatedly reassuring them that Esofi was just shy. But since several hundred people had watched Esofi fling herself into the mouth of a dragon, Adale's words did not carry much weight.

Adale had learned to disappear whenever she caught sight of a red-violet robe, and not just because of that. Since she and Esofi were both women, it would be the Temple of Dayluue's responsibility to aid them in the creation of heirs. Only Dayluue's priestesses knew how to perform the Change.

The Change was a magical ritual most frequently used by those who had been born into bodies that did not align with their souls. It wasn't uncommon for young people to try it out, even if they were content with their bodies. Most reverted to their original forms within a few hours. Some never did and had to pay for a second ritual to undo the first, if they were inclined.

The Change could also be used by couples like Adale and Esofi to conceive, though adoption was the most common way for two women to procure children in Ieflaria. The dragon attacks in past years had left many orphans, and part of Adale wished they could simply pick one of them. But she knew, when it came to royalty, people cared about lineage and blood.

To be fair, it was not just the priestesses who expected heirs from them. Everyone mentioned it at some point, from her parents' advisors to various ambassadors to her own friends. Some days it felt like it was the only thing anyone wanted to talk about. Adale and Esofi were always having babies pushed into their arms, as though everyone was hoping they'd be so overcome with maternal love that they'd immediately set about to creating one of their own.

But Esofi was in absolutely no hurry to begin producing heirs, difficult as it was for everyone to believe. The assumption had been that one so obsessed with duty would want to start on it immediately, and Adale could not blame them for that. Nor could she really blame them for assuming Adale was the reason why it *wasn't* happening. But the truth was, Esofi was far too busy to even consider such a thing.

Or at least, Adale thought that was the reason.

Some days she wasn't sure.

Obligations aside, Adale felt that Carinth's existence satisfied any desperate, urgent need for a child that might someday come upon her. But when she said as much, she could sense people's haughty dismissal. Some had even outright stated that a dragon really wasn't *quite* the same, now was it? The unspoken implication, that she did not love Carinth as much as she would love a child of her own species, offended her deeply.

When they arrived back at their room, Mireille and Carinth were there waiting for them, sitting on the floor and surrounded by a mess of toys. To Adale's eyes, Mireille got more use out of them than Carinth did. There was still no sign of Lisette, Esofi's other waiting lady, but Adale was used to that by now. Lisette came and went as she pleased.

Even after a year, Adale was not completely certain how she felt about Lisette, or how Lisette felt about her. On the surface, the woman seemed to have nothing but thinly veiled disdain for Adale, always looking at her as though she was a misbehaving child.

But Lisette had also been responsible for rescuing Adale from Albion's old room when Brandt and Svana had locked her in there, hoping to keep Esofi from selecting her as a spouse a year and a half ago. If she'd really hated Adale, she wouldn't have gone to the trouble. She would have let Esofi pick one of the twins and left it at that.

Adale's only guess was that Lisette's loyalty to Esofi was stronger than her dislike of Adale. Adale could not imagine what it must be like to have that sort of strength of character.

Adale crouched down to greet Carinth while Esofi went into the bedroom. He sniffed at her hands and bumped his forehead against hers, a habit he had picked up from the cat.

"He's more interested in hunting the dolls than playing with them," sighed Mireille, tossing one across the room to demonstrate. Carinth bounded after it and pounced, his claws digging into the soft fabric. He took it in his mouth and shook his head from side to side vigorously.

"I'm not sure if we should encourage that," said Adale.

Mireille's reply was cut off by the sound of Esofi screaming in pain. Adale leaped up and dashed into the bedroom, one hand to the short blade at her belt.

She found Esofi sitting on the floor, one leg held out in front of her. Blood poured from a long, narrow cut on the sole of her foot. A few inches away lay a silver dagger with a jeweled handle.

"Guards!" Adale screamed as blood began to pool across the carpet. "Esofi, what happened?"

"It was in my slipper," Esofi whimpered.

"Carinth," realized Adale. At the sound of his own name, Carinth chirped and went over to Esofi, sniffing at the floor. To Adale's surprise, Esofi reached out and slapped him across the nose. Carinth squeaked and scampered away from her.

"Esofi!" cried Adale. She took a few steps toward the baby dragon, intending to pick him up and comfort him, but the doors opened and two guards burst in, their swords ready. Carinth slipped out from between Adale's fingertips and darted past their boots, into the sitting room.

"We need a healer," Adale told the guards. One turned and ran, while the other knelt to press a handkerchief to Esofi's foot.

The healer, a white-robed acolyte of Adranus, arrived quickly. After the briefest inspection, he declared that the cut was clean and would be fixed easily. His hands glowed with white magic as he worked, the wounded flesh knitting back together without incident.

"There," he said, once the injury was healed. "Now, if it reopens or shows any signs of infection, call for me immediately. But you should be fine as long as you do not exert yourself."

"The carpet's ruined," sighed Esofi. But Adale found that she cared far less about that than she did Carinth. She went back out into the main sitting room to search for him but could not find him, even when she got down on her hands and knees to peer underneath the furniture. Then her eyes fell on the door that led to the outside hallway. It was not completely shut.

"I think Carinth ran off," Adale called to Esofi.

"He won't have gone far." In the bedroom, Esofi was getting back to her feet with the healer's help. She did not sound terribly concerned. Instead, she picked up the dagger and examined it. "Do you know who this might belong to?"

Adale did not, nor could she bring herself to care very much about it after what she had just witnessed. "I expect they'll find us once they realize it's gone missing," said Adale. The residents of the castle had quickly learned that any missing valuables had a good chance of turning up in Adale and Esofi's rooms. "I'm going after Carinth."

When Esofi only nodded, Adale pressed her lips together and left the room.

Adale knew all of Carinth's favorite places to hide and all of his favorite people. There was a good chance he'd be with her mother or Knight-Commander Livius. Or he might be in the castle's chapel, which was filled with lots of shiny things to admire. She decided she'd check there first. She did not want to explain herself to anyone just yet.

Unfortunately, Adale was so distracted by her own thoughts that she did not notice the archpriestess of Dayluue until she was nearly on top of her.

Birsgen's archpriestess of Dayluue was a middle-aged woman named Tofa, and Adale might have mistaken her for an ordinary priestess, if not for the fact that she knew her personally. Tofa wore the same red-violet robes the rest of the priestesses of her order did, with no special decoration or ornamentation to set her apart from the others. In lieu of any jewelry, she had a few daisies woven into her braids.

"Crown Princess!" cried the woman happily. "I was hoping I might run into you."

"Oh," said Adale, glancing around desperately for a distraction. "Uh, well, I...I'm in a bit of a hurry—"

"I'm here to see to Lady Catrin," Archpriestess Tofa went on happily. "She's due within the week. Perfectly healthy, nothing to worry about!"

"Oh," said Adale. "Well...good. Good. That's good."

"None of my priestesses have reported seeing either of you come in for a Change." Tofa moved forward even as Adale backed away. "We have all been expecting a visit from you for months now."

"Well, Esofi and I just want to focus on raising Carinth until he gets a little more independent. We wouldn't be able to give a baby the attention it needs right now."

"Have you at least discussed which one of you wants to do the carrying?" pressed the archpriestess. "I'd recommend Princess Esofi, she has those wonderful—"

"I am going now, goodbye!" yelled Adale, taking off in a sprint. Thankfully, Tofa did not pursue her.

In truth, Adale was still not completely sure how she felt about having a baby. In the long run, she thought she might be equally happy with or without one. The idea did not fill her with the same sort of terror or dread that it had a year ago. But she had not lied when she'd told the archpriestess that she and Esofi were simply too busy to consider it right now.

For while Esofi kept herself busy with overseeing the university, Adale was spending more and more time shadowing her parents, watching them work and learning what would someday be expected of her, making up for years spent running wild with her friends. Adale had been a miserable student since girlhood. Her tutors had tried their best to educate the young princess, but she was restless and unfocused and hardly retained anything she was told. And it was not as though she was incapable of learning: she picked up riding and hunting and falconry with ease. The trouble was that if a subject did not immediately catch Adale's interest, it might as well not exist.

But following her parents was different. With her tutors, there had only been laws and regulations and histories that felt as distant as the stars. Adale's parents dealt with things that were *real* and far more compelling than any book or lecture.

Once Adale was certain that Tofa really wasn't going to chase after her, she slowed back down to a walk. The Chapel of the Ten was not far, now. As its name suggested, the castle's chapel was not dedicated to any one god or goddess, though it was most frequently used for sunrise services. When Adale pushed the heavy door open, it was still and silent within.

The sole occupant was a young woman sitting on one of the benches, facing the altar. And when Adale approached, she saw that Carinth had laid his head on her lap like a loyal dog.

"Carinth!" His golden eyes flicked to Adale, but he did not move his head. "Oh, we're sulking, are we?"

The strange young woman laughed and gave Carinth a colorful boiled sweet of out her pocket. Carinth caught it on the end of his tongue and swallowed it whole.

"I'm sorry," said Adale. "He thinks everyone in the world should love him."

"And rightly so. He's just adorable, isn't he?" The woman rested her hand on his head. "You are very fortunate."

"I don't think I've seen you around before. Have you just arrived?"

"Only today. My name is Elyne of Otradosa."

"You're from Vesolda?"

Elyne nodded. "I came with Dame Orsina. She was delivering a message..."

"Oh, yes. I met her earlier." Adale noted that the other girl did not seem to be at all intimidated by her rank, which was uncommon for foreigners. Usually they were tense and awkward and bowed too often until they learned of Adale's carefree nature. "Will you be in Ieflaria long?"

"I'm not sure. It was quite a journey. I'd hate to leave so soon. There's so much to see." She stood up. Carinth shifted his head away but remained on the bench, his head pressed to the wooden seat. "I should go. Orsina worries about me if I'm gone too long, and she doesn't speak the language. I'm sure I'll see you again."

Once Elyne was gone, the heavy wooden doors of the chapel closing behind her, Adale sat down beside Carinth. His tail twitched, but he did not otherwise acknowledge her.

"You're planning to sleep in here?" Adale asked. "Only it's going to get cold after a while."

Carinth gave her another sidelong glance.

"You're mad Mera hit you. I was surprised too. I'll talk to her. I'm sure she's already sorry." Though Esofi hadn't really *acted* sorry. Nevertheless, Adale pressed on. "But you know not to leave things in shoes. You could hurt someone."

Carinth shuffled closer without getting up, like a snake slithering along the ground. Adale laughed.

"I wish you could talk to me. I wish I knew how much you understand."

Adale reminded herself that even if Carinth was an ordinary little boy, he wouldn't be able to speak at his age. She wasn't very good at guessing the ages of children, but she was certain that most one-year-old babies couldn't say more than one or two words and only barely knew how to walk.

She thought, yet again, of Esofi's hand reaching out to strike Carinth across the nose. Unease rose up in her chest. In that moment, Esofi had become someone that Adale did not recognize. It almost felt unreal. If someone told her she'd imagined the entire thing, Adale might believe them.

Esofi was *soft*. She was shy and gentle and covered her face with her hands when she giggled. She spent too long in the bath and always smelled faintly of flowers and...

And she'd hit Carinth in the face.

"I don't know what I'm doing," Adale said, more to the silence than to Carinth. He lifted his head and looked up at her. She rested a hand on his back, fingers playing with the strange leather of his folded wings. "But maybe nobody really does."

They sat in silence for a little longer. Adale glanced up at the altar and at the various statues of the Ten placed around the room. She felt no compulsion to pray. She hadn't in years.

The door creaked open, and Adale turned her head to see her own mother enter the chapel. She was alone, not accompanied by any guards or ladies, and so Adale knew she must be searching for her.

"What happened?" asked Saski. There was a distinct accusatory note in her voice.

"I didn't do anything!" Adale objected, more than a bit offended that her mother always assumed she was the one in the wrong.

Saski sat down beside Adale. Carinth immediately climbed into her lap to examine her necklace, sniffing at the gemstones.

"What did you hear?" asked Adale, almost afraid to know the answer.

"I heard that Esofi was injured and a carpet was ruined," Saski said unhelpfully. "Why don't you tell me what happened? Are you two quarreling?"

"I don't know," said Adale. "I don't think so? I think we just surprised each other. Carinth left a blade in Esofi's slipper, and she cut her foot on it. Not badly, the healer took care of it. But she struck Carinth's face when he went to her. I've never seen her do such a thing before." Though, belatedly, Adale remembered that Esofi had done far worse to dragons in the past.

"Have you two discussed matters of discipline?" asked Saski.

"Not exactly?" said Adale. They had never really needed to before. Carinth was generally well behaved, or at least better behaved than anyone would expect from a young dragon. When he did something that warranted punishment, Esofi always declared what it would be— whether that was being confined to his room for a little while, or not being allowed desserts. Adale never found a reason to disagree with her judgment. "But I don't want her hitting him. It...it doesn't seem right."

Saski looked thoughtful. "Has she spoken at all of her own upbringing?"

"Hardly ever." And the little pieces Adale had picked up along the way were not exactly pleasant. "I don't think she likes to."

"The way we are raised influences the way we raise our own children. I think you should make it a priority to discuss this with her."

"I should go to her now." She hadn't meant to leave Esofi alone. But in the moment, going after Carinth had felt more important. "Can you take him for me while I talk to her?"

Saski never really needed to be convinced to watch Carinth, and Adale knew he would be in good hands with her. Carinth was as spoiled as any grandson would be, but Saski did not let him run completely wild.

When Adale arrived back at their room, she found Esofi was still inside, sitting on a sofa and embroidering a handkerchief. Cream was sitting in her lap. He'd been a kitten when Adale gave him to Esofi as a courting gift. Now he was a fully grown cat and took up more than his share of space on the bed.

Adale had no patience or skill for embroidery, but Esofi claimed she found it soothing, even meditative. After long days, she could often be found with a bag of colored thread and a needle, building an enormous collection of linens.

Adale watched Esofi work and reflected on the fact that she had spent almost the entirety of her life believing that she would never marry, or if she did it would only be for her own amusement. Albion's death and Esofi's subsequent arrival had changed everything she had ever believed about herself and her future in a short amount of time.

Learning that Esofi expected her to be Albion's replacement had been terrifying, at first. Adale hadn't believed she was capable of being a good wife, or a good queen. But as they spent more time together, Adale's opinion changed. Esofi's presence brought something out in Adale that nobody had ever seen before, including Adale herself.

Esofi paused in her work to look up at Adale. "Where is Carinth?"

"He's following Grandmother around," said Adale. On its face, there was nothing abnormal about that. But she hoped that Esofi would comment on it, that she would realize that something was wrong and apologize.

But Esofi's eyes returned to her embroidery, apparently untroubled.

"I was...I was hoping we could talk."

"About what?"

Adale swallowed, silently questioning if she ought to let the subject drop for the sake of keeping the peace between them. But if Esofi struck Carinth again, Adale might never forgive herself.

"You seemed...angry. At Carinth. But you have to know it was an accident."

"Of course I do. Did you think I believed he did it maliciously?"

"I don't know. Maybe. I just thought you were very angry. Angrier than I'd have expected."

"Well, it wasn't your foot."

"Maybe not," Adale granted. "But you didn't need to strike him."

A concerned expression came over Esofi's face. "I didn't hurt him, did I?"

"No," said Adale. "I don't think so. But I don't think you should have done it."

"Why not?"

"Well..." Adale paused as she realized she didn't have a coherent reason *why* she felt Esofi should not hit their adopted son. She hadn't really counted on needing one. "It just seems wrong."

"Do parents in Ieflaria not discipline their children?" Esofi sounded legitimately confused.

"You can discipline children without hitting them," said Adale. "I don't understand why you'd *want* to hit one."

"It's not about wanting to," said Esofi. "It's just what you do."

"Maybe in Rhodia, but not here. Besides, we're meant to be raising him to be at least somewhat civilized, aren't we? If Talcia wanted him to be wild and violent, she'd have let him be raised by other dragons."

"He's not going to turn out wild and violent."

"He does what we do. What if he decides to go around hitting people who upset him? He could *kill* someone without even meaning to, someday."

Esofi's frown deepened, and Adale's heart sank. "Don't you think you're overreacting?"

"No," said Adale. "I don't. Esofi, he's so *little*, how could you hit him?"

"If striking children is culturally unacceptable in Ieflaria, I will not do it again. There's no need to make so much of it."

The finality in Esofi's voice was so decisive that Adale found herself dumbstruck. By the time she found her voice again, it was too late to say anything in reply. So Adale turned and went into the bedroom, her mind spinning.

She and Esofi had never really fought. They disagreed, certainly—their personalities were so different that it would have been silly to expect otherwise. But Adale had never stepped away from any of those disputes feeling so unsettled before.

Adale sat down on the bed. She wanted to go back out and confront Esofi, but maybe that would be a bad idea. Maybe that would only make things worse. She didn't want Esofi to think she was attacking her. But she did not want to sit and stew in her own anger for the next few hours either.

Adale paused to examine her own feelings. She was angry, yes, but beneath that was concern—concern for Esofi, as well as Carinth. Esofi only rarely spoke of her life before coming to Ieflaria, and always in very general terms. Adale was curious, but she made a conscious effort not to pry. Rhodia, and Esofi's childhood, were so far away that asking questions would accomplish nothing but satisfying Adale's own curiosity. It hardly seemed worth it.

But maybe those questions did need to be asked.

Esofi had first set foot in Ieflaria less than two years ago. On their wedding day, they'd known each other for ten months. At its core, their marriage was a political alliance and the fact that they'd taken so well to each other was viewed as nothing more than a stroke of good luck in the eyes of the Ieflarian court.

Adale did not doubt her own love for Esofi, but there were still things she did not know about her. There was so much Esofi did not like to talk about. And while Adale certainly didn't want to cause her pain by forcing her to recount the past, she could not help but feel she was missing some crucial element of who Esofi was. She wanted to love all of Esofi, not just the parts of her that she allowed the world to see.

And buried just beneath that was a faint but sharp terror that their relationship would sooner or later fall to pieces despite Adale's best efforts. Adale's past relationships—if they could even be called that—had never lasted for more than a few weeks. She never *meant* for them to last longer than that. Before Esofi, Adale had not believed she would ever want something as serious as a marriage.

Adale rested her hand over her heart, thinking of their wedding day. She vividly recalled the joy that had threatened to burn through her chest when Esofi smiled at her from the other side of the archpriestess of Pemele.

They'd initially hoped to marry at midsummer, only a few months after Esofi's arrival in Ieflaria. But planning the wedding was a time-consuming process, and Esofi's injuries from the battle with the dragons' Emperor needed time to heal. So a date was set for autumn, giving everyone room to breathe.

But the wedding plans grew more elaborate as time went on, and both Adale and Esofi's responsibilities increased with each passing month. They both devoted as much time as they could to Carinth. And while Adale shadowed her parents and listened to their advisors' concerns that the dragon attacks would begin anew as revenge for the Emperor's death, Esofi worked to accommodate all the newly blessed Ieflarians coming to Birsgen to train at a university that did not yet exist.

All of this meant that the wedding date had to be pushed back yet again, this time past Esofi's birthday, past midwinter, and into the new year. Adale had been afraid that postponing the wedding twice would provoke rumors that Esofi was rethinking the engagement. But instead, everyone was eager to see just how ostentatious the wedding would be. She'd overheard people speculating about what food would be served, which dignitaries would come to attend the ceremony, and how many gold coins Adale's parents would be passing out.

When the wedding day finally did arrive, it went without incident. Adale had not been allowed to drink, a rule handed down from her parents and enforced by everyone on staff. The ceremony had been an hour long, but the celebration afterward had lasted into the next day. Adale still believed that the entire event had been a little too extravagant, but Esofi had loved every minute of it, and so she would not have changed a thing.

Adale peered into the sitting room and saw that Esofi was in the process of packing away her embroidery bag. When she came into the bedroom, Adale went to the wardrobe and brought Esofi one of her nightgowns in a peace offering. Esofi accepted it without a word.

"Are you all right?" Adale asked.

The tension was so heavy that Adale almost regretted asking the question. It would have been *so easy* to say nothing, to fall asleep and then wake up tomorrow smiling as though nothing happened. But she did not want a fake peace. She wanted Esofi to be genuinely happy again.

Esofi pulled the nightgown over her head. "I'm fine," she said, somewhat muffled through the fabric, as though it was a shield she held between them and not just cotton and lace. She pulled the collar down and her head reemerged. Adale did not move.

"Are you angry at me?" asked Esofi.

"No," said Adale. "I'm just worried."

Esofi's eyebrows rose, but she said nothing.

"In Rhodia—" began Adale.

"We're not talking about Rhodia."

"We don't have to talk about it if you don't want to. But...I'm here if you do. It's easier to carry things together than alone."

Esofi sat down on the bed. She was silent, staring at the window for a long time. Then she said, "Have you ever seen an elf?"

"What?" Adale was not sure how this related to anything that had happened between them tonight and hoped that Esofi was not just trying to distract her. "An elf?"

"Yes."

"Once. When I was very young, two came to Ieflaria to petition my parents. What does this have to do with—"

"Thiyra stands between Domeysil and the rest of the world," said Esofi. "Our four nations—Rhodia, Eskas, Etrea, and Dossau—have a force dedicated to making sure the elves remain on their own lands. If not for us, they would be terrorizing the entire world."

"Are elves really that bad?" asked Adale. She remembered being frightened by them, but she'd been a child at the time.

"They eat people," said Esofi.

"Are you sure?" Adale could not keep the skepticism from her voice.

But Esofi nodded solemnly. "Talcia's magic is powerful in Rhodia because she means for us to keep the elves at bay. But we cannot take our blessings for granted. We must hone our skills for our entire lives. Complacency is weakness, and there is no room for weakness in Rhodia."

"Not even with your children?"

Esofi's fingertips played at the seams of the bedsheets.

"When I was nine years old, my mother got into a terrible argument with the archpriestess of Merla. I don't remember what it was about. I'm sure it was something absurd. But they decided that the only way to settle their differences was with a duel."

"Your mother dueled a priestess?" Adale was not sure which was more difficult to believe: that a queen would behave in such a way, or that an archpriestess would go along with it.

"Well, no," said Esofi. "My mother told the archpriestess that she wasn't worth fighting. She said, *'Beat one of my daughters first, and then I'll face you.'* I was sure the archpriestess was going to pick Esybele. But instead, she pointed at me. *'The fat one,'* she said."

"Did you win?"

"Of course I did. I don't think it even entered my mind that I might not. Looking back, though..."

"Yes?" prompted Adale when it seemed that Esofi was reluctant to say any more.

"When you're young, you think everything you experience is normal, because it's all you know. Then you grow up and get out and realize...maybe not." Esofi rubbed her eyes. "And your parents are kind, even when they're angry with you. I don't think I realized anyone could really be like that."

Adale reached out to touch Esofi's shoulder. "I'm sorry," she said. It felt weak and inadequate, but she could not think of anything else to say.

"Maybe I don't actually know what families are supposed to be like," said Esofi. "I always thought I did... until I came here. And now I feel like I hardly know anything."

"I don't think that's true," said Adale. "You're happy most days, aren't you? That is—you haven't been pretending all this time, have you?"

"No!" Esofi met her eyes. "I am happy. Happier than I've ever been in my life. That's what makes me think I'm doing it all wrong."

"You think you're meant to be miserable?"

"It's so foolish, isn't it?" Esofi shook her head. "I can hardly make sense of it myself. Of course I don't want to be unhappy. I came here hoping things would be better than they were at home. And they are! I ought to be grateful for that, not behaving like I'm still back there."

"It's not your fault," said Adale. "If it's how you were raised, if it's how you lived..."

"Maybe," said Esofi quietly.

She wanted to know more, but she knew she could not expect Esofi to recount her entire childhood in a single night—especially when uncovering just this little piece of it had been so arduous. She would have to be patient.

So instead of asking any more questions, Adale wrapped her arms around Esofi and pulled her closer before she pressed a kiss to her neck. "I'm so glad you're here now."

Esofi relaxed. "I am too. I think being sent away was the best thing that could have happened to me."

"Certainly the best thing that could have happened to me," Adale murmured into her hair.

Esofi laughed. "You're ridiculous."

Adale rested her chin on Esofi's shoulder and kissed her neck again. "I think you're the ridiculous one. For example..."

"Yes?"

"For example, you still don't believe you are the single most beautiful woman in Birsgen, despite the fact that I tell you so at least twice a week."

"Not this again."

"*At least* twice a week."

"Please."

"You think I'm lying?"

"I think you're mistaken." They were falling into a conversation they'd had many times before, a familiar old trek that led nowhere. "I think you think you're telling the truth."

"You missed your calling; you should have been a Justice."

Esofi gave her a halfhearted push. "Stop it. You're so embarrassing."

"Oh dear," said Adale. "You should do something to distract me."

Chapter Two

ESOFI

Three days after Esofi and Adale's wedding, Lexandrie announced that she was returning to Rhodia. Esofi was not sure what hurt more: the announcement or the timing of it.

She had always known her cousin would not remain in Ieflaria forever. But she had been expecting her to stay and serve as her waiting lady for at least a few more years. Esofi might have been popular with the Ieflarian people, but she still liked having other Rhodians near. And Lexandrie was her only blood relative on the entire continent.

Esofi could have ordered her to stay. But she knew that doing so would only have prompted several months of passive-aggressive pouting and complaining and sighing, and she did not want to live with that. Besides, she was not a jailor and Ieflaria was not a prison.

It seemed Esofi was the only one who was sad to see Lexandrie go. Adale had all but offered to pack her bags for her—but then, Lexandrie and Adale had never really approved of each other. Lisette hadn't given her opinion on Lexandrie's departure, but Esofi got the sense she didn't care very much. Mireille had cheerfully declared Lexandrie was welcome to leave, because she was no help anyway, but she had not said this to Lexandrie's face.

Esofi had been certain she would miss Lexandrie once she was gone. But it seemed she had been mistaken. Months passed, and Esofi barely ever thought of her cousin. And perhaps it was only her imagination, but she thought she might be happier too.

Adale always claimed that Lexandrie was too harsh, too critical, too cruel. But Esofi knew there was no changing Lexandrie's nature, and besides, she wasn't terribly different from most Rhodian nobles. They were a straightforward people, determined and pragmatic, hardened by thousands of years spent watching the mists of Domeysil for any sign of danger. What Adale saw as insults and pettiness, Esofi interpreted as opportunities to improve herself.

But the Ieflarians always made her feel as though she did not require any improvement.

That way lies complacency, Esofi warned herself. And for a queen, or queen-to-be, such a thing was dangerous.

Still, as she lay in the darkness with one of Adale's arms wrapped firmly around her midsection, she supposed it was nice to be loved.

Saski had offered to help her find another waiting lady to replace Lexandrie, but Esofi politely put her off. Mireille and Lisette were enough for her, at least for now. She trusted them both. And an Ieflarian waiting lady would be more loyal to Saski than Esofi.

Esofi trusted and respected Queen Saski, but sometimes she took a little too much interest in Esofi's relationship with Adale. Saski meant well and only wanted them to get along, but Esofi wanted *some* degree of privacy in her marriage.

There would be one benefit to having an Ieflarian waiting lady though. Esofi would always have someone on hand who could tell her when she was behaving in a way that her subjects would disapprove of. For Esofi was a foreigner, born and raised on another continent. Rhodia had sculpted her into a woman with values and priorities that sometimes felt diametrically opposed to the Ieflarians'. Yesterday's disagreement over Carinth was only one of them.

Nobody ever seemed to think much of them, but such incidents always left her feeling like an outsider. Even now, Esofi's Rhodian upbringing insisted that Adale had overreacted last night. Back in Rhodia, she had witnessed—and experienced—far worse than a quick strike across the nose. But if the Ieflarians saw it as inappropriate behavior, then Esofi would conform to their expectations without argument.

She had experience with that, after all. She'd reluctantly dropped the issue of the Temple of Adranus and their unorthodox approach to medicine that (in her opinion) bordered on sacrilege. She could not believe that Adranus would ever condone cutting people open, nor that boiling water would prevent plagues. But it had quickly become apparent that continuing to press the issue would damage her reputation.

Esofi consoled herself with the fact that if Adranus objected to these practices, he was more than capable of putting a stop to them. Besides, she'd been forced to spend some time at the 'hospital' after her fight with the Emperor, and found it was merely an inordinately clean temple, regardless of the impression that its name gave.

Esofi had not anticipated that she would struggle with her identity to such a degree after her wedding. She'd known she was going to be the queen of Ieflaria since she'd been old enough to understand the meaning of the words.

And she had been glad to leave Rhodia when the time came. She could not see herself returning under any circumstances. Something about the Rhodian court exhausted her, made her feel as though she must always be on her guard. And while Esofi acknowledged that this only served to make her stronger, she did not want to live her entire life on edge.

In marriage, she would have an unconditional ally. Someone she could confide in and rely on. That ally should have been Albion, but the gods apparently had other plans. Adale had certainly not been what she'd expected, but Esofi was slowly beginning to learn that sometimes surprises could be nice.

She was glad she'd picked Adale.

Adale was impulsive and uncertain and sometimes downright absurd. But Esofi knew that she could usually back up her more radical ideas with well-reasoned arguments if Esofi really pressed her. It had taken some practice, but Esofi had learned not to dismiss Adale's more ridiculous declarations out of hand. And in return, Adale was learning to explain herself rather than just make a statement and expect everyone to understand her reasoning.

She could have done without Adale's near-daily declarations of Esofi's beauty, or intelligence, or whatever other trait caught her interest, but she supposed nobody had ever died of embarrassment.

"I need to get up," she said aloud. In response, Adale merely groaned and clutched her tighter. "I mean it."

"Mm. No, you don't," Adale murmured. "You don't mean it. I know you don't."

And perhaps Adale had improved her as well. Adale would never believe it, of course. She always had such a difficult time thinking of herself as anything but an embarrassment, no matter how frequently Esofi reminded her of the progress she'd made in becoming an heir her parents could be proud of. Some of the older palace residents were no help in that, for they seemed determined to forever think of her as an irresponsible child, no matter what Adale did to demonstrate otherwise. Adale shrugged these critics off easily, but the disrespect grated at Esofi.

"You can't go," Adale mumbled into her shoulder. "You'll work yourself to death. And then I'll miss you *so* much."

Esofi laughed and began to squirm free of Adale's arms. "We need to go find Carinth."

"My mother's ladies are feeding him pastries and letting him try on their rings," predicted Adale. "And they'll all be extremely disappointed when you take him away."

That fit with Esofi's own experiences, but she got up anyway and began to dress, selecting another Ieflarian-style dress for her day. Her large Rhodian dresses and underskirts were all pushed to one side of her wardrobe, awaiting special occasions when Carinth would not be allowed to climb on her shoulders.

Today's dress was sapphire blue, a darker shade than what Esofi usually wore. It had short capped sleeves, and the fabric was thick and warm, suitable for the autumn temperature. She selected a pair of embroidered shoes (shaking each out carefully before she put her feet into them) and plain white gloves.

This morning, her mind was once again on the Temple of Talcia—though it was not the newly blessed Ieflarians who were occupying her thoughts. Rather, she was a bit concerned for the priestesses. The archpriestess of Talcia was a very old woman, and her health was failing. She was seldom seen in public these days, and everyone knew it would not be long before she departed Inthya for Dia Asteria.

Unfortunately, this meant some of the more ambitious priestesses were already jostling for her title. The new archpriestess would be chosen by a vote among the priestesses when the old one died. Even though Esofi would not be permitted a vote herself, she knew that voicing support for one or the other would be influential on the outcome. So far, she had not spoken on the matter.

In truth, Esofi was not certain which priestess she preferred. Both of the most prominent candidates had their own strengths and weaknesses, and either would make a suitable archpriestess. Esofi thought she would be happy with any outcome.

She did not want to see the old archpriestess die, but privately she could not help but admit she would be relieved when this period of uncertainty finally passed.

Esofi sifted through her jewelry box absently, distracted by her own thoughts. But her trance broke when a pounding came from the outer door.

"Go away," moaned Adale, drawing the covers up over her head. Esofi went into the sitting room just as Mireille pulled the outer door open.

Standing there was Ilbert, squire to the king. He looked a little bit winded.

"What has happened?" asked Esofi.

"A dragon has come to Fenstell," Ilbert said, naming Ieflaria's northeastern-most settlement that, in past years, had become home to one of the largest defense camps.

"What?" Esofi's heart skipped. "They were attacked?"

"No. It...*he*...is asking to speak with you, Princess."

"With me?" Esofi frowned. "When did this happen?"

"A courier just arrived. She has a letter for you from Lieutenant Vaseur." Lieutenant Helaine Vaseur was one of the battlemages that had accompanied Esofi from Rhodia to Ieflaria, and she commanded the Rhodians at Fenstell. "I can take you to her."

"Yes, of course," said Esofi. She turned to Mireille. "I must see to this. Please make sure Adale gets up. You have my permission to push her off the bed."

Couriers from the Temple of Nara tended to be female, just as paladins from the Order of the Sun tended to be male and those blessed with Inthi's fire tended to be neutroi. They were expensive messengers, though their prices were finally going down again now that the skies were safer.

This courier, standing in the middle of the throne room, did not appear to have undergone any danger on her journey to Birsgen. Her blue and white uniform was nearly pristine, and her beautiful gray feathered wings, folded neatly behind her back, did not appear to have any damage to them. Even her ebony braid was still firmly pinned around her head in a coronet, typical for Ieflarian women.

Gathered there were also Adale's parents, Saski and Dietrich, and Archmage Eads, as well as Captain Lehmann of the Ieflarian royal guard and Captain Henris, who commanded the battlemages who had come with

Esofi from Rhodia. Carinth was seated just between his grandparents, tail wrapped around his body and draped over his front claws.

Esofi crouched down, and Carinth came forward to sit beside her instead. Satisfied that he seemed to be back to his ordinary self, and no worse for the wear, she turned her attention to the courier, who bore a single sealed letter.

When Esofi opened it, she saw that it had been written in the Rhodian language. She tried not to interpret as a slight against their Ieflarian hosts.

Princess Esofi,

Our camp at Fenstell was visited by a dragon early this morning. He approached on foot and spoke to the guards stationed at the wall, indicating that he came in peace. He knew of the events that happened last year at Birsgen and said he wished to speak to the one who had killed the emperor.

He claimed that his name is Ivanedi, and he has been sent from the Silver Isles as an emissary of peace. He will remain at Fenstell until we receive word of what action you would like to take.

I leave this matter to your discretion.

Helaine Vaseur

Esofi looked up from the page, her mind spinning. There were so many possibilities to consider. Was this a trick? A clever way from a dragon to get inside Birsgen's walls without a fight? Or were they hoping to lure her to Fenstell, where she would be more vulnerable?

Or was Ivandei's claim legitimate?

"The dragon in Fenstell says he wishes to meet with me," reported Esofi. "It sounds as though he wants us to believe he has been sent as a sort of ambassador."

Nobody appeared to know how to react to this news.

"Perhaps it would be better to appoint an ambassador of our own," said Dietrich. "There is no need for you to risk your safety with such a task."

"Perhaps," said Esofi. But the dragon had asked specifically for her, and she knew from experience that they respected Men who were devoted to Talcia, as she was. What if they took offense to the Ieflarians sending someone else in Esofi's place? What if they saw it as a gesture of bad faith and renewed their attacks? "I will have to reflect on the matter."

There was also Carinth to consider. Did she want him around his own kind? Would this be a wonderful opportunity, or a terrible mistake? What if the dragons were a bad influence on him?

What if he decided he wanted to live with the dragons and leave Esofi and Adale forever?

She glanced down at Carinth, who was still sitting peacefully by her ankle. He gazed back up at her, untroubled by any of this.

"I don't like this," said Captain Henris. "If they wish to talk, why has it taken them nearly two years to request an audience? Your Highness, I feel certain that this is a trap."

"Under normal circumstances, I would agree," said Esofi. "But we have not had any attacks since the Emperor's death. I find that significant. Nevertheless…"

The door to the throne room opened, and Lady Lisette entered. As always, she wore a simple gray dress, and her expression was unreadable. Esofi saw less of her these days; she seemed to spend more time gathering information than guarding Esofi's back.

"Lady Lisette," said Esofi as she approached. "Is something the matter?"

Lisette did not reply, not until she was near enough to lean over and whisper in Esofi's ear.

"Your mother is in Valenleht," she murmured.

Esofi turned to stare at her, a smile frozen on her face. "What?"

"Queen Gaelle of Rhodia arrived in Valenleht's main port on a ship yesterday morning." Lisette's voice was still barely more than a whisper, so soft that Esofi could barely hear her over the sudden ringing in her ears.

Esofi shook her head, still smiling. "What?"

"Your mother is expected to arrive in Birsgen tomorrow." Despite her volume, Esofi detected a hint of impatience in Lisette's tone. "She is coming *here*."

The letter in Esofi's hand rattled as though it was in a thunderstorm. She looked down at it and frowned.

"Is everything all right, dear?" asked Saski.

"Of course," said Esofi. Her voice sounded like it was coming from somewhere very far away. "I just...I...I have made up my mind. I will go to Fenstell. There is no sense in bringing a dragon to Birsgen. Our people will not appreciate it, and it may very well be a trick."

"If that is the case, you must have guards," said Captain Lehmann. "I suggest at least—"

"Fine. That is fine. But be quick about it. I intend to leave today."

"Today?" Saski frowned and glanced at her husband. "So soon?"

"Of course. This matter is of the utmost importance." Her hands were still shaking. She shoved the letter into her pocket. "Please excuse me."

Before anyone could say anything else, Esofi fled. Carinth followed at her heels, his little claws clicking on the stone floors. She hurried through the halls, ignoring the confused and concerned looks she received from servants and nobles alike. She did not slow until she was safely back in her room.

"Mireille!" Esofi pressed herself against the door as it closed behind her, as though blocking out the entire outside world. Her waiting lady appeared in the doorway immediately, Cream draped over her shoulders like a shawl. "Call the maids. We are going to Fenstell and must pack immediately."

"Fenstell?" Mireille repeated.

"Fenstell?" That was Adale, emerging from their bedroom, finally upright and dressed. "What's going on?"

Esofi sank onto the sofa as her legs finally gave out. She pressed her hand to her forehead, wanting nothing more than to go back to sleep.

"Esofi?" Adale sounded deeply concerned. "What's the matter?"

Esofi opened her mouth to explain, but all that came out was a few deep, gasping breaths. Adale sat down beside her. She did not ask any questions or demand an explanation. She only pulled Esofi to her chest and held her close, stroking her hair.

"It's going to be all right," Adale murmured. "Whatever's happened, I know you're going to be fine."

Her nose was beginning to sting from the effort of holding in tears, and she turned her face away so that Adale would not see her cry. She did not know how to begin to explain what she was feeling, what she was thinking.

But Adale was patient. She kept a comforting hand pressed to Esofi's back and simply waited until Esofi was ready to speak.

"I need to pack," mumbled Esofi into Adale's shoulder. But she did not move.

"The maids can do it. Why don't we go riding?"

"I don't have time for that." Esofi fumbled in her pockets for a handkerchief. "I need to leave today."

"If you're going, I'm going too." Adale paused. "Why are we going to Fenstell? There's nothing interesting up there."

Esofi blew her nose. "A dragon is at the defense camp, asking to speak with me."

"Oh." Adale was openly puzzled. "Well...I suppose that's a good thing, isn't it?"

"If it's not a trick."

"Well, even if it is, you can handle it. I'm sure he's nowhere near as frightening as the Emperor was." Adale gave an encouraging smile. "Is that all?"

Esofi shook her head. "I don't care about the dragon. I know how to handle dragons."

"Then what's the matter?"

"My mother has come to Ieflaria."

"What? *How?*"

"By ship, I imagine."

"But *why?*"

"I don't know!" Tears were threatening to overwhelm her again. "And she's going to be here tomorrow! I need to be gone by then. I can't—I don't—I don't want to see her."

"Esofi," said Adale. "Listen to me. She can't do anything to you. You're not just a princess of Rhodia, you're a princess of Ieflaria by marriage. There's nothing she *can* do to you, and there's not a single person in

Birsgen who won't stand between you if she tries. You're not hers anymore. You're ours. You're mine."

Esofi just shook her head, unwilling to argue. "I need to go to Fenstell."

"Then we will go," said Adale. "Do you want to bring Carinth?"

The alternative was leaving him at the castle, where he might encounter Gaelle. "Yes. Yes, of course." Esofi folded her handkerchief and put it away. "Meeting another dragon might be good for him."

Adale squeezed her shoulders. "It's going to be all right."

"Didn't one of the empress's wives invite us to Anora?" asked Esofi. "Perhaps we should consider visiting them. Once I've sorted the situation in Fenstell."

Adale smiled. "Perhaps. But I have to admit I'm curious. Why would your mother travel all this way herself? That's a long time for a queen to be away from her throne."

Esofi's journey from Rhodia to Gennelet had taken three months, though that had been significantly longer than it needed to be because she had departed Rhodia in the winter, immediately after her birthday, when the sea was roughest and the monsters within were at their hungriest. She knew the Ieflarians would not have held it against her if she'd decided to wait until spring, but something inside her had been aching to leave.

Perhaps it had been uncharacteristically reckless. She'd been ready with the excuse that her marriage contract explicitly stated that she would leave Rhodia after her seventeenth birthday, and she intended to follow the letter of the agreement. But nobody had commented on her decision at all. Not the mages, nor her siblings, or even her father.

Further adding to the travel time had been the fact that Masim and Xytae were warring with one another in and around the Summer Strait. Though neither side had any hatred for Rhodia or Ieflaria, traversing the area could be extremely dangerous. Negotiating safe passage with both factions had been a tedious, time-consuming task, so much so that some of her mages had started quietly joking about blasting holes in any warships they encountered.

When they'd landed in Gennelet, it had been another month to Birsgen. A smaller party could have made much better time, but Esofi's retinue was extremely large, and the citizens of Ieflaria had wanted to see her. They had also been attacked several times by dragons, until they'd learned they were outmatched.

It was autumn now, so Gaelle would have had significantly smoother sailing. And she wouldn't joke about sinking Xytan warships.

She would just do it.

Esofi shook her head. No, not even Gaelle was that mad. Nevertheless, her journey had probably only been half as long as Esofi's. "Maybe she heard about Albion's death and assumed I never managed to secure another alliance? But she wouldn't need to come in person for that, she could send an ambassador. I don't know."

"Maybe she's been deposed and is seeking asylum," said Adale.

"That's ridic—" Esofi paused. Ridiculous or not, it was a legitimate reason for a foreign monarch to come to Birsgen unannounced. "Surely we would have heard already if such a thing had happened."

"Well, that's my only guess."

Esofi was certain her mother had *not* been deposed, for who could hope to stand against her, and Esofi's father, and all her siblings? Unless the dispute had been within the family.

Who would have the most to gain by deposing Gaelle? Eloisa? No. Gaelle favored Eloisa, and Eloisa knew it. Gael? But he was already set to be king, and he was not the sort to take risks. One of the younger siblings? All except Esybele were in advantageous marriages to other monarchs-to-be. Why would they seek control over Rhodia?

Well, the entire thing was a moot point because Esofi was certain her mother was still the queen of Rhodia. It was far more likely that she had travelled for months to berate Esofi for something.

Or maybe it had something to do with the Silence of the Moon.

The Silence of the Moon was not a chaos cult, regardless of the immediate impression that its name gave to outsiders. Its members worshipped Talcia, Goddess of Magic, and claimed that the goddess preferred it when they prayed to her in the wilderness, rather than man-made temples—though of course they attended all the temple services as well, just to prove their devotion.

Esofi had never disputed the philosophy of the Silence, and she did enjoy the time she'd spent in the Rhodian wilderness, focusing on her own gift and straining to sense Talcia's presence. But she privately felt that Talcia probably didn't care very much about where her followers worshipped. If nothing else, the goddess probably understood they were Men, not wild beasts, and did not hold it against them when they preferred to remain indoors.

There was no Silence of the Moon in Ieflaria. As far as Esofi knew, there was no Silence of the Moon anywhere in Ioshora. It was likely that she wanted Esofi to change that, to spread Gaelle's influence further still. But that mandate could have easily come in a letter, or via courier. There was no need for Gaelle to see to it herself.

As though she had heard these thoughts, Adale ran her hand down Esofi's back, over the tattoos inked onto her spine. Adale was the only Ieflarian who had ever seen them with her own eyes.

The tattoos depicted the phases of the moon, beginning with a waxing crescent, then a half moon, and a full, and a waning half moon, and then a final crescent. Innocuous to the casual observer but a little strange for a woman of Esofi's station.

Esofi was careful to never commission dresses that were too low-cut in the back. She was not ashamed of the markings or what they represented. It was just easier to not give people another thing to wonder about, to make her feel even more like a foreigner.

Esofi felt no pressing need to reestablish the Silence of the Moon in Ieflaria. The Temple of Talcia had grown in strength over the last year, aided by Esofi's efforts in establishing the University and the unexpected new blessings granted by Talcia since her arrival in Birsgen. Bringing the Silence back would only draw power away from the temple. And Esofi did not want to do that, even if it meant the power would be her own, because then...

...because then she would answer to Gaelle again.

There was a knock at the door, and Adale rose to answer it. Esofi expected to see Mireille, accompanied by maids to assist them with the packing. But instead, Saski stood there in the doorway.

Saski looked from Adale to Esofi and back again.

"What did you do?" Saski demanded.

"Me?" Adale sounded outraged. "I didn't do *anything*! I haven't even left this room yet today! Why do you always assume when something goes wrong—"

"Because I've met you, Adale!"

"That's—" Adale looked as though she planned to argue her point only a hand's breadth from her mother's face. Esofi decided to step in.

"It's not Adale's fault," said Esofi, getting up so she could take Adale by the shoulder and draw her back to a respectful distance. "I'm sorry to have worried you. I received some surprising news about my family. That is all."

"Your family? In Rhodia?"

"Yes. Well...not precisely in Rhodia..." Esofi turned to Adale for help. "You tell her."

"Apparently Queen Gaelle is in Valenleht."

"What? That cannot be. We received no word—"

"I expect that was deliberate," said Esofi.

"But whatever could she want from Ieflaria?"

"I don't think it's Ieflaria she's here for. I don't know what she wants, and I don't think I want to know. When she arrives, you can tell her you have no idea when I'll be back."

"You will not see her?" asked Saski.

"I suppose I will have to at some point, unless you can convince her to return home. But..." Esofi shook her head. "Not yet. Not now. I'm sorry to put you in this position."

"Have you written to her since your arrival in Ieflaria?"

Esofi shook her head again.

"I see," said Saski. "Well, once we determine why she has come here, we will send a courier to Fenstell."

"Thank you," said Esofi. She was glad Saski had not demanded any further explanations. Perhaps she already understood. "I must prepare for the trip."

BY THE TIME they left Birsgen, it was well past noon and the sun had begun its downward descent. She was asked several times by everyone from King Dietrich to Captain Lehmann to the castle hostlers if she was certain she wanted to leave so late in the day. But Esofi's mind would not be changed.

Northern Ieflaria was not completely foreign to Esofi. After their wedding, she and Adale had gone on a tour of the kingdom, visiting every major city and a few minor ones as well. Unlike southern Ieflaria, which was mostly farmlands, and the eastern coast, which was fishing and port cities, the north was made up of pristine forests and crystal lakes. It was popular with Adale's circle, who were fond of activities like hunting and riding and being out of reach of their parents.

But northern Ieflaria was also home to a thriving logging industry, and though the population was not nearly as high in that region, there were still several major settlements that Esofi heard of regularly.

Fenstell, located on the northeastern-most point of Ieflaria, was only notable due to its proximity to the Silver Isles, where the dragons came from. Once a humble fishing town, it had been nearly taken over by a defense camp in past years. Though the dragon attacks appeared to be a thing of the past, nobody was ready to disassemble the camp just yet. Tensions in Ieflaria were not as high as they had once been, but there was no guarantee that the informal peace would last forever.

Nevertheless, there had been no reports of any significant dragon activity until today. Immediately after the Emperor's death, Lieutenant Vaseur wrote to Esofi asking if they would begin an attack on the Silver Isles, but Esofi had firmly denied this request. In years past, she certainly would have considered it. It would have been an ideal time to cull the dragon population before they got the chance to regroup.

But that had been before she'd learned to think of dragons as anything more than dumb, dangerous animals, before she'd hatched a dragon egg in her own fireplace.

The revelation that dragons could speak, reason, and *think* had come as a complete shock. Esofi sometimes still wrestled with her guilt over having killed so many of them, even though Adale constantly pointed out that it was not truly her fault.

She looked down at Carinth, sound asleep in her lap. They all hoped that someday he would be able to communicate with his own kind, to serve as an ambassador to foster peace between their races. But Carinth was growing slowly. Perhaps his role—whatever it turned out to be—was something else.

If anyone was going to reason with the dragons in the meantime, it was probably going to have to be Esofi.

Her feelings surrounding that were complex. Certainly, she was eager to see one of Ieflaria's worst enemies become their allies. On a more personal level, she was intensely curious about how dragons lived their lives. Did they have a society of their own? A complex social hierarchy? Legends and lore?

But she had not really anticipated that they would respond well to her. After all, she was the one responsible for the death of their Emperor and those of many other dragons leading up to that, including one that had attacked Birsgen alone on the same day Talcia's blessing had been discovered. She expected they would view her as a murderer, a war criminal. Not someone to negotiate with.

Maybe it *was* a trap. Maybe this dragon—Ivanedi—was only here to break Esofi's neck and then fly home or die trying. Given Esofi's experience with dragons, it would probably be the latter.

Esofi had already killed the Emperor. She could not muster up very much fear of this new dragon. What a terrible waste of time it would be if the request for peace was insincere.

Still, she was grateful for the excuse to leave Birsgen.

Dread rose up in her stomach. She had almost forgotten the real reason she was going to Fenstell.

Adale sat, half-asleep, in the seat across from Esofi. How different their childhoods had been from each other! Sometimes it felt like the only commonality had been their stations.

But now they were both here. Together.

You're ours. You're mine.

If those words had come from one of her blood relations, they would have been chilling; a declaration of ownership, a demand for loyalty. But when Adale said them, they felt soft and protective.

She only hoped that Adale could live up to them.

Chapter Three

ADALE

It was three days to Fenstell by carriage. For the most part, the journey was uneventful. But on the morning of the second day, Adale awoke to find Esofi was not beside her, nor anywhere else in their too-large tent.

Rubbing at her eyes, Adale forced herself to get out from under the warm blankets and dressed as quickly as she could manage. Inside the tent was a comfortable temperature, but she knew it would be significantly colder outside until the sun had a few hours to warm the air. Pulling on her boots and fastening a heavy fur-lined cloak around her shoulders, she stepped out of the tent and into the weak sunlight.

The camp was still quiet, though some of their guards had already set to work taking down tents and preparing the morning meal. Mireille was by the fire, and normally Carinth would be anywhere food was happening, but it was too cold for him to be up yet, and so he remained in the tent, under the heavy blankets, waiting for someone to come drop breakfast directly into his mouth.

Adale looked around for any sign of Esofi and finally spotted her near the edge of the camp, quite near the main road. Directly in front of her was Lisette, mounted on a horse and dressed in leather armor instead of her usual grey dress. Adale could not hear what they said to each other, for they were too far away and spoke too softly. Before Adale could get near enough to listen in, Esofi nodded vigorously, and Lisette turned her mount in toward the road.

Adale watched curiously as Lisette directed the horse not toward Fenstell, but back in the direction of Birsgen. Once she was out of sight, Esofi turned around, only to jump in surprise when she saw Adale standing there.

"Where is she off to?" asked Adale.

"Oh...it's nothing," said Esofi. "Don't worry about it."

Adale frowned, uncomfortable that a secret was being kept from her. Esofi must have realized this as well because she added, "I am concerned that we haven't had a courier from Birsgen yet. Lisette believes it may be worth investigating."

"We've not been gone that long," said Adale. But Esofi only shrugged and said nothing more. Perhaps she was embarrassed by her own actions? That seemed the most likely thing, for there was no way that sending Lisette back was anything but a waste of time. It would take her a day to return to Birsgen and then three more to find them again at Fenstell. By the time Lisette managed to deliver any news to Esofi, they'd have already heard it from the courier.

If sending Lisette off made Esofi feel better, Adale wouldn't say anything more about it. But it seemed so very unlike her, so uncharacteristically irrational, that Adale could not help but suspect that there was more to the matter than just a delayed message.

Adale did not want to call Esofi a liar. She did not want to *believe* that Esofi was lying to her, whether directly or simply by omission. And besides, Esofi was not required to tell Adale every detail of her life. Married or not, they were still separate people, and there was nothing wrong with enforcing boundaries now and then...

But how could Adale possibly help Esofi if Esofi would not tell her what was wrong?

If they'd been at home, Adale might have pushed a little harder. But the camp was rather public, and if it turned into a real argument, she did not want their guards to overhear and spread gossip that the princesses were quarreling. Rumors like that could move like wildfire. It would be better to wait, watch, and hope.

But Lisette's departure did nothing for Esofi's anxiety. Every time Adale turned around, Esofi was watching the sky. She and Mireille worked together to distract her from her worries, but it seemed that Esofi was having difficulty focusing on anything but the expected courier.

Even Carinth had noticed something was wrong. He spent most of his time at Esofi's heels, watching her with worried golden eyes. Whenever Esofi spotted this, she looked down at him and asked, "What's the matter?"

But Carinth never answered.

On the morning of the third day, Adale emerged from their tent and found Carinth chasing a dragonfly across the clearing. Esofi had not risen yet and so Adale went to pick him up.

"Are we ready to *fly*?" cried Adale, tossing Carinth up into the air on the last word. The dragon unfurled his limp, awkward wings, as though attempting to catch the wind. He landed safely back in her waiting arms, as always, but Adale still glanced around guiltily to make sure Esofi had not seen this.

Esofi had not seen, but Mireille had. But she was laughing—she never scolded Adale for playing too exuberantly with Carinth. Sometimes she seemed so much younger than Adale and Esofi. Her exceptionally youthful face did not help matters.

"It's time for his breakfast," said Mireille. She was holding an oilskin bag that Adale knew had strips of dried meat inside. Carinth clambered across Adale's shoulders to sniff at it. "I know it's not raw, but..."

Carinth's tongue flicked out and wrapped around one of the strips. Before Mireille could properly react, he had swallowed it whole.

"Oh! Rude!" cried Mireille. "Carinth, you know better! He'd have never done that if Esofi was around."

"The wilderness is getting to him," Adale said, even though they were still within sight of the road. "He thinks he's a wild dragon."

"Wild dragons don't have their breakfast brought to them by beautiful young ladies," Mireille informed Carinth. "And they have to sleep out in the rain."

Carinth was clearly more interested in the bag than anything Mireille had to say. Adale set him down on the ground for fear she would drop him because he would not hold still.

"How is Esofi?" asked Mireille.

"The same as yesterday, I think," said Adale. "I'll be glad when we reach Fenstell. She needs a distraction."

Mireille handed Carinth another strip of dried meat. This time, he took it in his front claws and chewed it.

"You've met Esofi's mother, haven't you?" asked Adale.

"Only once," Mireille admitted. "She was there when they spoke to me to see if I was suitable to accompany Esofi to Ieflaria. I did not think I would actually be selected. My parents are Baron and Baroness of Aelora.

Not terribly...prestigious. But I suppose not many other girls wanted to make such a long trip. Her majesty didn't say very much to me, and I was glad for that. She is very frightening."

"I picked that up, yes," said Adale.

"She is very admired in Rhodia. In all of Thiyra, really. Her blessing is extremely powerful, and the elves know not to cross her."

Elves, again. Adale had questions about elves. But that could wait.

"She has this terribly intimidating air. Even if you didn't know her reputation, you'd sense it. Like an archpriestess or an eagle. And she's very tall for a Rhodian woman—but not for an Ieflarian, I suppose. If she didn't have Talcia's magic, I'm sure she'd have the blood rage from Reygmadra."

"She's violent?"

Mireille blanched. "I didn't mean it like that! It's just...she's...you have to understand; in Rhodia, it's different—"

"It's all right," said Adale. "I've been piecing it together."

"I should not have said anything." Mireille wrung her hands. "I've only met her once; what do I know? Don't take anything I say too seriously, please."

"I won't tell anyone you said anything," Adale promised. "I only want to protect Esofi. I'm not trying to start trouble."

"I don't see why Esofi is so anxious to meet her. She's done very well since she came here. She married you and ended the dragon crisis and the Ieflarian people seem fond of her. Queen Gaelle should not find any cause for complaint."

"You don't have any idea why she might have come?"

Mireille shook her head. "The journey to Ieflaria is so long. I worry something terrible must have happened in Rhodia, for her to have come herself. Is it possible all of the princes and princesses died, and Esofi is now her sole heir?"

"That would be inconvenient," said Adale. There would be no ruling Rhodia from Birsgen. Esofi would have to appoint someone to rule in her stead, or she and Adale would be forced to part ways.

"But if that were the case, we would have heard by now, wouldn't we? The couriers would be speaking of nothing else."

"I suppose there's no point in trying to guess," said Adale.

Mireille fed the rest of the meat to Carinth, one piece at a time. She was just finishing when Esofi emerged from the tent. Her make-up had been carefully applied, as usual, but Adale could still see the exhaustion in her face.

"Let's get you something to eat," said Adale, pulling Esofi into her arms.

"I'm not hungry," said Esofi. She had not been hungry yesterday either. She shook free of Adale's grasp and went to Carinth, resting one hand on his head.

"You have to at least have some tea before we go," insisted Adale.

Esofi did not answer. She only picked up Carinth, humming a little.

"I'll get you some," said Adale, trying her best to ignore the unease rising in her stomach.

When Adale returned with a teacup, Esofi was standing near the trees, staring into the dark forest and singing softly to Carinth in Rhodian. The trees smelled lovely, and Adale could see colorful birds flitting through the sunbeams.

Adale didn't know more than a handful of words in Rhodian, so she had no idea what the song was about. But it sounded like a lullaby.

Adale did not think she'd ever felt so disconnected from Esofi before. It was as though there was an invisible barrier between them, and Adale did not know how to overcome it. She wanted to respect Esofi's apparent need for space, but at the same time, she wanted Esofi to know everything would be so much easier if she just talked to her honestly and openly. In some ways, it was worse than a fight, because at least with a fight, Adale could identify where things had gone wrong.

Maybe it would have been better if they'd stayed at Birsgen. They would have found out what Gaelle wanted by now. Adale was starting to believe that Esofi's worrying was far worse than whatever Gaelle had come to say.

"I'll leave you alone if you just drink this," said Adale.

"I don't want you to leave me alone." Esofi's voice was faint.

"Then I'll leave you alone if you don't drink it."

Esofi looked puzzled. "What?"

"It was a joke!" Adale pulled the teacup closer to herself as Carinth attempted to stick his nose in it. "Captain Lehmann says we should be at Fenstell by noon."

Esofi set Carinth back down on the ground. "Make sure he doesn't run into the trees," she said and took the teacup from Adale.

Adale crouched down to Carinth's level. "Are you being good?" she asked him. He unfurled his wings and then folded them down again. "Maybe you'll get to meet another dragon today. How about that?"

"Don't promise him that," said Esofi. "I need to see if he's a suitable influence first."

As usual, there was no reliable way of knowing if Carinth understood her words, but Adale added, "*If* he's a suitable influence. Can't have him teaching you bad habits at your impressionable age. That's my job."

Esofi laughed into her tea, and Adale grinned hearing it.

True to Captain Lehmann's prediction, they arrived in Fenstell at noon. The camp was located outside of the town, higher up on the seaside cliffs and hopefully far enough away that the residents would not find themselves unduly imposed upon.

The camp was more fortress than camp now. It had a high wooden wall around it, constructed from tall Ieflarian pines. Guards had been posted at the entrance and at several checkpoints on the road leading up to it. It was cold up on the cliffs, the whistling sea winds making everyone pull their cloaks around tighter. Even in the carriage, buffered from the winds, Carinth was grumbling. He had never liked colder weather.

"Do we have any of his shirts?" asked Adale.

"They're in the luggage," said Esofi. Carinth had several knitted garments, all made especially for him. The trend had been started by a castle maid, who had given Carinth his first shirt with two long slits in the back during his first winter. Adale had been sure he'd hate it—he was a dragon, not a lapdog—but Carinth had worn it happily until he'd outgrown it.

These days, Carinth had as many shirts as Esofi had dresses, all of them gifts. And not just from the maids either. Her mother's waiting lady, Countess Amala, had been one of the first noblewomen to sew something for

Carinth. And as Adale knew, once the queen's ladies started doing something, it wouldn't be long before everyone else was following suit.

The carriage rolled into the camp, and the gates closed behind them. Adale stepped out first and turned to help Esofi. They both looked around together, evaluating their surroundings.

It really was more of a fortress than a camp. None of the structures were temporary, they'd all been built from the same Ieflarian pine as the outer wall. But before Adale could consider this further, two people, a man and a woman, approached them.

The man was Commander Gero, from the Ieflarian military, appointed by her parents to oversee the encampment. The woman was unfamiliar to her, but Adale supposed this must be Lieutenant Helaine Vaseur.

Like all of the Rhodian women Adale had met, Lieutenant Vaseur had light hair and she was not very tall. She wore a midnight-blue robe embellished with complex silver embroidery that reflected her advanced rank.

As soon as they were near enough, the woman began to speak to Esofi in the Rhodian language, barely acknowledging Adale at all. Esofi nodded along, frowning a little.

"So, where is the dragon?" asked Adale, tired of being left out. "And how big is he?"

Lieutenant Vaseur frowned at Adale as though she could not believe she'd dared to address her, and Adale felt herself immediately grow defensive in turn. But Commander Gero said, "He travels between the camp here and the forest to the west to hunt. I am certain he will return by nightfall, Crown Princess. We are grateful that you have come so quickly."

"Do you believe that he really wants to negotiate with us?" asked Adale. "Or is this just some kind of trick?"

"I...cannot say, Crown Princess. But his claim appears to be legitimate. As for his size..." Gero looked down at Carinth, who had become distracted by the silver clasp on Helaine's cloak. "Larger than this one, certainly."

To Adale's shock, Helaine removed the clasp and handed it over to Carinth. He accepted it eagerly and turned it over in his tiny claws to taste it.

"Oh, you don't have to do that—" Adale began. But Helaine paid her no mind.

"We have a room for you in the main citadel," said Commander Gero, gesturing to the largest structure in the camp. "I'm afraid it's not much. But you understand our circumstances."

"I'm sure it's fine," said Esofi. "By chance, has a courier come for me?"

"I am afraid not, Princess. But I will send for you if one arrives."

Commander Gero's assessment wasn't incorrect—the room that had been set aside for them was modest, but Adale had been expecting something like it. There was a single bed, two wardrobes, and a writing desk. It had no ornaments or decoration, and only a single small window that let in a little bit of daylight.

Esofi did not seem to be troubled by their accommodations either. She was sorting through one of the valises that had been brought in by a footman, searching for one of Carinth's knitted shirts.

Eventually she found one made from lamb's wool, dyed green, and called to Carinth, who allowed her to put it over his head without complaint. Adale watched as Esofi helped him get his wings through the long slits on the back, for Carinth would fuss if they were not allowed to be free.

"What do you think the dragon will be like?" asked Adale.

"I'm not sure," admitted Esofi. "I only hope he isn't holding a grudge."

"What, for killing the Emperor? I think he should be grateful for that. Now he doesn't have anyone forcing him to fly into danger."

The most unsettling thing Adale and Esofi had discovered during their research was the extent of the Emperor's power over his fellow dragons. The orders he issued were not followed out of fear or respect, but because there was magic in them, a sort of compulsion that the other dragons were apparently unable to resist.

Adale and Esofi speculated that dragons, known for their independence and solitary natures, were not inclined to band together in the face of an outside threat. Commanding a large group of them would probably be something like herding cats, so the Emperor's special ability was a necessity for the survival of the species.

But the most recent Emperor had used his ability aggressively, commanding his "subjects" to fly to Ieflarian towns and settlements and burn them to the ground. When Esofi finally had the opportunity to speak with him, he'd claimed that his plan was to rid the world of Men in retaliation for stealing Talcia's favor away.

Esofi had tried her best to reason with him, but in the end, the Emperor got the fight he'd come for.

Adale would have never said it aloud, but she wondered at the fact that Esofi could face fully grown dragons without flinching, but the idea of her own mother coming for a visit was enough to make her flee the capital.

Esofi fell asleep shortly after that, with Carinth settled beside her for warmth. Adale was inclined to explore the camp and perhaps even the town, but she found herself unwilling to leave Esofi's side. She wanted to be here when Esofi woke.

So, lacking anything better to do, she lay down beside Esofi and Carinth. Exhausted from the journey and worrying about Esofi, she was asleep within minutes.

She awoke a few hours later to someone knocking on the door and nearly fell out of bed. "Just a moment!" she called, struggling to readjust her clothing. Esofi was also up, rearranging her corset and her hair quickly. Once she was finished, Adale pulled the door open and found one of the camp's guards standing there.

"Princess," he said. "The dragon has arrived."

Esofi picked up her skirts and moved forward. "Wait here," she told Adale. "I will—"

"What? No, I'm going with you."

Esofi sighed. "I need you to watch Carinth."

Adale opened her mouth to tell her to make Mireille do it, but the girl was nowhere to be found. So instead she turned to the guard. "I'll give you five crowns if you watch over Carinth for me."

"I would be honored," said the guard quickly, his face lighting up.

"Fine." Esofi seemed to be too exhausted to argue. "Don't feed him anything, no matter what he tells you, and keep an eye to your pockets."

Adale had thought that perhaps the dragon would meet them outside the camp, away from all the guards and high walls. But when they stepped outside, he was the first thing she saw, crouched in the middle of the camp and nearly as large as the citadel itself.

His scales were pale silver-gray, much lighter than Carinth's stormy blue. He curled his tail around himself and laid it over his front claws, in the same way Carinth frequently did. As Adale and Esofi approached, he brought his head low to the ground, near to eye level with them.

"Greetings," he said, his voice surprisingly smooth. "I am honored that you have come to meet with me."

Esofi wasn't reacting yet, but Adale could still see the tension in her face and shoulders. She was still waiting for an attack, but her voice was very calm as she said, "I am told you are hoping to negotiate peace between our people?"

"That is correct," he said. "I wish to tell you what has transpired on the Silver Isles since you defeated our Emperor. I expect you will be surprised."

"Is there a new Emperor?" asked Esofi.

"No. We are not..." Ivanedi seemed to be struggling to explain. "We do not require an Emperor, usually."

Esofi did not say anything.

"Many of us now fear that you will lead your soldiers into our islands to destroy us," Ivanedi went on. "As revenge, or perhaps only to protect your own."

"I am not inclined to do so unless I am given no other recourse." Esofi's tone was still calm and neutral, but her eyes were uncharacteristically hard. "If you are without an Emperor, who has sent you here?"

"I was chosen for this task by majority after we conferred amongst ourselves. We have no ruler, and I doubt we will again for generations."

"I would like very much to trust you," said Esofi. "But you have to realize...after all that has happened between our races, it is difficult for me."

"I do not blame you for your hesitation." Ivanedi dipped his head low. "I cannot promise that none of my kind will ever encroach on your lands again. But without an Emperor, there will be no coordinated attacks as there were in recent years."

"Can you really guarantee that if you are without a leader?" asked Esofi.

"It must seem strange to you," said Ivanedi. "I understand that Men dislike it when they have no one to follow. But that is not our way."

"And what do you ask in return?"

Adale looked at Esofi in surprise. To her ears, it sounded like the dragon was pleading for his own survival. Why would Esofi offer him more than that?

"Zethe—our last Emperor—led us to believe that destroying Men would win us Mother's favor. We now realize that he was mistaken. But I am told that you spoke to him on the night he was killed. You claimed you could help us earn our magic back from Mother."

Esofi relaxed a little, and for the first time, Adale saw the hint of a smile on her face. "If I could ensure that my people would be safe, I would be honored to aid you with this."

"Esofi!" whispered Adale, horrified. "You can't—"

"This is for the safety of our people, Adale."

"You can't promise the safety of our people while you're putting a new weapon in the hands of their worst enemies!"

"But they won't *be* our enemies anymore."

"You don't know that! You can't promise that! And even if you could, don't you know what the Ieflarian people would do if they heard about you trying to help the dragons get their magic back? We'd have rioting!"

Too late, guilt and regret bubbled up in Adale's stomach. She had been too harsh, too exuberant. She'd embarrassed Esofi in front of a stranger. She should have kept her mouth shut until they were alone. Why hadn't she just stayed with Carinth? "Esofi, I—I'm sorry—" she began.

"Do not apologize. There is truth in your words," said Ivanedi. Esofi looked up at him in surprise. "I am not offended. I knew when I came here that I may have been asking too much, too soon. That you have not attempted to kill me on sight is better than many of us expected."

But he'd come anyway. Did Ivanedi's own life mean so little to him? Adale wished she could ask him without seeming rude. But she'd already embarrassed herself once today. It would be better if she remained silent for the remainder of the meeting.

"Perhaps, in time, the Ieflarian people will come to trust you," said Esofi. "And when that happens, I will aid you. You have my word on that."

"I also wish to extend an invitation to the Silver Isles," said Ivanedi. "I understand that you may be reluctant to set foot on our lands. But if you did, I promise that you would be welcomed as an ally. There is a large flight residing on the largest island, where we could receive you."

"I may have reason to take you up on that offer soon enough."

I thought we were going to Anora? Adale did not say, because she didn't feel like being beaten to death with a lace parasol.

"I thank you for your understanding," said Ivanedi. "I will return to my home with the news."

Esofi nodded.

"If any of my kind attack your lands in the meantime, know that we will bring them to heel," he added. "That is, if they survive."

"I will tell our king and queen what you have said," promised Esofi. "I hope our people will come to trust you quickly. If we continue to go without dragon attacks, I think they'll be more inclined to. And...if possible, I might ask you to stay here in Fenstell for a few more days. I have many questions about your race. I would like to understand you better."

Ivanedi regarded her with his enormous silver eyes, then gave a nod. "I will return tomorrow. I will tell you whatever I can."

As they walked back to the fortress, Adale said, "You didn't tell him about Carinth."

Esofi only shrugged. "It didn't come up. Besides, we don't know if we can trust him."

"You seemed to get along with him."

"That's called diplomacy." There was a bit of an edge in her voice.

"Esofi..."

"What?"

"I'm sorry. I didn't mean to embarrass you." When Esofi did not respond, Adale added, "I just...you surprised me. Only a few days ago you were saying it's not worth the risk to help Ioanna, and then you turn around and want to help the dragons."

"Given how many of them I've killed, I think helping them earn back their magic is the least I could do."

Adale paused. "You still feel guilty?"

"Why shouldn't I?"

"Because—Esofi, you can't be serious! They were going to destroy us! The only reason they're interested in talking now is because you showed them that they wouldn't be able to kill us all!"

"They couldn't have spoken to me before because the Emperor ordered their silence!" Esofi retorted. "Under the Emperor's command, they had no will of their own. I cannot hold them accountable for that!"

"Maybe, but that still doesn't make it your fault. I'd blame the Emperor before I blamed you. I'd even blame Talcia before I blamed you. She's the one who gave the Emperor his abilities."

"Don't say that!"

"What? It's the truth. Talcia gave the Emperor the power to control the other dragons."

"The Emperor's actions were not her fault."

"Then it's his fault! Blame him. But don't blame yourself. There's nobody in the world who would have done it differently than you did."

They arrived back at their room and found not only Carinth and the guard, but also Mireille and two other guards, all crouched down on the floor like Carinth was a particularly cute puppy. When they saw Adale and Esofi standing in the doorway, they all leaped back to their feet and saluted awkwardly.

"I'm only paying that one," said Adale, pointing to the guard that she'd assigned to the task.

The guards left and Esofi picked Carinth up. He settled his neck across her back and rested his head on her other shoulder.

"Do you think we want to introduce Carinth to Ivanedi?" asked Adale.

"I would like to," said Esofi. "But at the same time, I don't want to make a mistake by trusting him too quickly."

"Do you think he'd try to take Carinth from us?" asked Mireille.

"I don't know. I hope not. But I would be concerned if I learned two dragons were raising a child. I can imagine they'd feel similar about us raising a hatchling."

"I don't feel like those two things are quite the same," Adale said.

"Maybe not, but I still want to be cautious." Esofi sank into a chair, and Carinth readjusted himself.

Adale went to put her boots away, considering everything she had seen. Ivanedi seemed earnest, but then, ambassadors always did. Still, what would the dragons gain from lulling them into a false peace? The Ieflarians hadn't attacked the Silver Isles once, even though immediately following the death of the Emperor would have been the ideal time to strike. Surely they'd worked out that Ieflaria wasn't planning on attacking them?

No, it seemed far more likely that the alliance was the first step in the dragons regaining their magic.

Adale still wasn't sure how she felt about that. Unblessed by any deity, she had lived her entire life without magic and was glad for it. Magic seemed like a lot of responsibility, piled on top of the responsibilities of being a princess. And it added another layer of politics to everything. The temple of whatever god had blessed her would be expecting favors, support, preferential treatment. And all the other temples would be watching hawkishly to raise their objections when she did.

At the same time, she thought she understood the dragons' desire to have magic again, to know they had been forgiven.

When Adale emerged from the bedroom, Esofi was talking to Carinth while Mireille sat with her embroidery in her lap and did nothing. She could tell from Esofi's tone that she was telling him a story and settled into a chair to listen.

"The next night, the shepherd boy was feeling bored and lonely again," Esofi was saying. "He tried his best to amuse himself, but the moors were quiet and unfriendly. When he could bear the solitude no more, he shouted, 'Wolf! Wolf!' And just as they had the previous two nights, the townspeople ran to save him with their torches and scythes.

"When the boy saw them, he cried out in triumph, 'I've fooled you again!' And fell to the ground laughing at the trick he had played. As the boy laughed, the townspeople all looked around at one another with very solemn faces. Then one stepped forward with his scythe raised high..." Esofi raised her arms above her head to demonstrate, and Carinth watched, enraptured. "And with a single swipe—"

"Excuse me, *what*?" interrupted Adale.

Esofi turned to her, arms still in the air. "Do you know this story? It's a classic."

"Yes, I know it. But you're telling it wrong."

"Of course I'm not!" said Esofi. "This is how it goes in Rhodia."

"That's not how *my* mother told it," said Mireille meekly. "Well, in Ieflaria, the boy's sheep get eaten by the wolves," said Adale.

"Serves him right, I suppose, but it seems a bit contrived."

"The way I always heard it was the wolves eat the sheep, *and* the boy," said Mireille.

Carinth grumbled, clearly irritated that Esofi was no longer paying attention to him.

"Well, I suppose you get to decide for yourself how it goes," she said to him, running her hand down his back. "You have three endings to choose from. It's too bad Lisette isn't here. I wonder what version she's heard."

"The one where the ground cracks open and the entire village falls in."

"Adale!" scolded Esofi, but Adale could barely hear her over Mireille's shrieking laughter.

ADALE WOKE EARLY the next morning. When she turned over she was surprised to see that Esofi was already gone, though Carinth was still asleep on her pillow.

A little bit concerned, Adale got up and dressed as quickly as she could. By the time she was done, Carinth had woken as well and was watching her curiously.

"Come on, you," said Adale. "Let's go walk around."

Carinth bounded after her eagerly.

Since their arrival, Adale had been thinking of borrowing a horse and exploring the surrounding forests or maybe the town. Back home, she had a custom-made saddle with a little bucket on one side for Carinth to sit in so he could accompany her on rides, but they'd been in such a hurry to leave that Adale had not thought to bring it along.

The sun was just beginning to rise over the camp as they stepped outside. A few guards were patrolling the walls, but there weren't too many other people around. Adale supposed nobody was feeling very nervous after a year of no attacks and the peaceful meeting with Ivanedi yesterday.

Not far away, Adale could see a structure with a familiar insignia on it, a single sword pointed upward, indicating that the building was a temple dedicated to Reygmadra. Given the number of soldiers here, Adale knew there had to be at least one or two of her priestesses around.

Sometimes it could be difficult to tell where the Temple of Reygmadra ended, and the Ieflarian military began. Officially, they were two separate entities, and the priestesses were not ranking officers. But there was a great deal of overlap in resources and responsibilities, and Adale knew her parents had to work to keep things balanced. If the temple did not have enough influence over the military, Reygmadra's gifts would go to waste, for her priestesses had the power to bestow temporary blessings on the soldiers that increased their strength and resistance to injuries. But if the temple was allowed to grow too powerful, her parents would be rulers in name only.

The Temple of Reygmadra had not given them any trouble during Adale's lifetime, but one only had to look to Xytae to see just how influential they could become if a regent gave them free rein.

At the sound of voices speaking in Rhodian, Adale turned hopefully toward the sound. But it wasn't Esofi. It was two blue-robed mages who had noticed Carinth. Adale stood back and watched as Carinth bounded over to them eagerly so he could go through their pockets while they cooed to him in Rhodian and patted his head.

"Have either of you seen Esofi?" asked Adale after a moment. "I've lost track of her."

The mages exchanged looks, like they weren't sure if they wanted to answer her, and Adale wondered if she'd have to rephrase her question as an order. But then one of them said, "I believe she is in one of the indoor practice rings."

Adale frowned. "What's she practicing for?"

"I do not know, Crown Princess," said the mage, stepping back. "Good morning."

Adale did not know where the practice rings were, but she decided she'd ask a guard, not another mage. The interaction had left her feeling unbalanced. Adale certainly did not expect anyone to fawn over her because of her rank as crown princess, but she was beginning to sense that the Rhodian mages did not respect her very much.

The first guard she found was emerging from the mess hall. When he saw Adale approaching, he froze and saluted.

"I'm supposed to go to the indoor practice rings, but I don't know where that is," said Adale. "Can you point me?"

"Of course, Crown Princess," said the man.

"I ran into some of the Rhodian mages earlier, but I didn't want to waste their precious time," said Adale, rolling her eyes. "I hope you have separate barracks."

She could tell the guard was considering her words. Doubtless he did not want to speak badly of anyone in front of her, but he probably also hadn't been expecting her to be so candid. When he finally did reply, he spoke slowly.

"They have their own living quarters," he said. "I think...they prefer to live separately."

"I expect we'd all prefer that, wouldn't we?" asked Adale, keeping her voice cheery. She knew from experience that it might take a little bit of time, but she was confident she would be able to get the guard's real opinion on the matter if she remained affable.

Because it was difficult to get people to tell the truth sometimes. She knew people were afraid of angering and offending her. She wished they wouldn't be. She felt like she could solve so many problems if people would just tell her exactly what they wanted.

"I can't speak for everyone, Crown Princess," said the guard.

"No, that's my job, isn't it? Do they all pretend like they can't speak Ieflarian, or have I just been lucky?"

"No, that's about how it goes most of the—" the guard began, but then he seemed to remember who he was addressing, and his tone changed abruptly. "That is, I'm sure...I'm sure it's difficult. Being stationed in a foreign country."

"Well, maybe we can send them home soon," said Adale.

"I think they'd like that, Crown Princess."

Adale gave a bark of laughter that echoed around the quiet grounds. "I'm surprised that dragon was able to get near enough to even deliver his message. I'd have thought the mages would be on him in a moment."

"It might have been, but it was only us on patrol when it came walking up. We raised the alarm, but by the time the mages arrived, we'd realized the dragon meant no harm."

"You don't patrol together, then?"

The guard shook his head. "Commander Gero and the Rhodian woman keep us separate."

That did not strike Adale as particularly efficient, and she frowned. How well could Fenstell function if the mages and soldiers were essentially two different factions? "I wonder if I should ask Commander Gero about it, then."

"Let me show you to the training rooms," said the guard. "The indoor ones are only really used by the mages."

He led her to another building, much smaller than the main fortress but made from the same Ieflarian pines. Adale went in and found herself standing in front of a desk where another bleary-eyed guard was apparently keeping watch. He did not appear to be completely awake as he looked down at the schedule in front of him and said, "All the rooms except the last one are empty, so you've got your pick."

"I'm searching for my wife, actually," said Adale.

The guard peered up at her, then jolted to his feet so quickly he knocked the entire desk forward. "Crown Princess!"

"It's all right," said Adale, raising her hands in a pacifying gesture. "Did Esofi come in here? Someone told me she did."

"She is in room six. All the way at the end, there," said the guard, gesturing to the hallway behind him. "But...she asked that nobody be permitted to interrupt her."

"I'm sure she didn't mean *me*," said Adale. The guard did not say anything, but he appeared to be a little uneasy. Still, he did not stop her as she strode down the hallway and pushed the door open.

The training room was empty, devoid of any furniture, though a large circle had been painted on the floor. Adale supposed this was for practice fights. At the center of the circle was Esofi.

To Adale's shock, Esofi had her skirt knotted at her waist, so that her lower legs were visible. She also was not wearing shoes or stockings. They had been discarded and set neatly in one corner of the room.

"What in the *world* are you doing?" asked Adale, closing the door behind her.

"Oh!" Esofi jumped. "Adale! You're awake."

"What's going on here?" Adale bit back a laugh.

"Oh, it's nothing. It's nothing." Esofi hastily began to untie the knots in her skirt, letting it fall back to the ground, and went over to retrieve her stockings.

"I don't get to know what's going on?"

"As I said, it's nothing."

Adale frowned. "Well, if you wanted to keep me out, you should have assigned a mage to guard the door, not a soldier."

Esofi paused to give her a strange look. "What do you mean by that?"

"I think it's quite obvious that the mages respect you more than they do me."

Esofi frowned. "Has something happened that I need to address?"

"No," said Adale hastily. "No, nothing like..." Nothing like the sharp snubs that occasionally happened at home, the ones that Adale had shrugged off for so long that it was always a shock when Esofi came to her defense with the sort of righteous fervor one might expect from a paladin.

"If it helps," said Esofi, "I think the Rhodians are more comfortable with me because we all made the journey together. But they've no right to treat you badly."

"There haven't been any incidents. Just...a feeling I get. Perhaps it's only my imagination. Don't reprimand them for that." It wasn't quite true, but Adale always hated it when Esofi took offense on her behalf. Not because she was embarrassed, but because Adale felt that she did not deserve it. She'd behaved so poorly for such a long time. She had not earned anyone's respect, so what right did she have to demand it?

Esofi finished putting her shoes on and stood back up. "I should send a courier to your parents, shouldn't I?"

"My parents?"

"Informing them that I do not believe Ivanedi is a threat to us. I'd hate for them to think I'd been eaten."

"I doubt they think that." Adale paused. "Have we had a courier from Birsgen?"

"Not yet," sighed Esofi. "It would be just my luck if she was blown off course all the way to Anora."

"Well, hire one to go home and mention we haven't had any word of your mother. They'll send another."

They exited the training rooms together, Carinth bounding ahead of them and climbing onto the guard's desk to see if he had anything interesting on hand.

"Carinth!" scolded Esofi, but he did not even flick his ears in her direction. Adale went to retrieve him, gripping him around the waist and lifting him up onto her shoulder.

"Come on, you," she said. "That's not yours."

The sun was rising very slowly, and the camp was slow to warm. Adale found herself inclined to get back into bed and do nothing for the rest of the morning. She wondered how she might convince Esofi to do the same.

"When do you think Ivanedi will come back?" asked Adale.

"I don't know. I hope it's earlier than tonight. There's so much I want to ask him." Esofi breathed into her hands to warm them.

Adale and Esofi had probably done more research on dragons than anyone else in Ieflaria, even before receiving the egg that eventually hatched into Carinth, but their sources were limited to texts so ancient they were near to crumbling into dust. Being able to ask Ivanedi questions would be a relief.

And they could finally find out when they should expect Carinth to start talking. Adale only hoped it would be during her own lifetime. She did not really think it would be that long, but she knew that dragons could outlive Men by centuries, so it was not completely impossible.

Would Talcia do that to them? To Esofi, who had done so much for her? It seemed cruel. And what about Carinth? What if he was still a child when Adale and Esofi died of old age? Would he even remember them as an adult?

These were questions she never allowed herself to dwell on for long and she had never brought up to Esofi. Nor had Esofi mentioned them to Adale. It was as though they'd both simultaneously come to the decision that they did not want to worry over something they could not possibly control. Not when there was so much work to be done.

Chapter Four

ESOFI

Adale was worried about her.

Perhaps it was to be expected, given everything that had happened over the last few days. Adale was protective by nature, even as Esofi repeatedly insisted she did not require protection.

If she was honest, Esofi supposed that the heart of the problem was that she could not begin to explain the present without first explaining her past. And that was something Esofi did not want to do. Not only would it take hours—if not days, or even weeks—but there were many parts she did not care to think about, let alone describe aloud. And then at the end of it, she just knew Adale would stare at her with pity and confusion on her face, and that would make things even worse.

She imagined it was something like a soldier trying to describe the experience of war to one who had never known anything but peace. As soon as the thought entered her head, Esofi pushed it away. To compare growing up in a palace with the battlefield was disrespectful to every soldier who had ever lifted a sword.

She knew Adale wanted to talk to her, to understand. But right now, the cost of that understanding was more than Esofi was willing to pay. So instead she pretended like nothing was wrong and that she did not notice Adale growing more and more concerned.

"We should write a book of our own," said Adale over lunch. "Of everything Ivanedi tells us. So in ten thousand years, when someone else has to raise a dragon, they know what to expect."

"Do you think there will still be Men in ten thousand years?" asked Esofi, passing a chicken leg over to Carinth. He gripped it in his little claws and began to pull the meat off the bone.

Adale laughed. "Don't you? Why shouldn't there be?"

Esofi shrugged. "It was only a thought."

"Think about other things," Adale suggested. "Make a list of what you want to ask Ivanedi. I know the minute I see him again I'll forget everything I wanted to ask."

"I can't imagine Carinth ever being that size," Esofi sighed. "He'll have to live outside."

"Nonsense, I'll build a castle for him. Dragon-sized." Adale leaned back and waved her arm, no doubt envisioning something absurd. "Everyone who sees it will say... 'Oh! Crown Princess! What a terrible waste of money!'"

Esofi could not help herself. She burst into laughter, and Adale sat up and grinned.

"There," said Adale. "I knew I could make you smile."

Someone knocked at the door, and Esofi looked up. "Come in," she called. But the door was already opening. Mireille stood there, her face pale and stricken.

"Mireille?" asked Esofi. "What's the matter?"

From the expression on Mireille's face, Esofi nearly expected her to say that a dragon was in the process of attacking Fenstell. But the young woman merely stood there, staring with wide brown eyes, lips trembling.

"Mireille?" repeated Esofi.

"She's here," said Mireille.

"Who is here?" Adale asked.

"Her majesty, Queen Gaelle of Rhodia. She has come to Fenstell."

Esofi's eyes flicked toward the window. Even in an Ieflarian dress, she probably would not fit through it.

"What?" demanded Adale, leaping to her feet. "Why didn't they send a courier to warn us?"

"I don't know! I don't know anything! I just know that she's just arrived, and she's out there in the courtyard, and she wants to see you!"

"Wait here," said Esofi, getting up and adjusting her dress. "Both of you." She hurried to the door, brushing past Mireille. Adale caught her by the arm.

"I'm coming as well."

"I said to stay!"

"Who is the Crown Princess here?" Adale's voice was surprisingly forceful, and Esofi's mouth fell open. Adale had never once used her rank to overrule Esofi before. Esofi had all but forgotten that Adale even could. "I'm coming with you. Mireille, watch Carinth for us."

Esofi moved quickly down the hallways, her mind spinning. She was aware that Adale was speaking to her, but she could not process the words. As she approached the main doors to the fortress, a guard opened them for her.

Esofi stepped out into the frosty afternoon light and saw a carriage standing in the courtyard. Standing in front of it were two women, both blonde, both dressed in Rhodian gowns. Some of the Rhodian mages, including Lieutenant Vaseur, were already gathered before them.

Esofi reached for her skirts, only to remember she was wearing an Ieflarian dress. Feeling underdressed for the first time in over a year, Esofi moved forward with Adale at her side.

Gaelle did not look any different than she had the last time Esofi had seen her, on the day she departed Rhodia. Her sharp face still showed only a few signs of age, and her hair still had most of its pale blonde color. She wore a silver and white gown, still elaborate by Ieflarian standards but considered suitable for an older, married woman in Rhodia.

Esofi glanced to the other woman behind her mother and was surprised to realize that it was Lexandrie. Unlike Gaelle, Lexandrie did not seem at all like herself. Her hair was limp and badly styled, and she appeared thinner, so much so that she was almost lost in her own gown. When she realized Esofi was staring at her, she refused to make eye contact and stared down at the ground.

Esofi turned her eyes back to her mother, soft puffs of icy breath dissipating into the morning air. Naturally, Gaelle was the one to break the silence.

"Oh, good," she said. "You're pregnant."

Esofi found her tongue. "No, mother. Just fat."

Gaelle made a short, sharp sound that might have been a laugh. "Where is my grandson? I've travelled months to see him."

"What?"

"The dragon. Did you think I would not come as soon as I heard? Or had you hoped to hide it from me?"

Esofi swallowed, being careful not to show any trace of emotion on her face. "I did not think you would care. You showed no interest in Esolene or Matheo's children."

"Esolene and Matheo's children cannot fly."

"Carinth cannot fly yet either," said Esofi.

"Is that what you named him?"

Esofi nodded. "It is a name from Ieflarian legend. We—"

"I want to know exactly how you came to have him," Gaelle interrupted. "I am skeptical of Lexandrie's tale."

Esofi looked back at Lexandrie again. "I am surprised to see you here. It seems you only just left."

"I needed an attendant, and Lexandrie is already familiar with this country. She was the sensible choice."

Beside her, Adale cleared her throat.

"Mother, this is Crown Princess Adale," Esofi said, switching over to the Ieflarian language. "We were married last spring."

Gaelle's eyes flicked over Adale briefly. "It is too cold to talk out here. I'm going inside."

She swept past Esofi and Adale and into the fortress. Esofi turned to Lexandrie, who still did not meet her eyes. For a minute, she considered saying something, but then decided against it. Her mother required her complete and undivided attention. Hopefully, there would be time to talk later.

CARINTH SNIFFED GAELLE'S hands, examining each of her rings in turn. Tea had been laid out at a table for them, but Esofi remained standing, her entire body tensed, waiting to spring forward at the first sign of trouble.

But Gaelle seemed uncharacteristically pleased by him.

"So small," marveled Gaelle, tapping at the horns on his head. "How long before he is grown?"

"We're not certain. I am hoping the other dragons can tell us."

"Does he breathe fire?"

"Not yet."

"And he does not fly." Gaelle sounded more thoughtful than annoyed. "Well, I'm sure I can make something of him nevertheless."

"He is not yet two years old," Esofi reminded her. "If he was a child, he would still be in the nursery."

Gaelle did not respond to that. Instead she said, "When do you intend to return to the capital?"

"Within a few days, I think. You needn't have come all this way."

"Nobody could tell me when you were planning on returning. I do not have the time or the inclination to sit in a foreign castle waiting for you to remember your responsibilities."

Esofi fought down a frown. "This is not an excursion. Adale and I came to Fenstell to meet with a representative from the Silver Isles, to foster peace between our races."

"I can't be away from Rhodia forever," said Gaelle. "I want this business done with as soon as possible."

"And what business is that?" asked Adale. Gaelle pressed her lips together, openly disapproving. Adale's entire body tensed, and Esofi glanced over at her worriedly. Adale was frowning, and her hands were curling into fists.

But Gaelle did not reply to the question. Instead she petted Carinth's head again and said, "Have there been any threats against him? I'd think perhaps some people might want revenge, given Ieflaria's history with dragons."

"We were afraid of that, at first," said Esofi, moving to sit down in the chair beside Adale. "When he was still an egg, I didn't trust anyone but our Rhodian mages to guard him. But nobody has expressed any desire to harm him. In fact, he seems to be popular."

"What about the Xytan Empire?" Gaelle pressed. "They must be concerned."

"We hear very little from Xytae. Their ambassador sent congratulations, but I don't know if the news has truly reached Ionnes. He spends more time in Masim than at home."

Gaelle looked discontented, so much so that Esofi wondered if she truly was worried about Carinth's safety. That would be very much unlike her. But then, Carinth was a dragon, not a child. So perhaps there was no knowing what to expect.

"How are things in Rhodia?" asked Esofi, eager to change the subject. "Is Esybele still at home?"

"She is off sailing with the Alliance. Perhaps I ought to find her a husband. Though I do not know who would ever agree to marry her."

"What is the Alliance?" asked Adale.

"It is the force that deals with threats from the Elven Lands," explained Esofi. "All of the Thiyran nations contribute to it. We are also aided by the Mer."

"Two elves came to Ioshora when I was a girl," said Adale. "I didn't think much of it at the time, but now I'm surprised they managed to get past you."

"Men do trade in Domeysil. There's not much we can do to stop them, unfortunately. Perhaps they booked passage on a merchant ship," suggested Esofi.

"What did they want?" Gaelle's eyes narrowed.

"I'm not sure, I was too young to really understand. I think they just wanted access to our lands. My parents could tell you better than I." Adale shrugged. "In any case, they didn't get what they wanted. I never saw another elf again after that day."

"You had one in the castle?" The disdain in Gaelle's voice was like poison.

"Two, actually," said Adale. Either she was oblivious to Gaelle's reactions, or she was enjoying them. Esofi suspected it was the latter. "I don't think they stayed long. Nobody liked them very much."

"Elves may not set foot in any of the nations of Ioshora," said Gaelle harshly. "And yet you had two in your capital? In your castle? How was this allowed?"

"Don't blame me, I was a child at the time."

"It was a single incident, I am told." Esofi hurried to quell Gaelle's temper. "I believe they were trying to establish diplomatic relations. But their offer was rejected, and they never returned."

"They tried Xytae and Vesolda and Ibaia as well," Adale added. "Nobody took them up on it."

"Why didn't you arrest them?" demanded Gaelle.

"I don't know. You'll have to ask my parents. They didn't do any harm while they were here though."

"As far as you know," said Gaelle.

Adale just shrugged, untroubled.

"Lexandrie," said Esofi, desperate to change the subject. "How was your voyage?"

Lexandrie looked up from her teacup, surprise in her face. It seemed she had not been expecting anyone to address her. "It was fine," she said, her voice barely more than a murmur. "Uneventful."

"I'm glad to hear that," said Esofi, forcing enthusiasm into her voice. But Lexandrie did not reply.

The silence stretched on painfully. Beside her, Adale was starting to fidget, a sure sign that she was about to do something absurd for her own amusement.

"You have been speaking with dragons?" said Gaelle at last.

Esofi nodded. "Yes! It was a great surprise to learn they are capable of speech. When Ivanedi returns tonight, I am hoping to ask him some questions about Carinth's development."

"How do they feel about you two raising one of their own?"

"We have not told him yet. But...I do not believe he would attempt to take Carinth from us."

"No?"

"I should start from the beginning," said Esofi. "So much has happened since I arrived here."

Gaelle listened impassively as Esofi described her arrival in Ieflaria and the first dragon attack at Birsgen, where she had learned that they were capable of speech. Esofi skipped over the complicated mess that had been her courtship with Adale, and the research they had done together. She knew her mother would have no interest in that.

She described the Emperor's attack on the night of her betrothal and how he had blamed Men for the fact that Talcia was no longer granting magic to his kind. With his death, the attacks on Ieflaria had stopped, and they had heard nothing more until a few days ago, when Ivanedi arrived in Fenstell.

"I know they want their magic back. They're hoping I can help them with that," concluded Esofi. "That is why I don't believe they'd risk stealing Carinth from me."

Gaelle looked down at Carinth again. There was something calculating in her eyes. She got up out of her chair, and Esofi tensed again.

But then Gaelle crouched down so that she was level with Carinth. Esofi frowned and readied herself to lunge across the table at the first sign of trouble.

Gaelle held her hand out between herself and Carinth, only a short distance away from his own nose. Carinth sniffed at it, then settled back, assured that she was not hiding anything good in her palm.

Gaelle curled her fingers and a little spark of blood-colored magic flashed to life, dancing like candlelight. Carinth sniffed at her hand again but didn't seem terribly interested. If he could not eat it or hoard it, it wasn't important.

But Gaelle did not move. She frowned and shook her hand meaningfully. After a brief pause, Carinth raised his front arm in the same way she had, little claws curling inward.

Esofi felt her lips part to ask a question just as a little spark of azure light flickered at the edge of Carinth's silver claws.

Adale spat her tea out onto the table, and Esofi jumped up so quickly that she nearly knocked her chair over. She was beside Carinth in a moment, but the magic was already gone. He looked from Esofi to Gaelle, who was now sipping her tea calmly. His ears flicked, like he was not certain if he was in trouble or not.

Esofi took Carinth's claw in her hand very gently, waiting to see if he would summon his magic again. But he only looked in the direction of the table, clearly more interested in the sugar bowl than what had just transpired. Heart racing, Esofi took a few deep breaths. What did it mean, that Carinth had magic? Was Talcia giving magic to all newborn dragons? Or was Carinth a special case because he was being raised by her? Would only the young dragons be granted magic, or would it be a repeat of what had happened in Birsgen two springs ago, when grown adults found themselves suddenly blessed?

"Did you not attempt to see if he had been granted magic?" asked Gaelle scornfully.

"I did not think..." Esofi shook her head.

"Evidently not. Well, I think this settles the matter. I must bring him to Rhodia."

"What?" Adale interrupted. "No!"

But Gaelle was not even pretending to care about anything Adale said. "You can't expect anyone here to be worthy of the task of teaching him, let alone competent enough to do so. Letting him remain here would be negligent. I will not allow it."

Esofi's mouth had gone dry. She wanted to speak, but it seemed she had forgotten how. She gathered Carinth in her arms and stood up, trying to think of something to say, acutely aware of the lump rising in her throat.

"Carinth isn't going anywhere," Adale said. "He was given to us, and he's staying with us. Esofi is more than capable of training him."

"You did not even know he had magic," Gaelle waved her hand dismissively. "I won't let you two raise him to be an embarrassment to my family."

"Then it's a good thing we don't need your permission." The venom in Adale's voice surprised Esofi. "I don't have to sit here and listen to this. Esofi, let's go."

"What?"

"We're leaving!" Adale got up and walked to the door. "The food isn't nearly good enough for me to put up with this conversation."

"But..." Esofi looked from Gaelle to Adale. "We can't just—"

Adale seemed to realize Esofi was not going to leave of her own free will, so she walked behind her and put her hands on her shoulders. "Come on," she said, steering

Esofi toward the door. Carinth licked her nose. "Hey. Stop that. I'm trying to be serious here."

"We're not finished here, Esofi!" Gaelle called after her in a warning voice.

Esofi did not respond, but her arms tightened around Carinth. If not for Adale's hands on her shoulders, she knew she would have turned around and gone back to the table.

"Esofi!" She heard silk rustling and knew Gaelle was finally getting out of her chair. "I'm not going to tell you again!"

Adale dipped her head closer to Esofi's ear. "It's fine," she whispered. "Just keep walking."

"I'm sorry," said Esofi, and she was not certain if she was addressing her mother, or Adale, or Carinth.

Esofi had been expecting Adale to push her all the way back to their room, but it seemed she had a different destination in mind. She guided Esofi to the fortress's main entrance, and they went outside, where the carriage was still standing.

Esofi barely felt the cold. She couldn't feel her legs at all, and if not for the fact that she was holding Carinth to her chest, she knew her hands would be shaking.

"Esofi!" Gaelle had followed them out. "Where do you think you're going?"

Esofi faltered, even as Adale tried to spirit her along. "Keep moving," Adale murmured. "Come on. You'll be fine."

"Stop!" cried Lexandrie, and Esofi finally did. She turned, curious to hear what her cousin might have to say.

But Lexandrie had not been speaking to Esofi at all. Both her hands were gripping Gaelle's arm, and Esofi realized why. Gaelle's hand was glowing once again, blood-colored magic gathering like an angry storm.

"Your majesty, please," Lexandrie said, desperation in her face. "They will arrest you."

That got Adale's attention, and she turned around too. Her expression changed from irritated to incredulous as she took in the scene before her. Esofi watched her lips part, but no sound emerged. Adale was at a loss for words.

Eyes alight with rage, Gaelle stepped toward Lexandrie and brought her hands to the other's throat. Lexandrie's eyes widened and she grabbed at Gaelle's hands, gasping and desperate.

"Guards!" screamed Adale. A few people ran up, but they were all Rhodian mages. And when they saw Gaelle, they froze, uncertain.

But then, a burst of emerald green magic hit Gaelle in the chest. Her fingers came free of Lexandrie's neck and she staggered backward. Esofi spun around to see who had been foolish—or mad—enough to attack Gaelle and found herself staring at not one of her fellow Rhodians, but a rare Ieflarian mage, a young woman with her braids in two coiled buns. Just behind her was another mage, this one a young man with the same dark hair.

Both wore high-necked blue robes, similar to the ones the Rhodians wore. But these robes were ordinary blue instead of midnight-blue, and they had none of the silver embellishments the more experienced mages had. Esofi recognized them in an instant, and her mouth fell open in shock.

"What—what are you doing here?" demanded Adale before Esofi could say anything.

"We're stationed here," said Brandt unhelpfully. Meanwhile, Svana had gone over to Lexandrie and was helping her back to her feet, her body a shield between Lexandrie and Gaelle.

Esofi had not seen or heard of the twins since the day they'd been sent away from Birsgen. She had assumed they were staying in Valenleht. But there was no time to reflect on that, because Esofi could see blood-colored magic gathering at Gaelle's hands again. She would have to act quickly if she wanted Svana to live.

Esofi thrust Carinth into Adale's arms. Then she hurried forward and stepped between her mother and Svana, squaring her shoulders and setting her jaw.

"You need to stop," she said in the calmest voice she could manage.

"Get out of my way," snarled Gaelle.

"That mage is the daughter of Duke Raldfur," Esofi said, even though she knew that would not be enough to quell her mother's rage. As predicted, Gaelle tried to push past her, but Esofi took a step back to block her.

"I want her arrested, then!" cried Gaelle. A few of the Rhodian mages began to move forward.

"Hold!" snapped Esofi. "She has done nothing worthy of arrest."

The Rhodian mages all looked around at one another, uncertain. Esofi felt a little bad for putting them in such a position. She knew it could not be easy for them, deciding who to follow. They were on Ieflarian soil, and Esofi was paying their salaries. Nevertheless, Gaelle was their queen.

But now the Ieflarian soldiers Adale had called for were arriving. And they did not appear indecisive at all.

"I want her *arrested*," Gaelle said again, but she seemed to realize that this was not going to happen. "Fine, then. I demand a duel with her, for the insult she has dealt me."

Svana opened her mouth, but Esofi spoke first.

"That will not be possible," she said. Her mind was spinning, but her voice was surprisingly steady. "For you see...I have decided to appoint Lady Svana as...my waiting lady."

"What?" said Gaelle.

"What?" said Svana.

"What?" cried Adale.

Esofi swallowed visibly. "You and Queen Saski are always saying I should select an Ieflarian waiting lady. I think you're right. Lady Svana, do you accept this position?"

Svana looked at her brother, as if seeking confirmation that she was hearing Esofi's words correctly. Brandt just shrugged, then nodded.

"I...do?" said Svana.

"Excellent. Then my first order to you is that you may *not* accept any duels until you have achieved master rank. Do you understand?"

"But—"

"Good." Esofi grabbed Svana by the arm, digging her fingers in so that Svana realized she was serious. "Here, come with me. I need someone to press my..." Esofi faltered. "...stockings."

"Esofi!" hissed Adale. "What are you *doing*? Is this a joke?"

"Oh," Esofi gave a high, fake laugh. "Stop teasing me. Please excuse us, Mother. I must show Lady Svana where we are staying."

Chapter Five

ADALE

In Adale's opinion, she had tolerated a great deal of absurdity over the course of the last week. And as they returned to their room in the main citadel, she felt she was finally on the verge of boiling over.

The only thing that kept her temper in check was the fact that Svana was being quiet. Adale had been expecting her cousin to start gloating as soon as they were away from Gaelle, but Svana seemed uncharacteristically subdued.

Esofi shut the door behind them and locked it, breathing heavily. Adale set Carinth down on the floor, and he immediately went to sniff at Svana's earrings.

"This is your fault," Adale informed Svana.

"Actually, I'd say it's *yours*," Esofi interrupted before Svana could retort.

"Mine!" Adale felt as though she had been slapped. "How in all the planes in all of Asterium is any of this my fault?"

"If we'd just stayed at the table—"

"And let her insult us?"

"Yes!"

"No. She has no right to speak to us that way. I don't care where she's queen of or how many cults she leads."

"She is my mother."

"Well, she's not very good at it, is she?" Adale retorted. "She's come here to steal Carinth. I don't see why I shouldn't tell my parents to put her on the next ship out of here."

"Perhaps if *your* parents had spent any time educating you, you would know why that cannot be done!"

Adale was dumbstruck. Yes, she knew she had neglected her education as a girl, and her parents had let her get away with it because they had Albion to be their heir. But that wasn't *their* fault, it was hers. And perhaps it was irrational, but she resented the implication that her parents had been inadequate—especially given what she had just seen of Gaelle.

Adale stormed past Svana and Mireille and went out into the hallway. Esofi did not follow her.

She was only a handful of steps away from their door when she nearly collided with Brandt. Like Svana, he seemed uncharacteristically subdued, and did not greet her with the haughty smirk that she had come to expect from him. It was unnerving.

"What was all *that*?" he asked. For a moment, Adale wondered if he'd heard her fight with Esofi, but then she realized he was referring to Gaelle's behavior. Adale gave a shuddering shrug in reply. "Are we sure that's Esofi's mother?"

"What are you doing here?"

"I'm searching for my sister."

"What are you doing *in Fenstell*?"

Brandt seemed to collect himself. He gave a weary sigh and ran his fingers through his hair. "If you must know, our parents were...cross with us...after that terrible misunderstanding at the betrothal party. They said we could join the defense in the north or be disinherited. We chose to come here."

"That's—"

"It's not as bad as you'd think. We haven't actually had any dragon attacks. And the Rhodian battlemages know all sorts of interesting techniques. I'd take this sort of training over boring temple meditation. Don't tell Esofi I said so."

"So you're not being punished at all?"

"Of course we are! The food is dreadful, my best socks were stolen a week after we arrived, and they force us to wake at dawn even if we're not on duty. Furthermore, I'm certain that half these Rhodians are in some sort of cult."

Adale rubbed her forehead. As if Gaelle's sudden appearance wasn't enough, now she had her cousins to contend with once again.

"We were sorry to miss your wedding," added Brandt. "We sent a gift. Did you receive it?"

"Seeing as I have not been poisoned, I can only assume it was lost in transit," said Adale.

"Oh, don't be so melodramatic! You got what you wanted in the end, didn't you?"

Continuing this conversation would require both time and patience that Adale did not currently possess, so she said, "Svana's in there. If the two of you try anything with Esofi, I'll kill you with my own hands."

"What are you talking about?" Brandt scoffed, incredulous. "Neither of us have any reason to harm Esofi. We never have. You need to move past your petty grudge."

Before Adale could formulate a response, Brandt pushed past her and knocked at the bedroom door.

"Hey!" cried Adale, but the door was already opening. Mireille peeked out anxiously.

"Hello," said Brandt with a winning smile. "Is my sister about?"

"Ummm. Yes," said Mireille.

Adale did not want to go back into the room so soon after her dramatic exit, but she did not want Esofi alone with the twins, either. So she gritted her teeth and followed Brandt in.

Esofi was sitting on the sofa with Carinth settled in her lap. Her eyes were distant and unfocused.

"Brandt is here," announced Adale, mostly for lack of anything better to say.

"Oh," Esofi looked up at him. "Brandt."

"It is good to see you again, Princess," he said. "Congratulations on your wedding."

"Thank you," said Esofi, in a very subdued voice. She did nothing as Brandt reached forward and touched Carinth's head tentatively. "How long have you two been here?"

"About a year and a half," said Brandt. "It hasn't been easy, but we're learning a great deal from the Rhodian mages."

Brandt and Svana had not been born with Talcia's magic. It had been granted to them later in life—something Adale had not even known was possible. They'd been among the hundreds of Ieflarians granted magic shortly after Esofi's arrival.

Unfortunately, one of the first things they'd used their magic for was kidnapping Adale and locking her in Albion's old room in an effort to prevent her engagement to Esofi. Adale still was not sure why Talcia thought giving them magic was a good idea.

"I hope Helaine hasn't been making you too miserable," said Esofi. Adale bristled. She hoped the opposite!

"She is strict," agreed Brandt. "But she was impressed when she learned the two of us can share our magic."

"You two can share your magic?"

"Well, we share everything else," said Brandt.

"We won every fight we were challenged to in the first month before the others caught on." Svana smiled. "That was a good month."

"Gods," muttered Adale, rolling her eyes.

"Did someone teach you the technique, or did you discover it yourselves?" asked Esofi, who apparently found the whole thing far more interesting than Adale did.

"We discovered it by accident," said Brandt. "It seemed useful, but we didn't think to report it to anyone. Helaine threw a fit when she found out. She seemed to be under the impression that we'd accidentally kill ourselves and she'd have to explain it to Father. Naturally, I told her not to worry. Father would be thrilled if we died."

"Brandt!" objected Esofi.

"So we spent a few weeks learning how to not drain each other. It wasn't terribly difficult."

"If I bring you back to Birsgen, will your parents still disown you?" asked Esofi.

"If it was by your command, I doubt they would be able to object," said Brandt. "We would not mind leaving Fenstell."

Adale groaned. Everyone ignored her.

"But what has happened to Lady Lexandrie?" asked Svana. "Is she well?"

"I don't know," Esofi admitted. "She went back to Rhodia after the wedding. I never expected to see her again. But my mother forced her to accompany her here. She does not serve me any longer."

"I am sorry to hear that," said Svana.

Adale gave her a strange look. "What do you care?"

Svana appeared to be legitimately surprised by the question. She seemed to struggle with an answer. "Why— well, why shouldn't I?" she asked at last. "I'd be worried about anyone employed by that woman."

"I don't know if there's anything I can do for Lexandrie," said Esofi.

"Queen Gaelle cannot treat anyone in that way. Not while she is in Ieflaria," insisted Svana. "Even if Lexandrie is her subject, we have laws against attacking one's servants. You should have let me accept her challenge."

"You'd have me witness a murder so soon after breakfast?"

Either Svana had become an excellent actor in the last year, or her body had been taken over by some kind of trickster spirit. Adale was not sure which was more likely. Maybe she would ask a priest to check her for signs of possession.

"I think we *should* go back to Birsgen," said Adale. "There's more guards, and my parents will keep her busy. Once she sees we're not giving her Carinth, she'll leave."

"Is that what she wants?" asked Brandt.

"So it seems," said Esofi.

"Tell her to go to the Silver Isles and steal an egg of her own if she wants one so badly," suggested Svana.

"Do not give her that idea." Esofi shook her head. "She might do it."

It was difficult to keep her anger up when Esofi seemed so subdued, even with her cousins in the room. Adale was not sorry for what she had said, but she was sorry Esofi was so miserable. She decided she would back down, for now. Besides, she did not want the twins to suspect something might be seriously wrong, for fear they might try to twist it to their advantage.

"When did you want to start teaching Carinth to use his magic?" asked Adale.

Esofi cheered up a little at the reminder. "I don't know. Can you believe it? I don't think it even occurred to me that he might have magic. Maybe that was foolish of me—"

"No," said Adale. "Don't listen to her. How could you have guessed that? And we'd have figured it out sooner or later."

"Well, I should probably start with some mediation exercises," said Esofi. "I doubt he'll be capable of much until he gets older. But it won't hurt for him to become accustomed to it."

Carinth seemed to realize they were talking about him and looked from Adale to Esofi with curiosity in his golden eyes.

"What if we enrolled him in the University?" asked Adale. There were only a handful of children in training, those rare few that had been born with Talcia's magic before Esofi had arrived in Ieflaria. Adale knew that, if not for Esofi, most of them would have neglected or outright ignored their gifts.

But Esofi had been instrumental in changing people's minds about Talcia and her magic. The creation of the University had not hurt, either. Nowadays, a blessing from Talcia was seen as honorable and prestigious, rather than a mark of a chaotic nature.

"Perhaps," said Esofi. "I don't know if he would learn in the same way as an ordinary child, but I suppose it couldn't hurt to try."

Adale sat down beside Esofi, wishing the twins would leave so they could talk. But she could hardly order them out of the room—and right now, it might even be dangerous to do so, given they could easily encounter Gaelle again. Adale wouldn't admit it out loud, but she did not really think they deserved whatever Gaelle wanted to do to them. Besides, they'd acted to protect Lexandrie. That was something she would never have expected from them.

She thought of Gaelle's hands around Lexandrie's throat and wondered if she'd ever done the same to Esofi. The idea filled her with rage, and it must have shown, because Esofi gave her a strange look.

"What's the matter?" she asked. Her eyes were pretty, Adale realized for what had to be the thousandth time, soft brown and framed by long, pale lashes that made her seem so very delicate.

"It's nothing," Adale said. Then, so Esofi would know that she was not being deliberately noncommunicative, she glanced over at her cousins to indicate she did not want to speak in front of them.

Esofi lowered her eyes again and nodded minutely. Adale set her hand on top of Esofi's in what she hoped was a reassuring gesture, rather than oppressive. It might have only been wishful thinking, but she thought she felt Esofi relax just a little bit.

IVANEDI RETURNED AFTER midday but before sundown. This time, when Adale and Esofi went out to meet him, they brought Carinth with them.

In the meantime, Adale had sent a courier to Birsgen, explaining that their meeting with Ivanedi had been successful, and they would be on their way home the following day. She'd also added a strongly worded note at the end asking why no courier had come to warn them of Gaelle's arrival.

There had been no other signs of Gaelle, and Adale hoped it would stay that way. She did not want Gaelle to have a chance to be alone with Esofi. There was no guessing what the woman would do or say if Adale wasn't there to step in.

Adale could not begin to understand the dynamics of Esofi's family. It seemed Gaelle had no interest in any of her children, and her children were not overly fond of one another, and Esofi's father ignored all of it. Was that really just how Rhodian families were? Esofi seemed to think so, but Adale could not believe it. Surely the entire nation would fall apart if everyone hated one another?

Ivanedi was waiting for them in the same place where they'd met before, every bit as intimidating as Adale remembered. But when he spotted Carinth, Adale saw his eyes soften, and he lowered his head to sniff at Carinth.

Carinth was absurdly small beside Ivanedi, small enough to climb onto his nose and settle there if he wanted. But he did not do this. In fact, he seemed nervous and stayed securely in Esofi's arms as Ivanedi inspected him.

"His name is Carinth," explained Adale. "It was the only dragon name we knew."

"But...where are his parents?"

"We are his parents," said Esofi. "After I defeated the Emperor, Talcia came to me in a vision. When I awoke, I was holding an egg. We have cared for him since that day as best we can."

"She spoke to you?" Ivanedi tilted his head to the side. "What did she say?"

"I told her I was sorry for killing so many dragons. I did not know that you were capable of thought. She didn't seem angry with me. She seemed...sad. I know she wants the dragons to improve. I don't know exactly why she gave me Carinth, but we were hoping he might be a bridge between our races, when he gets older."

Ivanedi's reptilian face was difficult to read, but Adale thought he seemed pensive.

"Our knowledge of dragon development is limited," said Adale. "We're doing our best with him, but we don't really know what to expect."

"I would never advise raising a dragon among Men, but if you say it was our mother's will... Still, do you not believe he would be better among his own kind?"

"I'm not sure," said Esofi. "I worry that he will grow up feeling like an outsider, not a Man but not really a dragon. I don't want that for him. But I do not believe Talcia gave him to us simply for her own amusement. And...perhaps it is selfish to say, but I do not wish to give him up. It would be like losing my own son."

"I would urge you to bring him with you, if you do visit the Silver Isles," suggested Ivanedi. "He can be among his own kind and meet other hatchlings. And we will teach him our language."

"Do you know how soon we might expect him to learn to fly?" asked Esofi. "The books we've found have told us he ought to have started trying at a year old, but he seems to be lagging behind..."

"All hatchlings develop at their own pace. I would not begin to worry until he has reached five years of age. It is the same with speech. He may begin tomorrow, or he may remain silent for a few years yet."

That was simultaneously a relief and disappointing. Of course Adale was happy that there wasn't anything wrong with Carinth. But four years seemed a terribly long time to wait for him to begin speaking.

"And how long do dragons live?" asked Esofi. "From what we have read, it seems your lives are considerably longer than ours."

"The eldest among us have reached three hundred years old," said Ivanedi. "I, myself, am one hundred and ninety. But this is rare, for we are more likely to be killed long before reaching old age. Life is harsh in the Silver Isles. Parents may expect only one or two of their hatchlings to survive to adolescence. After that, the greatest threat to a young adult dragon is other dragons. Fights over territory or food or hoarded treasure are the most common causes of death. Those adventurous ones who leave the Isles to live in the lands of Men are in even greater danger."

"What is killing them as hatchlings?" asked Esofi.

"When they are at their smallest, even a wildcat can carry one off," said Ivanedi. "It is not uncommon for hatchlings to have only a single parent as a caretaker. When the mother leaves to hunt, the hatchlings are vulnerable to everything else that dwells on the Isles. The greatest threat to a hatchling's life, though, is a gryphon."

"Really?" Adale did not know very much about gryphons, besides the fact that a few families depicted them on their coat of arms. Gryphons could be found in parts of northern Ieflaria and were known to be dangerous when provoked. But few ever saw them, because they tended to live deep in the wilderness or high up on mountain peaks and did not make a habit of attacking Men. "I'd think you'd be allies. You have the same mother, don't you?"

"The matter is complex," said Ivanedi. "Over the last few centuries, our race has managed to alienate not only your kind, but all of our cousins."

Adale was beginning to understand why Talcia had taken the dragon's magic away.

"So they attack your hatchings?" asked Esofi.

"It is unfortunate," said Ivanedi. "We kill them where we find them, and they do the same to our young. I cannot say who first began the cycle of violence, but it seems it may never end."

"Do you think you could beat a gryphon?" Adale asked Esofi. Interesting as the Silver Isles sounded, she didn't want to go there if Carinth's life would be in danger.

"I imagine so. They're supposed to be much smaller than dragons. But I've never seen one myself."

"They still have their magic," cautioned Ivanedi. "Some of them can be quite formidable."

Adale tried to imagine a gryphon balancing on his hindquarters while his scaly bird claws wielded Talcia's magic. Surely it would tip over?

"There is something else I'd like to understand," said Esofi. "I've been trying my best to piece it together, but your last Emperor...how many years did he reign? I understand that Ieflaria has withstood dragon attacks for all of recorded history, but they only began to escalate within the last few decades."

"Zethe was granted the Emperor's Song approximately one hundred years ago," said Ivanedi. "But he did not begin by ordering attacks—if he had, he would not have remained in power for long. One of his first commands was to forbid us from speaking to Men. At the time, we wondered why he bothered. Very few of us had any inclination to speak with Men in any case."

"It's not just dragons," said Esofi. "The unicorns, and all the other creatures that Talcia made—they do not speak to us, either."

Ivanedi lowered his head in what Adale was beginning to understand was his version of a nod. "We all take after our mother."

"How far does the Emperor's influence reach?" asked Adale. "Was he able to control dragons all over the world, or is there a limit to his range?"

"The Song has an impressive reach, but it is not unlimited. Zethe was able to call dragons from as far as Ibaia and the northernmost parts of Aquuim. But you've nothing to fear. As I said yesterday, I doubt we will have another Emperor for generations."

"I believe you," said Esofi. "I'm merely curious. It's such a strange blessing, I've never heard of anything like it."

"Some say that it is not truly a blessing, and I might be inclined to agree," said Ivanedi. "Mother revoked our magic long ago; that is not a secret. But we retained our breath of fire, as well as the Emperor's Song. Some point to this as evidence that we have not been completely abandoned. But I suspect those are skills intrinsic to our kind, no different than flight."

"They certainly seem like a blessing to me," said Esofi. "But if they were, I suppose we might see more races with those abilities. Still, I do not like to think she has abandoned you. If it is any consolation, we have just learned that Carinth has magic of his own."

"What?" Ivanedi started. "Are you certain?"

"Yes. It was my mother who managed to draw it out of him, only just today."

"Your mother?" Ivanedi interrupted.

Esofi nodded. "Yes, she was always good at—"

"Is she here?"

"Well...yes." Esofi blinked up at him in confusion. Ivanedi was shifting, and Adale pulled Esofi back out of the way of a massive claw as his feet adjusted. "Is something the matter?"

"I must go," said Ivanedi.

"Do you...do you *know* her?" Esofi frowned. "How could you possibly—"

"My invitation stands. Bring your hatchling to the Isles. You will be safe there. Now I must bid you farewell." Ivanedi inclined his head slightly, then unfurled his wings. Within a moment, he was in the sky, shrinking in Adale's vision until he was nothing more than a black speck on the horizon.

"What just happened?" asked Adale, dazed.

"I'm not certain." Esofi set Carinth down on the ground. "Do you think I might have offended him?"

"It almost sounded like..."

"Like he knew her. But that's impossible. My mother has never come to Ioshora before now."

"Well, maybe Ivanedi has been to Rhodia," suggested Adale. "Back when he was young and adventurous."

"I don't think so. My mother would never face a dragon and allow it to live. And if one was ever her ally, we'd have never heard the end of it."

They began the walk back to their room together, just as they had yesterday. Carinth ran ahead of them, occasionally pausing to examine things that caught his interest. When he returned to them, he had a silver coin clutched in his claws.

"What's that?" asked Adale. She took it from Carinth and turned it over in her palm. "Oh, it's not Ieflarian. Is this Rhodian?" She showed it to Esofi.

"Yes," said Esofi. "One of the mages must have dropped it."

Carinth looked up at Adale expectantly, and Adale gave the coin back to him. "Don't put it in your mouth," she warned because Carinth had swallowed coins in the past. The first time it had happened, they'd panicked. Carinth had been much smaller then, and even though the healers said that he was showing no signs of choking or poisoning, Esofi had insisted they feed him something to make him throw it back up.

Unfortunately, the serum that the healers used to induce vomiting didn't work on Carinth. Apparently dragons had stronger stomachs than Men. The healers had shrugged and said that if the serum did not make him sick, it was unlikely a single coin could harm him.

Adale had been prepared to accept that answer, especially since the healers assured her that small children swallowed coins every day. But Esofi had pried Carinth's mouth open and forced her fingers down his throat until he spat the coin—and everything else he'd eaten that morning—out onto the healer's table.

It had taken her at least a month to admit she may have overreacted.

"Do you want to go to the Silver Isles?" asked Adale in a low voice.

"What if she follows us?" Esofi whispered back.

"Well, then you could fight her, couldn't you?"

Esofi made a strangled noise that was somewhere between a gasp and a laugh. "No!"

"I think you could win."

"I'm not going to fight her!"

"Why not?"

"Because I don't want to leave you a widow. You should be thankful for that."

"You killed the Emperor. How is it that she's more powerful than he was?"

"The Emperor didn't have any magic at all," Esofi reminded her.

"He was the size of a house and breathed fire!"

"Maybe so, but that is nothing compared to what she is capable of. I *would* like to go to the Silver Isles, though. I am eager to forge a diplomatic relationship with the inhabitants, and I want Carinth to meet other dragons. I am also curious about what precisely caused Ivanedi to flee."

"I am too," said Adale. She paused. "Would the twins be coming with us?"

Esofi gazed up at her. "Are you angry at me?"

Yes. No. Not when Esofi looked at her like that.

"I'm worried," said Adale. "I'm so worried. Not about the twins, just—I've never seen you like this before, all secrets and avoiding and... and I don't want to pry and make things harder for you but..." Her nose began to sting. Was she about to cry? She breathed in sharply to calm herself, but when she blinked, she could feel a little pearl of a tear gathering in one eye. Irritated with herself, she swiped at it with the back of her hand. This was not what Esofi needed from her right now.

"There's no secrets," said Esofi. "Just things that aren't worth the trouble to explain."

"I don't think that's true."

"Well, you're not the one who has to explain them."

Adale might have recoiled from that, but what would that have accomplished? More silence, more backing away. Instead she reached out and pulled Esofi to her chest, resting her chin on the top of Esofi's head.

"We're in public," Esofi mumbled faintly into her shoulder.

"Oh no. Someone might think I love you," said Adale. But then, so Esofi would be reassured, she added, "Nobody's watching. It's so cold, the only ones out here are the guards on duty and we lost their interest after Ivanedi left."

Nevertheless, Adale loosened her grip a little so Esofi could pull herself to freedom if she really wanted to. But Esofi did not move. Instead, she remained there, breathing softly into Adale's neck.

"Will you be angry if we brought your cousins back to Birsgen?" Esofi asked eventually.

Adale pulled back a little bit so that she could look Esofi in the face. "What?"

"I don't think they'd be suited for the Isles, but I'd feel better if they were in Birsgen, at least until my mother returns home. I know you don't care for them. And maybe they deserve your hatred. But Talcia blessed them, which means she has plans for them. I feel compelled to keep them alive."

"If your mother is coming back to Birsgen with us, then they might actually be better off staying here," Adale pointed out.

"I am not so certain of that."

"What do you mean?"

Esofi said nothing, but her eyes drifted to a pair of Rhodian mages, who were crossing the grounds together.

"You think they'd—"

"I don't know."

That was concerning. Adale wasn't fond of her cousins, but they were still the children of Duke Raldfur, and niece and nephew to the King and Queen. If the Rhodian mages were willing to turn on them at Gaelle's command, Adale was not so certain of her own safety.

"Well," said Adale. "I think I can tolerate them for a little while. Especially if the alternative is..."

Esofi glanced away.

"Let's walk around a little," coaxed Adale. "I think the surrounding forests should be safe enough. I feel like we've had no time to ourselves lately. I've missed you."

"I have not gone anywhere," said Esofi very quietly, but perhaps even she realized this was not completely true, because she nodded. "Just not too far, and not for too long."

None of the guards tried to stop them from leaving the camp. Adale thought that Carinth might refuse to come along, given his low tolerance for cold weather, but he gave no indication that he wanted to go back to the citadel and kept close to his mothers' ankles.

They walked in silence for a time, around the eastern side of the outer wall. In the distance, Adale could see the town of Fenstell, and the grey ocean just beyond it. If it hadn't been nearly winter, she might have suggested they go down to the water.

Carinth wandered through the long grass and climbed over rocks, occasionally unfurling his wings when the wind hit them the right way. Adale called to him, warning him not to wander too far, but he only flicked his tail at her. Adale had always thought of his color as a little impractical, but he blended in well with the grey stones.

She looked over at Esofi, but Esofi was still watching Carinth.

"Is Lexandrie going to be all right?" Adale asked. Lexandrie had spent years picking at every one of Esofi's flaws, real or imagined, and so Adale would never feel any affection for her. But it was as Svana had said—she was concerned for anyone within arm's reach of Gaelle. And it was the best way she could think of to turn the subject back to Esofi's own experiences.

"I think so," said Esofi. Then she glanced sidelong at Adale, openly suspicious. "It is different in Rhodia."

"Yes, I've picked that up," said Adale, thinking once again of Gaelle's hands on Lexandrie's throat, of Esofi striking Carinth across the nose. "But I'm not trying to criticize you, I just...I'm trying to understand."

"What do you want me to say to you?" asked Esofi. "That Rhodians live in a way that Ieflarians would find shocking at best and unbearable at worst? That I left home in the dead of winter to escape it? That my younger sister has apparently decided that she'd rather risk a brutal death at the hands of the elves than sit at the same table as our parents?"

Adale struggled, not sure which point to address first. "I'm not—that's not—I didn't mean—"

"I don't know what you want from me," Esofi whispered, and now there were tears in her eyes too. She turned away, toward the cliffs and the sea.

"I want you to know that I love you," said Adale. "No matter what. And I won't let her hurt you."

"You can't stop her."

"We'll see about that," said Adale.

Esofi gave a little shudder and Adale stepped nearer, pulling her close. Esofi pressed her cheek to Adale's chest. "I don't want you to be hurt, either."

"If she does, she will no longer be welcome in Ieflaria," said Adale. "I know you don't believe that, but my parents won't tolerate her treating either of us badly. Or threatening to take Carinth."

"Ieflaria cannot afford to make an enemy of Rhodia."

"Why not? We barely trade with them, and the most valuable thing they've ever owned is already mine." Adale let her fingers tangle in Esofi's curls. "Or would you return home if she demanded it?"

"Of course not," whispered Esofi.

"Then what are you afraid of?" There was far too much land and sea between their two nations to really go to war, unless their armies agreed to meet at some absurd midpoint in western Xytae.

"She can order the battlemages to go back with her," said Esofi.

"Let them go, then!"

"And if the dragons begin attacking us again?"

"We know they won't! Ivanedi has promised—"

"The dragons are without a leader. There is no telling what they'll do, regardless of Ivanedi's promises. I believe his intentions are good, but the dragons are wild creatures and we cannot predict how they'll behave."

"Let's plan to go to the Silver Isles, then," suggested Adale. "We can verify Ivanedi's claims for ourselves. And Carinth will enjoy it too."

"Maybe," whispered Esofi. Adale rested her hand on Esofi's back and pulled her close once again.

"I hate feeling like there's distance between us," said Adale. "And I hate not knowing how to fix it."

Adale was afraid Esofi might try to deny anything was wrong. But she said, "It's not your fault. This is my problem, and now I've made it your problem too."

"Your problems are my problems whether you intend them to be or not. That's what it means to be married."

Esofi breathed in very, very deeply and then exhaled. "I know," she whispered in a very small voice. Then, "I'm scared of her."

Adale nodded.

"And telling me not to be won't fix anything."

"Then I won't," promised Adale. She brought one hand to Esofi's face, brushing gently at her cheek with her thumb. "Just...let me help you. Even if I'm no use at all, I still want to know what you're thinking."

"If I told you everything, you'd only be upset," said Esofi. "You'd be upset, and you'd pity me, and I wouldn't be able to stand it."

"But I can't go on like this!" Adale's voice broke on the last word.

"Don't cry," pleaded Esofi. "Please. If you cry, I'll cry too and then—"

Adale tilted her head down and pressed her forehead to Esofi's, shoulders shaking from the effort of holding back tears.

"I'm sorry," Esofi said weakly. "I've been a terrible wife."

"You don't have to tell me everything. I know there're things you don't want to talk about, and things that are none of my business. I just need to feel like you trust me. Or at least, that I'm not a burden."

"I'd never think of you as a burden, I promise. This is all my fault. I've handled everything so badly. There's not a thing you could have done to make it come out differently. And I do trust you. I'm just not accustomed to relying on people, I think. At least, not for things like this. In Rhodia, it was...dangerous...to do so."

Instinctively, Adale opened her mouth to say she was sorry. Then she realized her pity was not what Esofi wanted. So she didn't say anything at all, only allowed her hand to trail down Esofi's back.

They stood and watched the ocean roar until it became too cold to remain outside any longer.

CARRIAGES HAD NEVER been Adale's favorite method of transportation. She preferred to ride outside, either up with the driver or on a horse of her own. But for the sake of being near to Esofi and Carinth, Adale decided she would endure it.

Svana and Mireille were both with them, though Brandt was riding outside with the guards. He had been tasked with informing them immediately if Gaelle's carriage stopped or showed any signs of trouble. Adale was still not delighted that Esofi seemed to be acting like Svana's new post was an official appointment instead of a silly ruse, but Svana had been uncharacteristically well behaved.

She turned to Mireille, wondering if Gaelle's appearance and the Rhodian mages had at all made her homesick.

"You weren't planning to go back to Rhodia, were you?" asked Adale.

"No," said Mireille. "That is...you don't want me to, do you?"

"Of course not! But we should probably get on with finding you someone to marry if you're going to stay here."

"Oh, well..." Mireille looked embarrassed. "Maybe."

"Did you have someone in mind?"

"Um. Not really."

"Do you care if it's a husband or—"

"I don't think so," said Mireille. "Maybe a husband would be better. But I'm not sure."

Adale had always felt a little sorry for people who had strong preferences regarding the gender of their romantic partners. It sounded like an inconvenience. It reminded her of Lady Brigit, who simply refused to consider anyone who was taller than her. But then, Brigit's restriction was self-imposed. People with strong preferences weren't being silly or contrary; they could not help the way they'd been made. Still, Adale was glad she was not one of them.

Preferences or not, members of the nobility tended toward pairings that could have children easily, for the sake of heirs and bloodlines. The Temple of Dayluue always offered help to those couples who couldn't have children together, but there was no guarantee they'd be successful. Some nobles seemed to feel it was not worth the risk. She wondered if that was why Mireille might want a husband over the alternatives. But it would be rude to ask.

Esofi had been betrothed to Albion with the expectation they'd be able to have children together without needing the priestesses to help them. Though their betrothal had been at such a young age, there'd been no guarantee one of them wouldn't get permanently Changed long before the wedding.

Adale wondered what Gaelle would have done if Esofi had wanted to get Changed. Would she have tried to talk her out of it, or at least urge her to put it off until she'd had children with Albion? It struck Adale as the sort of thing Gaelle might do.

"Don't worry, we'll find you someone," Adale promised Mireille.

"Who do *you* know who isn't an embarrassment to the entire country?" asked Svana.

"Don't make me put a shield up between you," warned Esofi. "Anyone who starts a fight can get out and walk."

"It's all right," said Mireille quickly. "I don't want to get married right away. I like things how they are right now. And I'd hate to have to leave you or Carinth."

Adale understood. She hadn't wanted to marry, either. Or maybe Mireille didn't feel that kind of attraction? Not everyone did.

Belatedly, she felt a little embarrassed for taking such an interest in Mireille's preferences. None of it was really any of her business. Normally she wouldn't really care, but there was nothing to do in the carriage, unless she decided to try her hand at Esofi's embroidery, and she would never be *that* bored.

The trip to Birsgen was uneventful, even with Gaelle travelling with them. She remained in her carriage, with Lexandrie, for the majority of the journey. When they camped, Adale was on high alert, waiting for Gaelle to say something terrible to Esofi or maybe try to grab Carinth in the night and run, but nothing of the kind happened. In fact, Gaelle seemed determined to pretend that Adale and Esofi did not exist.

Brandt and Svana were behaving themselves too. Adale still did not trust either of them, but she had to admit they were being more civil than she'd ever seen them in her life. It was probably just the fact that Esofi was around, or maybe the tight-laced Rhodian mages had finally managed to knock some manners into them. Whatever the reason, Adale had a feeling the change was not permanent.

When they came within sight of the castle, Adale felt her annoyance with her parents flare up again. They'd seen how distraught Esofi had been at the news that her mother was coming to Birsgen. Why had they not sent a courier to warn them Gaelle was on her way? It was uncharacteristically thoughtless of them.

Her mother was waiting for them when they stepped out of the carriage, along with a few of her ladies. Saski hugged Esofi in greeting, then leaned down to say hello to Carinth.

"Did you receive my letter?" asked Adale pointedly.

"Yes," said Saski. She glanced over at the other carriage, where Gaelle was just stepping out and leaned in quickly to whisper in Adale's ear. "We sent a courier the moment she announced she was going to Fenstell."

"Well, they never found us," Adale said. She knew her mother was telling the truth, which was frustrating because now she had nobody to blame. Adale reached out and rested her hands on Esofi's shoulders, hoping to steer her away before Gaelle could get out of her carriage.

But it seemed Esofi wasn't in a hurry. "Has anything happened in Birsgen since our departure?" she asked.

"Your mother's arrival was the most excitement we had, but she left so quickly," said Saski, a hint of disapproval in her face. "I told her you would be returning soon, but she insisted."

"I'm sure she did," sighed Esofi.

"But your meeting with the dragon went well?"

Esofi nodded. "I will deliver a full report tomorrow. But I do not think we need to worry about any more attacks, at least for now."

Saski looked back to the carriage, where Svana and Mireille were still disembarking. Her lips pressed together at the sight of Svana, and even more so when Brandt stepped around the carriage, leading his horse behind him.

"Oh, I forgot," said Esofi. "Brandt and Svana were stationed at Fenstell with the Rhodian mages. I thought Lady Svana might make a good waiting lady."

"You what?"

"And of course, it seemed cruel to separate her and Brandt. They're both so close to each other, you know. You don't mind, do you?"

"Well..." Saski appeared to be at a loss for words. "I..."

"It's a complicated story," said Adale, raising her eyebrows meaningfully.

"I should like to hear it, I think. But after you have rested." Saski paused and glanced over at Gaelle. For a moment, Adale wondered if she would address Esofi's mother. But instead, she said, "Lady Catrin has had her baby. She is taking visitors now. I am sure she would be pleased if you went to see her."

Lady Catrin was only a few years older than Adale and Esofi, but they had never really spoken to one another beyond basic pleasantries. She had never run in any of the same circles as Adale and her friends. Still, if Saski was mentioning it, it meant they were expected to be polite and bring a gift.

"We will visit her as soon as we are able," promised Esofi.

Adale risked a glance back at Gaelle, but she was now being swarmed by servants eager to take her parasol and her gloves and her cloak.

"Is Lady Lisette here?" asked Esofi. "She separated from our party on the journey to Fenstell, and we've not seen or heard from her since."

"I do not know," said Saski. "I have not noticed her about. Shall I ask the guards?"

"No, no, that's all right," Esofi reassured her. "I'm sure she is fine."

Chapter Six

ESOFI

The next morning, Esofi awoke to Adale's body pressed tightly against her, as usual. It would have been nice to stay there all day and just enjoy the warmth of the blankets and the fire and Adale's unfaltering affection. But they both had matters to attend to, and so Esofi forced herself to get up and dress.

Though her day would be busy, there were no formal or ceremonial events on her schedule. Nevertheless, she selected a Rhodian gown for the first time in what felt like a month, feeling a little bit like a bird trying to fluff up his feathers to drive away predators. Adale did not comment when she pulled the dress from her wardrobe, and even got up to help her with the complicated lacing in the back, even as Esofi protested that she could call Mireille for the task. Even with the continued presence of her mother, it was a relief to be back in Birsgen. Gaelle had certainly managed to take her by surprise in Fenstell, but Esofi liked to think that she had the advantage now, if not simply in the sheer number of people loyal to her—even with Lisette's absence.

For Lisette had never made it back to Birsgen, or if she had, she hadn't reported in to their majesties or anyone else at the castle. Esofi forced herself to be rational. Lisette had warned about this exact possibility the morning she'd left their camp and specifically told Esofi not to send people to search for her if she disappeared.

Esofi would respect Lisette's wishes for now. But if she did not reemerge soon...

She would much rather see Lisette angry with her than see her dead.

Esofi pushed those thoughts away. They had only been gone for a little over a week, but there was a great deal to catch up on. Foremost among them was the priestess of Talcia. Last night, shortly before sundown, Archmage Eads had sent her a short note suggesting she might visit the temple and try to quell a dispute brewing between two of the priestesses before their majesties were forced to step in themselves. Esofi had sighed at the words, for even without any further details she knew precisely which two priestesses the court mage spoke of. Without a doubt, it was Asta and Eydis, the two most prominent candidates for archpriestess.

Asta was an experienced senior priestess, popular among both her colleagues and the university's students. Some of the priestesses were openly disdainful of the newly blessed, viewing them as lesser due to the fact they had only been granted their magic in adulthood, rather than at birth. Asta had been the loudest opponent of this philosophy, and Esofi appreciated her for that.

Eydis was younger—too young to be named archpriestess, or so Asta claimed. Esofi was not so certain of that, though perhaps she was biased due to her own youth. Unlike Asta, Eydis was soft-spoken and had a reputation for settling disputes the old archpriestess did not have the energy to deal with. From her sweet nature, one might not guess she had one of the most powerful blessings in Birsgen. If it came to a duel, Esofi expected that Eydis would win over Asta through sheer brute force.

But then, Ieflarians were not as inclined to duel as Rhodians were.

Esofi tried to imagine how the most recent dispute between them had gone. Perhaps Asta had criticized Eydis loudly, and Eydis had responded by making some vague comment about women who claimed to understand Talcia's serenity but bellowed like a street vendor, and the only reason it *hadn't* come to a duel was the fact Asta knew that she would lose...

Esofi sighed and mentally prepared the lecture she'd already delivered several variations of. The Temple of Talcia had gone neglected for so many decades, it seemed the priestesses sometimes forgot they were once again in the public eye. And even with all that had happened in the last two years, not everyone trusted them the way they trusted the other temples, mostly due to Talcia's association with dragons.

She wondered if threatening to cast them both out of the city and appoint herself archpriestess would carry any weight. Probably not, since the Temple of Talcia mandated that anyone seeking a rank beyond acolyte was required to renounce any titles they might hold, nor could they acquire any afterward. Most temples had similar policies, though not all did.

But before she could see to that, she had to meet with Queen Saski and King Dietrich. Ostensibly, it was to report on her time at Fenstell and her interactions with Ivanedi, and Esofi had dutifully composed a formal report that they could pass along to their own advisors. But she knew they were equally curious about the reappearance of Brandt and Svana. Esofi was still debating how exactly she would describe her mother's actions in a way that would not offend their Ieflarian sensibilities.

Esofi had not given much thought to the twins after they'd been sent away from Birsgen in disgrace. She'd assumed they were still back at home. To learn that their parents had been angry enough to banish them to a defense camp was...surprising. Esofi had always had the impression that Ieflarians were exceptionally permissive parents.

She'd known from the very start that Adale didn't like her cousins much. But until the kidnapping, it had seemed more like a petty rivalry than a cause for concern. As far as she could tell, there had been no single inciting event to cause the schism between them. If that had been the case, Esofi might have been more inclined to take a side. But at the time, she'd just viewed it as a silly grudge that ought to have been left behind in childhood.

To an extent, she still did.

She could not help it! Adale swore Brandt and Svana were awful, but Esofi had seen far worse behavior in Rhodia. They had only crossed the line when they had kidnapped Adale. And even then, they had not injured her or starved her or demanded a ransom. Life at the Rhodian court was not nearly so idyllic.

Perhaps she ought to resent them for attempting to steal Adale away from her. If they had been successful, if Mireille and Lisette had not uncovered their plot and corroborated Adale's story, her life might be very different right now. But it was difficult for Esofi to get angry about something that had not happened. When she thought about what the twins had done to Adale, all she felt was annoyance and a little bit of disgust. That they would do something so childish, so foolish!

But the fact of the matter was, they were members of the royal family. Someday, one or both of them would control Valenleht, arguably Ieflaria's most important port city. Esofi did not want them to be her adversaries.

Nor did she believe she or Adale was in any danger from them. If they'd wanted to murder Adale, they would have done so at the betrothal. If anything happened to Adale or Esofi now, they would be the first suspects. Even if Brandt and Svana were completely innocent, there was a fair chance they would still take the blame for anything that befell the princesses.

Certainly she would keep an eye on them, but she could not muster up any suspicion or hatred.

If she'd hated them, she would not have stepped between Svana and Gaelle.

She only hoped that Saski and Dietrich would be able to see it from her point of view.

Why *had* Talcia given the twins magic? It was something Adale had asked multiple times, and Esofi always retorted that perhaps Adale ought to ask her, which in turn prompted Adale to shout her question up at the ceiling. No response ever came.

Esofi entered Saski and Dietrich's private rooms about an hour later. Stepping inside, she looked around to realize she was alone—there were no advisors or aides with them today. That could only mean they wanted to speak to her candidly. Esofi was not worried, though— they were always kind and understanding, even when she confused them.

"We're so glad to have you back," said Saski, taking Esofi by the hands. "Come, sit. We have questions for you."

Esofi sat down at the table, where tea had been set for three.

"Adale told me that our courier never reached you?" Queen Saski asked.

"I'm afraid not," said Esofi.

"I find that extremely odd. Our couriers are never anything but reliable, and it is not a terribly long distance between Birsgen and Fenstell. I wonder if something befell her?"

"I hope not," said Esofi. "But I know you wish to understand why I have added Brandt and Svana to my retinue?"

"We know you would not do such a thing on a whim," said Dietrich. "Nevertheless..."

"I promise, it was strictly necessary. When I met with my mother, we had...a bit of a disagreement regarding Carinth. Adale was so offended she made us leave. My mother is not used to being ignored. I believe she intended to challenge me to a duel." A lie. "Lady Lexandrie stepped between us, and... my mother struck her. Before I could act, Svana stepped in. This offended my mother further, and she demanded Svana duel her. Lady Svana is a very talented mage, especially considering how late her blessing came, but she is nowhere near my mother's level of skill. I can say with complete certainty that Svana would have been killed if she had accepted the challenge. So I appointed her my waiting lady on the spot and forbade her from accepting any duels."

Dietrich and Saski both looked at each other. She could not tell what they were thinking.

"I do not mean to keep her in my service permanently," added Esofi. "But I have found her conduct so far to be exemplary, as well as that of her brother. I believe their assignment in the north may have been good for the development of their characters."

"Do you believe they may be in danger from your mother?" asked Dietrich pointedly.

"I..." Esofi floundered, knowing they would never understand. Saski's frown deepened, and Esofi pulled herself together. "She will respect Ieflarian laws while she is here."

"That is not terribly reassuring," commented Dietrich.

"Rhodian culture is very different from the culture here," said Esofi. "We are...not so forgiving, sometimes. And perhaps a little quick to anger."

"Are you not a Rhodian, then?" asked Saski.

Esofi shrugged helplessly. "Not a very good one, some might say."

"I disagree with that. We have had your ambassadors here in the past, and none of them ever behaved questionably. And what about your waiting ladies? Mireille is a very sweet girl, and Lisette is so quiet I hardly remember she exists."

"Well, my mother may be in her own class of women," Esofi granted. "I do apologize for anything she may have done before leaving for Fenstell."

"She departed quickly when she learned you were not here," said Saski. "We were surprised. We thought she might have urgent news for you. Some were even speculating something had gone terribly wrong in Rhodia."

"No. She was just very eager to see Carinth. My mother is extremely devoted to Talcia, as you may have guessed. I think...she may still be trying to make sense of it."

"What is there to make sense of?" asked Saski. "You restored her worship, and saved our nation. Why should Talcia not favor you?"

"Well, she is a quiet goddess," said Esofi. "My mother has never been favored personally. So…"

"You think she is jealous of you?" asked Dietrich pointedly.

It sounded so terrible when he put it that way. Esofi shook her head. "Not jealous, precisely. Just…confused. She is certainly more devout than I and brings more worshippers than I have, and…I don't think anyone in the world venerates Talcia as much as she does. I am sure she is wondering why I was favored before she was."

"What use would Queen Gaelle have for a dragon egg?" asked Dietrich. "Rhodia is not threatened by their kind. My understanding has been that we intend for Carinth to bridge the gap between our races, to serve as an ambassador. Rhodia has no need for that, do they?"

"Well, no," said Esofi.

"Carinth is not a symbol of your status with Talcia," said Saski. "She did not give him to you as a trophy for defeating the Emperor. She gave him to you because we need him. He is your son and my grandson, and someday he will accomplish great things for Ieflaria and the Silver Isles."

"I don't disagree," said Esofi. "But the heart is not always rational. I can see her perspective. But let me tell you of the dragon who came to Fenstell."

Saski and Dietrich were willing to let her change the subject, and Esofi described her interactions with Ivanedi, including his invitation to the Silver Isles. She did not mention his abrupt departure when he learned about Gaelle's presence. Esofi had not yet made sense of it, and Saski and Dietrich would only assume the worst.

"I *would* like to go the Silver Isles," concluded Esofi. "I think the danger would be minimal, and Carinth would benefit greatly from it."

"Perhaps in the spring?" suggested Saski. "Our people would be devastated if you were not here at midwinter, and I cannot imagine there are any accommodations for you there that would protect you from the weather."

"Perhaps." Esofi had not thought about where she would stay. The Silver Isles was nothing but forests and mountains and caves. There would not even be temporary structures unless she brought along workers to set something up quickly. But what if the dragons found such a thing offensive, or presumptuous? She did not want to cause an incident on her first day there, but she did not want to die of exposure, either.

Still, springtime was quite a long time to wait. Esofi wondered if she could visit the Isles and return safely before winter struck.

The meeting came to an end, and Dietrich had to leave, but Saski did not seem to be in a hurry. Servants brought in more tea, and Esofi thought it would be rude to leave in a hurry. They sat in peaceful silence for a while longer. Then Saski finally spoke.

"There is something I would like to tell you," she said. "Though if you tell anyone I told you, I will deny it until my dying day."

Esofi was intrigued. "All right," she said, a half smile working its way across her face.

"I mean it," said Saski. "I might even caution you against telling Adale until the time is right. I know she still sometimes struggles with discretion."

"What is it, then?"

Saski seemed to hesitate a moment longer. Then she said, "What do you know of Irianthe Isinthi?"

Esofi had not been expecting this topic of conversation. "Emperor Ionnes' mother?" she asked.

"Yes, the dowager empress," Saski confirmed.

"I've never met her," said Esofi. "But I have heard she is...secretive, or at least a bit shy. She gave her throne to her son the moment he came of age. I might have thought he coerced her into it, but by all accounts, she never cared for her title."

"You are correct," said Saski. "If she were any other woman, I might think Ionnes tricked or threatened her to gain the throne. But I knew Irianthe, if only a little. You never saw a woman so uncomfortable to be the center of attention. Men have killed and died for that throne, but she would have traded it all in an instant in exchange for a quiet library—and in the end, she did exactly that. I understand that she is much happier now."

"Well, that is good, I suppose," said Esofi, wondering what any of this odd story had to do with her.

"And what do you know of Ionnes' father?"

"His...?" Esofi paused. "Emperor Ionnes has no named father."

It was a rare thing for a noblewoman, let alone an Empress, to refuse to name a co-parent, but Esofi supposed the former Empress had been in a position to do whatever she wanted. Irianthe had never married, either. If Esofi had to guess, she would assume Ionnes' father was perhaps a Xytan noble or perhaps a Companion that Irianthe had only used for the sake of having a requisite child. But really, it was none of her concern. Ionnes was Irianthe's son, and now he was the Emperor.

"Empress Irianthe found the thought of giving birth to be repulsive," said Saski. "So when she announced her pregnancy, it was quite a surprise. She spent the duration of that time in seclusion, though nobody knows precisely where she went. Even her closest confidants were each told the names of different cities. She claims it was because she feared assassins, but I do not believe that was the truth of the matter."

"You do not believe Ionnes is Irianthe's son?"

"Oh, there is no question that he is her son. The resemblance between them is unmistakable. But I do not believe she gave birth to him."

"You think she was Changed?"

"No," said Saski. "Else there would be no need for secrecy. I believe the Xytan priestesses of Dayluue did something that has never been attempted in Ioshora. I believe they created Ionnes using magic."

"*What?*" Esofi had never heard such a thing in her life, and she was not certain if she was more offended by the idea that priestesses would attempt to twist Dayluue's will in such a way, or the implication that the experiment had been a success. "Why—how—"

"It was not precisely a secret that Irianthe Insinthi felt no attraction to anyone, man or woman or neutroi. I believe that it was not just pregnancy that she found repulsive. But at the same time, she knew that an heir would be the only way she could free herself of her title without leaving Xytae in chaos."

Esofi shook her head. "I am sorry. I do not mean to be rude, but I cannot believe such a thing. Children cannot be created by magic. It is impossible."

"Not purely by magic," agreed Saski. "I believe the priestesses took something from Irianthe, some part of her essence, to create her child. If anyone could attempt such a thing, let alone succeed, it would be the Temple of Dayluue, wouldn't it? But I am not telling you this story so that we may discuss rituals."

"Why, then?" asked Esofi.

"I merely want you to know of all the possibilities that exist in this world," said Saski. "You and Adale are young. You are caring for Carinth. I do not expect grandchildren immediately, especially given how busy you are keeping yourself. But if you ever find that you relate to Empress Irianthe's circumstances—"

"No!" said Esofi, horrified.

"Then I shall not mention it again," said Saski. "I only wished for you to know that you are not without options. And even if you do not require it for yourself, perhaps someday you will be able to aid someone else with this knowledge."

IT WAS QUIET and very warm in Lady Catrin's room. She was sitting upright in a chair with a very small bundle in her arms and smiling brightly when Adale and Esofi entered.

"Thank you for coming," she said, clearly very happy despite the exhaustion in her face. "It's so good to see you. I hope your journey went well?"

"It did," said Esofi. "I think the dragons are feeling more amicable now than they were when we last saw them." She leaned in to look down at the baby. It was no different than any other baby Esofi had ever seen. Only a few days old, it was as red and scrunched-up as any newborn, with a slightly asymmetrical head. When it squinted up at them, she saw dark grey eyes.

"We named him Michi," said Catrin.

A boy, then. Probably. There was no telling what he'd end up as in the end. For now, they could only give their best guess.

Neutroi usually declared themselves in childhood or early adolescence. It was rare for one to be born, though when it did happen, it was considered extremely good luck. Of course, a neutroi baby might very well declare themselves to be male or female later in life. But people never turned down an excuse to celebrate.

"Would you like to hold him?" Catrin asked Esofi.

Esofi did not. She did not want baby spit on her dress. But it would have been rude to refuse, so she awkwardly took the child into her arms. Adale, meanwhile, went to find a place to set down the gift they'd brought, a little package wrapped in simple red fabric. The table was full of similar things.

"Just set it anywhere!" said Catrin. "You can put it on a chair, if there's no room—oh! Here, you can move that plate..."

Catrin lurched to her feet, despite Adale and Esofi's protests, and took a dish filled with unusual-looking round pastries from the table. Adale set the gift down in the space it had occupied.

"Now I have a good excuse to finish these," said Catrin, glancing down at the dish. "Here, try one—they're from Coplon. I haven't decided if I like them or not."

Trying to pick up a pastry while working very, very hard to not drop a newborn baby on the floor was not something Esofi would ever want to try again. Adale immediately realized the problem and came over to aid her. Luckily, this baby was peaceful and did not begin screaming, not even when Esofi adjusted her grip on him a few times before she found a comfortable way to hold him with only one hand.

"I wonder if he will have a blessing," Catrin mused. "I know it's far too early to tell, but I can't help but be curious."

"He seems so fragile," Esofi observed. "I hardly trust myself with him. It's strange. At three days old, Carinth was already climbing my skirt."

Catrin laughed. "I do not know if I am envious of you or not. Perhaps after a week of screaming, I will be. But I am sure you will have a child of your own soon enough. A little prince, maybe?"

"Perhaps," said Esofi.

"Is that why your mother has come?"

"Oh, no, nothing like that. She only wished to see Carinth."

"Oh, of course. Still, if you did, it would be nice to have her with you. It can be frightening, the first time."

"My mother does not care much for babies, I'm afraid," said Esofi. "I expect I'd find her about as useful as a priestess of Reygmadra. But never mind. I'm far too busy to think about such things now. Perhaps next year, or the year after."

"Don't wait too long, or people will worry."

But they already were worrying.

Esofi looked down at the baby again. He was about as handsome as a lump of firewood. She felt nothing for him, no stirring of maternal love. But then, perhaps that was to be expected? He was not hers, after all. Still, she knew some people adored babies, no matter who the parents were.

She could only hope that when it came time to have her own, she would feel differently.

More visitors came in, and Adale and Esofi took advantage of the opportunity to excuse themselves. Esofi did not realize that she'd fallen into a pensive silence until Adale slipped her hand into Esofi's and whispered, "Are you all right?"

Esofi did not reply, wordlessly signaling that she didn't want to discuss what was on her mind until they were safely alone. When they arrived back at their rooms, Mireille was playing with Carinth, as usual. Brandt and Svana were both gone, and Esofi hoped they had the sense to stay away from Gaelle. There was still no sign of Lisette.

Mireille called a cheerful greeting without getting up off the carpet, and Esofi realized that this was because Cream was sitting in her lap, rendering her trapped. Esofi managed to keep a neutral smile on her face until she and Adale were safely alone in their own bedroom.

"What's the matter?" asked Adale, once the door clicked shut behind them. But Esofi struggled to find the words to explain.

"Was it Catrin's baby?" asked Adale. "I've already forgotten his name."

Esofi nodded.

"We have time," Adale assured her. "I know women who have children when they are past thirty, and the priestesses say most women are safe until thirty-five, and some even later than that!"

"It's not that," said Esofi.

"Then what's wrong?"

"What if I don't like it?" she whispered. "What if I *hate* it?"

"Why would you?"

"I don't know. Why do any mothers hate their children?"

"Well..." Adale struggled, "I think...that's rare."

"But it does happen. What if I hate it so much that I kill it?"

"What!" Now Adale was alarmed. "You'd never do something like that!"

"You don't know that. None of us can know that. It might happen."

"You love Carinth. You'd never harm him."

"Carinth is different! Babies are different from dragons! We both know that!"

For hatchlings did not scream at all hours of the day and night. They did not require the constant care newborn babies did. They seemed to be cleaner, and more self-sufficient as well. Having Carinth was more like adopting a child that was already out of infancy.

Their rank meant that Esofi could probably get away with letting nursemaids and priestesses raise their child, but she did not want that. Children knew when their parents did not love them.

"I don't think you'd hate a baby," said Adale very slowly. "Let alone hate it enough to kill it."

What kind of people killed their own children? The stereotype for that sort of behavior was uneducated chaos cultists out in remote areas who did unspeakable things in the name of evil gods. But Esofi had spent enough time studying the law to know this was not always the case. Most murderers did not spend their days wearing hooded capes indoors and rubbing their hands together gleefully like characters in a stage-play. Most of them lived ordinary lives until they were caught. To think of them only as monsters nobody sensible would ever trust was tempting, but it was not true to reality.

Besides, Esofi knew strange things could happen to mothers after they gave birth, a sort of temporary melancholy that occasionally turned to madness. The priestesses of Pemele and Dayluue swore that it could happen to anyone and was not indicative of a wicked nature. She did not really know anything about it beyond that.

"Well," said Adale. "Your mother never killed any of hers. And you have a much better temper than she does."

"She might have, if she hadn't been allowed to hand us off to the nurses. I hardly saw her until I was old enough to begin learning to use my magic."

Adale drew Esofi into her arms. "You are not her," she whispered. "I promise you're not. But if you're that frightened of it, we don't have to. We'll find someone else to pass the throne to."

Unacceptable, said Esofi's upbringing. *If you can't produce heirs, you are not worthy of your title.*

"I don't know what I want," said Esofi aloud.

"Good, then we match," Adale smiled. "Look at everything you've done. You haven't even been in the country two years and you've already accomplished so much. Nobody can criticize you for not wanting a baby."

"Of course they can," said Esofi. "And they will."

"All right, they can. But that's all they can do. And nobody ever died of criticism. But if it means that much to you, I know we can bribe the Temple of Dayluue to claim I'm infertile."

"You can't bribe a temple!" Esofi cried, scandalized.

"Of course you can. You can bribe anyone."

"What if *you* want a baby?" asked Esofi. "What if you hate me for not wanting one?"

Adale laughed. "I don't think there's any danger of that. Besides, I could never love something that doesn't exist more than I love you."

It was not the first time Adale had said these words to her, but hearing them again was reassuring. She sighed and rubbed at her eyes. "I wish I could just go back to sleep. But I need to see to the Temple of Talcia next."

"I'd go with you, but my parents are expecting me to review a few cases that are going before the Temple of Iolar soon," said Adale. "There's been a development in that case with the counterfeiter. Sorry, the *alleged* counterfeiter. They think he might have once had Inthi's fire—which explains why the fakes were so good—but his magic was revoked."

"Revoked?" Esofi's eyes widened in surprise. She had heard stories of such things—rumors and legends with varying degrees of credibility—but never encountered the phenomenon herself. It was supposed to be very difficult to displease the gods enough to have one's blessing rescinded.

"I need to review the details," said Adale. "But yes. The Temple of Iolar is taking it to mean he's guilty of *something*, counterfeiter or not. And I hate to agree with them, but..."

"Would counterfeiting be enough for Inthi to rescind a blessing? Or should we be looking for evidence of something worse?"

"That's what I thought, but having your blessing taken away isn't against the law, so we might have a hard time justifying another investigation. At least, that's what my father said. I think he wants me to try to find a legal loophole. I'm sure he already knows one. He just wants to see if I can work it out for myself." Adale rolled her eyes. "Want to trade? You deal with this, and I'll tell the priestesses to stop pulling each other's hair."

Esofi went to her mirror to check on her hair and make-up, to verify that they had not been damaged by Lady Catrin's baby. She adjusted her curls and retrieved a cloak suitable for the colder weather. Adale, meanwhile, settled herself at the desk with a stack of papers and set to work. Not wanting to disturb her, Esofi pressed a very soft kiss to the top of her head before setting off.

Esofi stepped out of the room and shut the door behind her. As she turned to lock it, she heard a familiar voice from behind her say, "Let's see about this University of yours, then."

Esofi had seen nothing of Gaelle since their return to Birsgen. Now she stood before Esofi again, so tall and thin and terribly cold. She wore a heavy fur-lined cloak over an emerald green dress, and one hand clutched a pair of gloves.

"The University?" Esofi repeated. Her eyes darted, briefly, to the bedroom door. Adale was just on the other side of it. She would probably hear Esofi if she called. But Esofi didn't want to make a scene. Besides, Adale had work to do.

And Esofi was a grown woman. She could handle dragons, and she could handle her own mother.

"Why shouldn't I be curious?" asked Gaelle. "And since I've little else to do, I thought I might tell you what you're doing wrong."

"Well there's not much to see—" began Esofi, and that was the truth. The new university at Birsgen was still under construction, with just enough of it standing to hold classes if one did not mind exposure to the elements and the noise of the laborers.

"Regardless," said Gaelle blithely. "I know you're going to the Temple of Talcia now. Aren't you?"

"Yes, but—"

"And the University is on the same grounds?"

"Yes."

"Then it's settled," said Gaelle. "Honestly, Esofi, I don't understand why you make these things so difficult."

Esofi allowed herself a tiny sigh. "Is Lexandrie coming?"

"No. I'm tired of looking at her." Gaelle adjusted her cloak. "Don't just stand there, I don't have all day."

Rhodian dresses were a little inconvenient for meandering through half-completed buildings, but since she was trapped with her mother for the next few hours, Esofi was glad she'd decided to wear one. It was irrational, but she really did feel more formidable in it.

The day was cold, and when Esofi stepped out of the carriage she thought of how much Carinth would hate it, followed by a great deal of relief that she'd decided to leave him behind with Adale before Gaelle intercepted her.

Was that wrong of her? Despite everything, Gaelle *was* his grandmother as much as Saski was. And she did not seem to mean him any harm—certainly she'd shown him more kindness than any of her children. But her declaration that she would take him back to Rhodia disturbed her. She had not raised the subject again, but even knowing she was contemplating it put Esofi on edge.

Esofi pushed those thoughts away and looked at Gaelle. She was surveying the half-constructed building with a critical eye.

"I know it must seem small, but we had to work with the land available. We're planning to build upward, instead of outward." Esofi gestured to the high, half-completed walls. "The largest part of it will be like a tower, when it is complete. They have the designs in the temple, if you'd like to see."

Gaelle did not respond, so Esofi pressed on.

"The lower levels will be for instructing the newer students. Then we'll have the library. I am already gathering materials for the collection." Though the priestesses of Talcia were refusing to part with some of the older tomes in the temple's possession, even as Esofi protested they were giving up nothing, as the University would be under their own guidance.

It seemed they did not entirely trust her, even now.

Nevertheless, Esofi thought her relationship with the temple was good. They all knew it was due to her arrival in Ieflaria that Talcia's worship had been restored, and there were more attendants at the monthly Lunar Services than there had been in decades.

"Am I meant to be impressed?" asked Gaelle.

"Why start now?" Esofi replied evenly, surprising herself with the words. Gaelle stared at her in confusion and Esofi curled her fingers, ready to call up a shield if she needed one. But after a moment, Gaelle laughed. Esofi exhaled through her nose.

"Well, let's visit the temple," Esofi said. "Perhaps the archpriestess will be about today."

The Great Temple of Talcia was only minutes away from the University-to-be. When Esofi and Gaelle ascended the dark marble steps to the courtyard, there were a few younger acolytes tending to the flowers and those few birds that had not fled to Vesolda when the weather turned. When the acolytes spotted her, they all leapt to their feet and crowded around her, chattering excitedly.

"Did you bring Carinth today?" asked one.

"I'm afraid not," said Esofi. This received a chorus of disappointed sighs.

"I want a baby dragon of my own," said one of the girls. "Every night I ask Talcia to give me an egg."

Esofi had to laugh at that. "It's more work than you'd think."

"I don't mind! I don't!"

From behind her, Gaelle made an irritated noise. Esofi forced herself to keep smiling. "Is the archpriestess about today?"

In unison, all the girls shook their heads.

"We haven't seen her in *ages*," whispered the eldest one. "She doesn't come to meals anymore. Eydis sings the moonrise songs for her now. And Asta is leading this month's Lunar Service again."

"That is to be expected. She has served Talcia for so many years. She has more than earned her rest." Esofi smiled comfortingly. "I will bring Carinth next time I visit, if it's not too cold."

But the girls had caught sight of Gaelle and their smiles were fading. A few of the younger ones edged back in the direction of the temple. Esofi wasn't sure how much they had heard about Gaelle, but it was evident they had been told *something*.

"Well, I need to go," said Esofi, and the relief on the girls' faces was a little insulting.

Inside the temple's atrium was quiet, but Esofi knew a class for the newly blessed was happening in the large, open area where services took place on a monthly basis. The students were learning quickly, more so than expected. It seemed that being granted magic later in life was less of a disadvantage than she'd initially presumed it might be.

"Princess!" yelled a familiar voice. Esofi turned to see Asta striding toward them, her heavy silver bracelets clanging against one another. "You did not tell us to expect you!"

If there was one thing Esofi disliked about Asta, it was the fact that there was little difference in the voice she used to lead services and the voice she used to address others. Esofi tried to whisper around her, in hopes that she might catch the hint and adjust her own volume, but Asta never did.

"It's all right, Asta. We were just hoping to view the plans for the university."

"Then this must be..." Asta's eyes narrowed before she sank into a rapid curtsy. "Your Majesty."

"Is everyone here so familiar with you?" asked Gaelle in Rhodian.

"It's different here, Mother," replied Esofi in a voice a little sharper than she had intended. Asta lifted her head, frowning. "It's all right, Asta. Let's have a look at those drawings."

"I will bring them for you." Asta turned and strode from the room, in the direction of the staircase that led to the temple's private library. This was unusual because normally Esofi would just go up to the library herself. But it seemed the acolytes were not the only ones uncomfortable with Gaelle's presence.

Just as Asta disappeared up the stairs, the doors to the main area of the temple opened and another young woman stepped out.

"Oh, Princess," said Eydis. "You've returned from Fenstell!"

"Yes, but don't let me interrupt you if you're teaching."

"Oh no, I'm not teaching today. I'd only stepped in for a moment to oversee." Eydis smiled and glanced down toward Esofi's feet. "You didn't bring Carinth today?"

"No, I'm afraid not."

"That's too bad," sighed Eydis. "Well, never mind. I'm sorry the archpriestess is not taking any visitors today. She has been...a little confused, these last few days."

"I understand," said Esofi. "And it's fine. I just sent Asta to bring the plans for the University. My mother wished to see them."

"Actually, I don't really care," came Gaelle's voice from somewhere behind her.

"The construction is coming along so quickly!" Esofi said to Eydis, determined to ignore both her mother's words and the way they'd made her heartbeat falter. "How have things been here?"

"Oh..." Eydis wrung her hands together, eyes locked still on Gaelle. "We're fine. We're all fine. How was your meeting at Fenstell?"

"It went very well, I think," said Esofi. Or at least it *had* until the impromptu ending. "I don't think we'll have to worry about dragon attacks for a very long time."

Eydis clearly wanted to say more, but perhaps Gaelle's presence was too intimidating. Fortunately, Asta was quick to return, bearing the familiar drawings in her hands. Once she arrived, Eydis mumbled something about tea and vanished again.

Esofi had known from the start that there would be no way to pull Eydis and Asta aside and remind them of the temple's fragile reputation without her mother overhearing. And she could just imagine what Gaelle would say if she found out the priestesses had been bickering in public. Esofi would never hear the end of it. She would have to try again another day or hope they got the message from her presence alone.

"There's a room this way," Esofi said to Gaelle, gesturing off to the side. "We can sit there, instead of standing out in the open."

The room was small and would not fit more than three or four people at most. It had been used for storage until the resurgence of Talcia's worship. Some of the newly blessed students had started studying there when classes were not in session. It was empty today, save for the little table and few chairs that were always there.

Despite her mother's words to the contrary, Esofi could see the interest in her eyes as she looked over the drawings. For a few minutes, they sat in peaceful silence, until Gaelle set the designs down on the table between them.

"You should support the younger one," said Gaelle idly.

"What?"

"The younger priestess. For archpriestess. She is soft. She will be easier to control."

I do not wish to control her. Esofi did not say it aloud because she knew that would only get a scornful laugh from Gaelle. Instead she glanced to the door to make sure it was truly closed and said, "You may be right. But even so, that is no guarantee she will be named."

It was not so in Rhodia. In Rhodia, Gaelle's support was more akin to a mandate, and everyone knew it. No archpriest had been appointed that she or Esofi's father did not publicly support first.

"I want a Silence established here," said Gaelle.

Esofi stared at her hands.

"Did you hear me?"

"There are not enough worshippers," said Esofi, clenching her fists in her lap.

"Esofi, what have you been *doing* for the last two years?" Gaelle snapped. "You failed to identify Carinth's blessing, your 'university' is a pile of stones, and you have no heir! I should have known the moment you were out of my sight, you would revert to your old ways."

There was no point in arguing. There never was. But Esofi's silence seemed to annoy Gaelle further.

"There is no reason for you to not have at least one child by now," Gaelle went on. "Unless, of course, you are failing to keep the Crown Princess's attention."

Esofi nearly jumped out of her seat. It was only the small size of the room that kept her in place. *"What?"*

"Well, let's be realistic, Esofi. I know her reputation. And—well, just look at you. I'd hardly call you two an ideal match."

"We're—"

"You need to give more thought to your appearance before you lose her completely."

"That isn't going to happen!"

"I know you believe that, but I've seen how these things go." Gaelle sat back in her seat. "I suggest you take my words to heart before it's too late to salvage things."

"Stop it," said Esofi, her voice rising sharply. "You don't even believe what you're saying! You're only trying to hurt me!"

The door opened, and Esofi's mouth snapped shut. An acolyte in pale blue robes held a tea-tray in one hand, her eyes wide and face stricken.

"I—I'm sorry—" squeaked the girl. Esofi rose and took the tray from her hands before Gaelle could reprimand her for entering without knocking first. The girl turned and fled, her footsteps echoing on the stone.

"I'm the only one who will tell you the truth. You should be grateful for that," said Gaelle as Esofi set the tray down on the table. "Look around you! By the Ten, do you think there's a single Ieflarian who would tell you something you didn't want to hear? They all know you will be their queen someday!"

"All this just because I don't want to establish a Silence?" asked Esofi. Her nose stung with the effort of holding back tears, and she turned to sit down so she could calm herself without Gaelle seeing. Then she took one of the teacups from the tray so she would have a good excuse to not look her mother in the eye.

She *knew* her mother was only grasping wildly at anything she thought might get a reaction out of Esofi, that the words themselves were meaningless. But for some reason, that did not make it hurt any less. Gaelle might be correct, if only by accident. She'd been pushing Adale away, so much so that Adale had begged her to stop.

How much more could she except Adale to tolerate?

"Oh, so now you're ready to talk about the Silence?" asked Gaelle.

"The Temple of Talcia is still weak! If I pull it in two, neither organization will be an asset to me, or to you!"

"To me?" Gaelle repeated. "Is that what this is about?"

Esofi fell silent, but a thin smile stretched across Gaelle's lips.

"I shouldn't be surprised," said Gaelle. "You left Rhodia so quickly, after all. That's hardly remarkable, all my children seem to run from me, but...yes. You think establishing a Silence here would give me a foothold. And you don't want that. You're having such a lovely time, after all. If I was around, trying to hold you to my standards, it wouldn't be nearly as much fun."

Esofi said nothing.

"You thought you'd outrun me, hadn't you?" asked Gaelle. "Don't you realize I'm the one who sent you here in the first place? You're exactly where I've always intended you to be. But do not flatter yourself. My desire for a Silence has nothing to do with you. It is purely for the veneration of Talcia."

"I do not believe you."

"What other motive would I have? You think I care anything for this miserable country of mud and sheep and impertinent peasants when my own kingdom is so very near to perfection? Or did you think I sought power over you, as though I do not have that already?" Gaelle reached forward, and Esofi flinched away instinctively, all thoughts of calling up a protective barrier scattering like frightened mice. But Gaelle's hand had not been raised in anger. Instead, she curled her fingers around Esofi's chin and held it.

"I could break you so easily," said Gaelle. There was no malice in her voice, only calm certainty. "But what in the world would I do with the pieces?"

Chapter Seven

ADALE

When Esofi returned, she looked so unwell that Adale thought someone might have died. At the sight of her, Adale dropped the papers she'd been reading and leapt to her feet, but Esofi waved her away, saying she was only exhausted.

Nevertheless, Adale helped her to the sofa. Once seated, Esofi rested her head back and closed her eyes. "It's just been a long day. I'll be fine."

"Are you sure?"

"Yes, just..." One of Esofi's hands struggled, listlessly, with the clasp at her cloak, then appeared to give up and flopped down into her lap. "It's so warm in here."

"Let me help you," Adale said. "Have you eaten yet? I'll have someone bring us something."

"I don't think I'm hungry," said Esofi, standing up partway so that Adale could pull her cloak free. Once it was done, she sank down onto the pillows again.

"Well, I am, so you may have the privilege of watching me eat." Adale paused when this elicited no response. "Esofi?"

Esofi's eyes stared blankly ahead at nothing.

"Esofi?" repeated Adale.

"It's so warm in here," mumbled Esofi.

Then she tilted forward and collapsed onto the floor.

Adale cried out in shock and lunged forward, struggling to lift Esofi off the floor. To her horror, Esofi's skin was icy cold to the touch.

"Mireille!" Adale cried. "*Lisette!*"

But Lisette was gone. Adale clenched her hand into a fist and punched the floor in frustration. The door flew open, and Mireille and Svana both stared down at her in shock.

"I'll—I'll get a priest!" cried Mireille, bolting from the room immediately, stumbling over her own skirt in her haste. By contrast, Svana appeared as though she was still taking in the sight before her.

"Don't just *stand there*!" snapped Adale.

"What do you want me to do, then?" Svana retorted.

Adale hesitated, realizing Svana had a point. But she would never admit that. "Help me get her up," she said. "Onto the couch."

It was not easy work, but by the time Mireille returned with a white-robed priest of Adranus, Esofi was laying on the couch instead of the carpet. Adale crouched beside her, one hand feeling desperately for the pulse in her neck.

"What happened?" asked the priest, coming to kneel by Adale. She shifted out of the way for him.

"I don't know. She was sitting with me, and then she fainted."

The priest did not respond immediately, but she could see white light already gathering at his hands. He pressed his fingers to Esofi's forehead, then her neck, and then her stomach.

Adale was used to priests examining injuries, nodding, and recommending bed-rest or some other treatment. But this time, the priest did not nod.

"Send for an alchemist," he said.

"What?" Adale's stomach lurched. "Why? Can't you heal her? Why do you need an alchemist?"

Instead of answering, the priest pulled a glass bottle from his bag. Adale watched as he removed the lid, which had a long glass rod protruding from the underside, not unlike a perfume bottle. He held it just below Esofi's nose.

Esofi's entire body shuddered, and she spat up an ugly yellow bile. The priest did not seem at all disturbed by this and simply turned her head so that she would not choke on it. Behind Adale, Svana gasped.

"This is not an illness," the priest said. "I am not an alchemist, Crown Princess. That is why I have asked for one. And I hope she tells me that I am incorrect in my suspicion. But I believe Princess Esofi may have been poisoned."

Adale's head swam. She dug her fingertips into the carpet to right herself. "What?"

"An alchemist could tell us for certain," the priest was infuriatingly calm. "And she would know better treatments than I. I sincerely hope I am mistaken. But I do not believe I am."

"That can't be right," whispered Adale. "Who would—why would—" Everyone *loved* Esofi. What would anyone stand to gain from her death? Rage gathered inside Adale's chest like a fire.

"I'll send for an alchemist," Mireille said quickly, hurrying back out of the room.

"We need to lock down the castle," said Adale, more to herself than anyone else. "The whole city. Once I find out who did this..." Her voice trailed off as her eyes fell on Svana. "Maybe it won't be much of a search."

"What?" cried Svana. "You think I—how *dare* you—"

"Who else would have done it?" demanded Adale.

"Why would I poison Esofi? How would that help me?" Svana retorted.

"As though you need a reason!"

"If I was going to poison someone, it would be you!"

"Maybe you meant to," said Adale. "Maybe Esofi ate something meant for me. Is that it? You thought maybe if you got rid of me, she'd marry one of you?"

"You're mad," said Svana. "I'm not going to stand here and let you accuse me of—"

"Princess Esofi needs peace if she is to recover," interrupted the priest. "Please, take your dispute elsewhere."

Adale stormed out of the room. Svana followed her, but Adale was not thinking about her anymore. If Svana had poisoned Esofi, there would be time to kill her later. But if Svana was innocent, the castle needed to be sealed off. She *would* catch the culprit, even if she had to hunt him down herself.

"Where is Captain Lehmann?" Adale demanded of the first set of guards she found, posted at the end of the hallway. "We have an assassin in the castle." At least, Adale sincerely hoped they were still in the castle. Perhaps they had fled hours ago. But she refused to consider that possibility. "I don't want anyone leaving the grounds until we've caught him, no matter what their station." If anyone took issue with her edict, they could complain to Adale directly.

Looking back on the day later, Adale knew that things had happened very quickly. People all over the castle had been unceremoniously ushered out of the halls and entire areas were closed off. And Captain Lehmann was beside her in minutes. But those minutes had been crawling, sickeningly slow as Adale struggled not to imagine some awful poison sinking deeper and deeper into Esofi's heart.

"We will find the one who did this," Captain Lehmann swore. "No matter the cost."

"Bring them to me," said Adale. "I want to kill them with my own hands." Her voice felt like it was not her own. Her body felt like it was not her own. Perhaps she was dreaming.

A strong hand wrapped itself around her shoulder, and she stared up into her father's face.

"Is it true?" he asked.

Adale nodded.

"Come with me," he said.

"But I need to—"

"There is nothing you can do that is not already being done," Dietrich interrupted. "Trust our healers and our guards. We must discuss this immediately."

Adale reluctantly followed him. They had never had an assassin at Birsgen in Adale's lifetime. Accidents happened, certainly, along with fights with both magic and blade when tempers ran hot. But never attempted murder. Never *assassins*.

Dietrich led her to her parents' room. The outer chamber was surprisingly empty, but he brought her to their private bedroom anyway. Her mother was waiting for them there.

Once the door was closed behind them, Saski pressed her hands to it, murmuring words too soft for Adale to catch. Soft lavender light, Pemele's magic, glowed at her hands for the briefest moment. The light spread out, enveloping the entire room for just a moment before vanishing.

Adale did not frequently think about Saski's blessing. She had only ever really seen her use it to make little charms or sew protective magic directly into her children's clothes. Pemele's magic was soft and subtle, just like Pemele herself. Some of it was so unremarkable that Adale wondered if it was really magic at all. And it had limitations too. Much of it only worked on members of Saski's own family.

"Tell me what happened," commanded Saski.

"I don't know. She was fine...she was sitting...and then she just collapsed. The priest said he thought it was poisoned, so I called the guards. I want to question everyone in the castle. Someone has to know who did this."

"Do you have any suspicions?" asked Dietrich.

"I...I think it might have been the twins." But deep down, she did not believe that, not really. It was only her dislike of them that made her name them. "Maybe. I don't know."

"Breathe," said Saski. "Think. Who would benefit from this?"

"Nobody!"

"That is not true, Adale," said Dietrich. "There is no one in this castle so unimportant that nobody could benefit from their death."

"I don't *know*. Everyone likes her, don't they? Nobody's ever threatened her." Adale shook her head. "Were they hoping that if they got rid of her, they'd be able to marry me and rule Ieflaria?"

"That is one possibility," said Saski. "But I believe the timing of this is significant. What has happened in the last week? The dragons sent a messenger to us, and Esofi's mother arrived in Ieflaria."

"Gaelle." Adale's eyes narrowed. "You think Gaelle did it?"

"No, I—"

"To steal Carinth," Adale realized. "Of course. She knows Esofi will never let her take him, so she—"

"Adale!" Saski snapped. "Listen to me! If Gaelle wanted Esofi dead, she would be dead already! For once, consider the situation. Chasing every whim that comes into your head will not bring anyone to justice."

Adale could feel the heat rushing to her face. "If you've just brought me here to insult me, there're better ways I can be using my time."

"I am attempting to communicate with you," said Saski. "You think you're the only one who loves Esofi? She is my daughter as much as you are. I want to see this assassin caught, and that will not happen if we are not careful with our next moves."

"You think you know who it was, don't you?" asked Adale.

Her parents both glanced at each other, and she knew she had guessed correctly. "Who? Tell me!"

"No," said Saski. "I won't have you rushing to confront them before we have evidence and undermining—"

"Just tell me!" cried Adale. Tears leaked down her cheeks, and that only made her angrier. She wiped them away furiously. But Saski was not impressed.

"I. Will. Have. Justice," said Saski. "What I will *not* have is your determination to turn this investigation into a farce, do you understand me? It was my hope that you could be a part of this process, but now I see you are too close to the situation for such a thing to be possible."

Adale turned on her heel and stormed from the room, unable to keep her tears in any longer.

But if the culprit wasn't Gaelle, and it wasn't the twins, then who could it be?

When she entered her room again, Mireille was hovering just outside the bedroom, twisting a handkerchief in her hands.

"I didn't know which temple you wanted, so I got them both," she said. "I hope that's all right."

As Adale pushed past her, she saw what Mireille had meant. Two women stood at Esofi's bedside. One was young and dressed in a pale-green robe, her hair in a single strict braid and coiled around the back of her head. Slung across her chest was the strap of a large leather satchel. The other woman was middle-aged, and her robe was such a dark shade of green Adale initially mistook it for black. A short, hilted dagger hung at her waist.

"How is she?" asked Adale.

The two women glanced at each other, and the one in the lighter robe stepped forward.

"Crown Princess, I am Linza, priestess of the Temple of Adalia," she said, bobbing her head as she bent her knee slightly. "I am happy to tell you that Princess Esofi will live. She did not ingest enough of the poison to do serious damage to herself."

Adale swallowed. "Do you know anything else?"

"The plant is called the Bone Rose, though it is not a true rose. The blossoms are yellow or white in color and harmless. The roots can be made into a slow-acting poison. It was probably powdered and mixed in with something she ate today," said the other woman. Then she nodded her head respectfully. "I am Githea, of the Temple of Rikilda."

"How did this happen?" whispered Adale. Neither of the women answered, perhaps knowing the question was not meant for them. "Both of you—will you stay here, until she is recovered?"

"We will examine everything she is brought for further attempts at poisoning," said Githea.

"I'll send guards as well," said Adale. But could guards be trusted?

Adale shook herself. She had to be rational. If they couldn't trust the guards, they couldn't trust anyone. Nevertheless, she would specifically ask for senior members, those who had proven themselves time and again over the years.

How many people were in the castle? Hundreds? It would take weeks to interview them all. Not just servants and guards, but nobles and merchants and ambassadors and artists and visiting dignitaries...

Adale moved closer to Esofi. She appeared to be asleep, and her skin was unnaturally pale. Adale rested one hand against Esofi's face and nearly recoiled at how cold she was. Rage flared up in her chest again. She would *kill* whoever was responsible for this crime, no matter what her parents said.

"Crown Princess?" said Githea.

Adale looked up. "What?"

"Where is her attendant?"

"What?"

Githea glanced over at Linza, as though she was reluctant to speak in front of the other priestess. Then she said, "Where is the girl who protects her?"

"You mean Lisette?" Adale's eyes narrowed suspiciously. What would a priestess from a minor temple know of Esofi's waiting ladies? "Why do you ask?"

"If she is gone, the temple will provide a replacement."

Linza gave a small, disapproving sniff, but did not say anything.

"Then you..." Adale supposed it made sense. Rikilda was secretive and dispassionate and possibly evil, just like Lisette. "Was Lisette a priestess?"

"No," said Githea. "Am I to take it she is no longer in Birsgen?"

"Esofi sent her off on an assignment over a week ago," said Adale. "She should have been back by now, but..."

Githea pressed her lips together disapprovingly. "For shame. On behalf of the Temple of Rikilda and the Nightshades, I apologize for the lapse in service. You will have a replacement by sundown."

"No—that—that won't be..." Adale shook her head, overwhelmed and more than a bit confused. "No replacement. Not yet." Despite Githea's apparently earnest desire to help, Adale could not quite bring herself to trust the Temple of Rikilda or whatever sister organization Lisette was affiliated with. And she did not want to bring yet another stranger in while Esofi was so weak. "Our guards will be enough for now."

She turned away from the bed, already thinking of what she would say to Captain Lehmann when she found him. Out in the hallway, the sight of all the extra guards posted should have reassured her, but for some reason it only made her feel worse.

"Crown Princess?" said a voice from behind her. Adale turned to see that Githea had followed her out.

Adale held in a sigh of impatience. "What?"

Githea gestured for her to come nearer. Once Adale was close enough for her to whisper, she said, "Two of the women Queen Gaelle brought with her from Rhodia are also Nightshades."

Adale's eyes narrowed.

"One is dressed as an Archmage," said Githea. "And the other a serving-maid. But fabric falls differently when there is leather armor hidden beneath it. I only saw them once, when she entered the city for the very first time."

"Are you allowed to tell me that?"

"Certainly not," said Githea. "But I think Rikilda will forgive me, since I am telling you for the benefit of her temple."

"You want something from me?"

"Yes," said Githea. "In two or three decades from now, when you sit on your father's throne and the Temple of Iolar tells you they believe Rikilda ought to be classified as a chaos goddess, I want you to remember this day."

Adale must have appeared unconvinced because Githea added, "We are gardeners, Crown Princess. Leave us to our flowers. We work at dusk, but we are not evil. We keep our promises, and we are loyal to the crown. The Temple of Iolar struggles with nuance, and so they cannot see the good we do."

"The Temple of Iolar wants you gone?"

"Of course they do," said Githea. "And it's not just us—anyone who doesn't fit into their narrow idea of lawfulness. I don't expect your patronage or your favor. I just want you to know we are not what some might claim."

"I need to go," said Adale, pulling away. This time, Githea did not follow her.

Adale moved past the guards, her mind already back to what she would say to Captain Lehmann. Her parents weren't cooperating, but maybe they'd shared their suspicions with him. She could probably get the names out of him if she leaned on him hard enough.

"Crown Princess?" A young woman was standing there at the end of the hallway. Adale recognized her—Elyne, the Vesoldan woman who had come to Birsgen with the paladin.

"What are you doing in here?" Adale frowned. "*How* did you get in here?" This area of the castle was restricted to the royal family. There was no legitimate reason for Elyne to be here, especially now.

"You need to find Carinth," said Elyne.

"How did you get in here?" Adale closed the gap between them and seized Elyne by the wrist. "Guar—"

"*No,*" said Elyne.

Adale's jaw clamped shut, her teeth locking together so tightly it ached. Try as she might, she could not free herself. Panic began to rise in her chest, and she tried to back away, only to find that her legs would not move either. The only thing she could manage was tightening her grip on Elyne's wrist.

"I am trying to *help* you," said Elyne impatiently. "Gaelle has Carinth. You need to retrieve him from her now, or you may never see him again." She pulled her arm free and stepped back. Adale felt the pressure on her jaw dissipate as she regained control over her mouth.

"What are you?" Adale whispered.

"*Go!*" cried Elyne, and Adale ran past her, mind spinning.

It was as though her legs were not her own. She ran down the stairs, past servants and more guards, stopping to acknowledge no one. She was not sure what room Gaelle was staying in, but it couldn't be very far away from where they kept other visiting dignitaries.

Adale rushed through the halls, stopping only when she came to the wing where important foreigners usually stayed. Looking around, she spotted one door guarded by a Rhodian mage, one Adale did not recognize.

Throwing back her shoulder, Adale strode forward. "I am here to see Queen Gaelle," she said.

"Queen Gaelle is not accepting any visitors," began the mage, but Adale shoved past her and wrenched the door open without knocking.

The room was spacious, nearly as large as the one Adale and Esofi shared. Gaelle sat in plain view, in a large chair by the fireplace, with Carinth in her lap. Not far away, Lexandrie was kneeling in front of an open trunk and folding dresses quietly.

Gaelle pressed her lips together, as though the sight of Adale offended her. "What are you doing here?"

"Looking for Carinth. I see you've found him. Thank you." Adale stepped forward to remove him from her arms. Gaelle's entire body tensed, like she wanted to struggle to keep him, but Adale moved quickly and pulled Carinth free before Gaelle had time to react properly. "I expect you've already heard that Esofi has been poisoned."

"Yes," said Gaelle. "I am surprised. Do your parents not employ poison-tasters?"

"We have never had a need," said Adale defensively. That wasn't completely true—there were some, but they only came to the castle for events when there would be a great many people in attendance. "This sort of thing does not happen here."

"Evidently it does."

Adale glanced around the room. Lexandrie had stopped folding clothes and was standing, stock-still, in the corner. "Are you going somewhere?" asked Adale.

"What?"

"You have her packing. Are you going somewhere?"

Gaelle glanced over at Lexandrie. "I have her *un*packing. I have only just arrived." She flicked her wrist as though swatting at a bee.

"I haven't seen you at all today," said Adale. "I was sure you'd want to spend some time with Esofi."

Gaelle pressed her lips together and lifted her chin. "Didn't she tell you? We saw the...university...today." Her nose wrinkled disdainfully. "If that is what you insist on calling it."

Adale's tightened around Carinth. "No. She did not tell me."

"I can't imagine why," said Gaelle, and something in her voice gave Adale the impression that she was just barely holding back laughter. "Was there anything else you wanted?"

Adale swallowed. There were *many* things she wanted to say, but she remembered her mother's warning about not alerting Esofi's poisoner to their suspicions. "No," she said through gritted teeth. She turned back toward the door and left without another word.

Once outside, she set Carinth down on the ground. "I don't know why you like her so much," she told him. She rubbed her eyes, exhausted. She still wanted to meet with Captain Lehmann, but she also wanted to be back with Esofi.

And now there was the question of who—or what—Elyne was.

Adale remembered the way her jaw had frozen up at just a word from the other girl. What sort of magic was that? It seemed unlike anything she had ever heard of before. Could it possibly be chaos magic, from a minor god? Was she a cultist?

But she'd come to Ieflaria with a paladin.

Adale began moving back in the direction of her rooms, thinking of Esofi again. She'd left Elyne standing there in the hallway. Logic dictated that the guards had escorted her out, or possibly even arrested her. But...for some reason, Adale was not certain. What if she was still there?

What if she'd gone into the room with Esofi?

Adale broke into a run, heart racing once more. But when she burst into the bedroom, she found it no different than how she had left it. Esofi was still in bed, asleep, and the two priestesses were on either side of her. Adale let herself breathe, shoulders slumping in relief.

"How is she?" asked Adale.

"She will recover," said Linza. "But it will be a few days before she is back to her full strength."

"Can you wake her?"

"I can, but I do not recommend it. Bodies heal more quickly when they are allowed to rest."

Adale opened her mouth to object—she wanted to *see* Esofi, to speak to her, to reassure her. But she knew Linza was probably right. "Call me if she wakes?" she asked.

Linza nodded. "We will, Crown Princess."

Adale went out into the sitting room. Brandt and Svana were both sitting on the sofa together, and Mireille was between them, crying loudly into a handkerchief. Carinth climbed into her lap and licked at her cheek.

"It's going to be all right," said Adale. "The healers say she just needs rest."

"I never thought something like this could happen here," sniffed Mireille. "It's always seemed so safe. Lisette is going to murder me."

"This is not your fault," Adale assured her. "Nobody was expecting you to do Lisette's job for her."

"We haven't seen her since the journey to Fenstell." Mireille wiped at her nose with her sleeve inelegantly. "Do you think something's happened to her too?"

"I'm not sure," said Adale, thinking of her conversation with Githea. "I can't imagine anyone getting the better of her. But she's never been gone this long before, has she?"

Mireille shook her head, and Adale wondered if she should send guards out to search for Lisette. But she had no idea where Lisette had gone. Maybe Esofi had some ideas? She would wait until she woke. Lisette could survive on her own for a day or two more.

"You don't *really* think we did this, do you?" asked Brandt.

"I don't know," said Adale. The twins both looked offended. Normally, Adale would be pleased by that, but for some reason, she couldn't muster up any real emotions. "Probably not."

"Aren't your parents going to demand an investigation?" asked Svana.

"Yes. But that's going to take ages. I want answers now!" Adale began to pace the room. Could she hire a truthsayer? But truthsayers were so *rare*. She had never even met one. Was Ioanna really one of them?

"Why bother?" asked Brandt. "We all know who did it. We all know it was her mother."

"I'm not certain of that," Adale muttered. Her instincts were the same, especially given that she had found Gaelle with Carinth. But her parents had seemed so *certain* that Gaelle was innocent.

Could she invite Ioanna to Ieflaria? Would it arouse suspicions? Would Ioanna even accept the invitation? The Xytan royal family had not even come for Adale's wedding; it seemed unlikely that they'd come for whatever ridiculous event Adale dreamed up.

Adale chewed her lower lip. As far as she knew, there were no truthsayers in Ieflaria.

But no! That was not true! A year and a half ago, when Esofi first came to Ieflaria, Adale's cousins had courted her with the gift of a live unicorn, captured from their mother's estate. Esofi had rejected the gift, though not because she had disliked it. Rather, she had not wished to see a wild creature held captive in a city.

But before the unicorn could be sent home, Birsgen had been attacked by dragons, led by their emperor. Esofi had gone in search of a horse to ride to the city gates, and had found the unicorn still in the stables. It spoke to her, she claimed, and she'd learned that it was a truthsayer, blessed by Iolar despite being one of Talcia's children.

As far as Adale knew, she was the only one Esofi had told about the unicorn being a truthsayer. She'd been afraid that if too many people learned the truth, they'd try to hunt him down again and he would never know peace.

But why would Iolar give a unicorn his best blessing, the sort of blessing he usually reserved for kings and heroes? It seemed a waste of magic, especially considering the unicorn did not appear to have any ambitions beyond galloping around and eating grass. She did not imagine that the creatures of the forest frequently called upon him for judgment or guidance.

"Do you remember the unicorn you brought Esofi when you were courting her?" Adale asked.

"Yes," said Brandt. "What about him?"

"I need you to go find him."

Svana's eyebrows shot up. "What? Why?"

"Because I need you to bring him here!" Adale cried impatiently. "Don't worry about why. You don't need to know why! Just *do it*."

"Esofi will only make us send him back again," pointed out Svana.

"That's not your concern. Capture him or bribe him or cry until he is so embarrassed that he agrees to come. I don't care how you do it. I need him here. Esofi's life may depend upon it."

"You *have* gone mad," said Brandt. "But never mind. We'll do it. Just know we're not taking the blame when Esofi gets upset."

"Go!" cried Adale, pointing to the door.

"What, now?" Svana asked.

"Yes, now!"

"They're not going to let us out, the entire castle has been locked down," pointed out Brandt.

"I'll deal with that! Go pack your things!" Adale flapped her hands at them. "We don't have any time to waste!"

The twins got up, reluctantly, and left the room.

"Now we're alone," Mireille said mournfully.

"We'll be all right," said Adale. "Esofi will be better in no time. And I'll have Daphene and Lethea stay with us tonight." Daphene and Lethea were Adale's waiting ladies, though she hardly required them for anything these days. They had remained in Adale's old rooms when she married Esofi, enjoying all the benefits of their station and almost none of the responsibilities.

Adale did not begrudge them their happiness. They had been good friends to her for many years. She knew her parents wanted her to find replacements, ladies suitable for a queen-to-be, but Adale was not concerned about that. She had never really felt like she needed waiting ladies in the first place. There wasn't any task she'd ever needed done that she could not do herself.

So in the meantime, Daphene and Lethea could stay in Adale's old rooms, far enough from Esofi that they would not irritate one another but near enough to Adale that they would be on-hand if she needed them.

Restless, Adale went back into the bedroom and sat down on the other side of the bed, next to Esofi. She stroked her hair gently, watching her face for any sign that she was about to wake.

ADALE COULD COUNT on one hand the number of Sunrise services she'd attended since she was a girl. They were tedious, and she couldn't imagine that Iolar really expected people to sit through them every single day. Most people only attended once a week. Only the most devout also attended the Sundown services at the end of each day.

And yet, that day she found herself waking just before dawn, dressing clumsily and kissing Esofi's forehead very gently before shuffling toward the chapel.

When she arrived, she found both her parents sitting near the front and went to join them. They both had identical expressions of surprise on their face as she drew near, but neither said anything. They wouldn't, not in public.

She turned her face toward the altar and let them think she was only here to beg Iolar for justice. It was easier than explaining.

The Sunrise service lasted an hour and was just as boring as Adale remembered. She occupied herself by peering through the crowd to see who was in attendance. As expected, the paladins were all seated together. With them was the Vesoldan woman who had delivered Ioanna's letter. She wore no armor today, only a dress so simple and plain Adale might have mistaken her for a maid if she didn't know any better.

But there was no sign of Elyne. Adale was not sure if she was surprised or not.

She shifted impatiently, and her mother gave her a stare of disapproval.

The moment the service ended, people began to crowd her and her parents, clasping her hands and offering their sympathies. Adale shook them off, her eyes locked on the Vesoldan paladin, who was already making her way out.

She caught up with the young woman in the corridor just outside, catching her by the arm. As Orsina turned to face her, Adale grinned broadly.

"Hello," said Adale brightly in Vesoldan, recalling that the paladin did not speak Ieflarian. "Dame Orsina, wasn't it?"

Orsina glanced back at her fellow paladins, then nodded.

"Let's talk!" Adale linked her elbow with Orsina's. "Don't worry, you're not in trouble. I just want to ask you some questions. It won't take long."

Orsina nodded again, but from the stricken expression on her face, she was not reassured.

"Let's go out to the gardens," said Adale. "It's so dark in here."

Orsina could have broken free easily—from the looks of her, she could probably lift Adale with one hand. But Adale knew she would not do anything of the sort.

"I'm sure you heard about what happened yesterday?" asked Adale as they emerged into the cold morning light.

Orsina nodded. "I am very sorry. Our prayers are with Princess Esofi."

"She'll be all right," said Adale. "And we will catch the one who did this. But that's not what I wanted to talk to you about."

"Crown Princess—" Orsina sounded deeply uncomfortable.

"What is she?" asked Adale.

Orsina froze. Adale knew the expression on her face well. It was the same one that all paladins got when they couldn't respond to a question without lying. Adale had always found it hilarious.

"Oh, I knew it!" laughed Adale. "Don't be cross with me, it was obvious. I'm surprised nobody else has noticed. So what is she really? No, wait, don't tell me. I want to guess."

"Crown Princess—"

"Does Knight-Commander Glace know?"

Orsina nodded vigorously. "She is not dangerous."

"Oh, I don't think she is," said Adale. "And even if she was, I can hardly criticize. I'm raising a dragon."

"Her true name is Aelia. I encountered her this spring during my travels in Vesolda. She was...keeping villagers in thrall. A chaos goddess."

Adale raised her eyebrows. "She's a chaos goddess?"

"Only a goddess, now," said Orsina. "Please, do not be angry with me for not informing your family. We do not wish to attract undue attention. And she is not as powerful as you might expect."

"Do you know who poisoned Esofi?"

Orsina shook her head. "I'm sorry. I do not."

"But Gaelle was planning to take Carinth."

"That is what Elyne told me."

"That's what she told me too. And I found Carinth in her rooms, and it looked like she was packing, though she denied it."

Orsina gave a helpless shrug. "I am very sorry that I cannot tell you any more than I already have."

"You're sure she didn't say Gaelle was the one who poisoned Esofi?"

From the stricken expression on Orsina's face, it was clear that she had not even considered the possibility before this moment. "Do you believe she would do such a thing to her own daughter?"

"Would she? Yes, I think so," said Adale. "The question is if she *did*."

"I do not wish to believe any mother would be capable of that," Orsina bit her lip. "But I have been told that I am too idealistic."

"Orsina!" cried a voice from behind them. They both turned to see Elyne hurrying toward them, a heavy cloak wrapped around her shoulders. "There you are!"

"You are awake early," said Orsina. Adale could not help but notice how her eyes softened when she looked at Elyne, how the worry left her face.

"You didn't come back to the room. I was afraid you'd gotten lost. Or fallen asleep at the service." Elyne smiled mischievously as she came nearer.

"Stop that," said Orsina. "The Crown Princess doesn't know you're joking."

"You don't like services?" Adale asked Elyne.

Elyne shook her head. "I can't stand them!"

Adale thought this was an unusual stance for a goddess to take, but then, Elyne clearly wasn't an ordinary goddess. In fact, if not for the fact she knew paladins could not lie, she'd have laughed in Orsina's face at the claim.

Adale studied Elyne's face. She was not beautiful, but she was not plain, either. She was...ordinary. The only thing that set her apart from anyone else at the castle was the fact that she was Vesoldan—or at least, appeared to be. Adale supposed she could look however she wanted.

But then, Adale had seen Talcia twice. And both times she had appeared to be an ordinary woman, if not a bit unusual. Perhaps the gods were not as foreign and unapproachable as the temples made them out to be. It was something to consider.

Now Elyne was curling into Orsina's chest like a lover might. "It's too cold out here. Let's go back to bed," she murmured.

"We were going to go out today, to see more of the city," Orsina explained to Adale. "But it seems nobody is allowed to leave until the investigation is complete."

Adale nodded. "I'm sorry. I know it's inconvenient, but..."

"No, I understand," said Orsina. "I'd do the same in your position."

"If there is anything more you can tell me about who poisoned Esofi, it would be appreciated."

Elyne's face became solemn. "Whoever it was, I don't think they're in the castle."

Adale frowned. She had been afraid of that. "What makes you say that?"

"Just...nobody seems to know anything." Elyne shrugged. "Of course, I might have just missed them. But I don't think so."

"Then it really wasn't Gaelle?"

Elyne shook her head. "I don't think so. Or if it was, she's very good at not thinking about it."

"She was my only real suspect." Adale sighed and rubbed her forehead. "I hate this. I hate not knowing. And I hate the idea that it was an Ieflarian who was behind it."

"If I learn anything more, I will tell you," promised Elyne. "But if it helps...everyone I've encountered in the castle is worried for her. She has far more friends than she does enemies, I think."

Chapter Eight

ESOFI

The sky was clear and perfectly blue. Esofi lay on the grass, gazing upward. She knew that if someone saw her, she would be scolded for ruining her hair and dress. But the sun was warm, and she was feeling lazy and careless.

She closed her eyes and breathed in the scent of the garden, hardy Rhodian flowers that didn't mind the rugged soil and mountain air. A shadow fell over her, and she opened her eyes again.

"Where are you going, Princess?" asked a woman's voice. Esofi could not make out her face, for she eclipsed the sun.

"I'm going to the Silver Isles," said Esofi, raising one hand to block out the harsh rays that slipped out from behind the woman's head. "To meet with the dragons."

"You're running away, then?"

"No!"

"Yes," said Talcia. "How far will you allow her to chase you before you turn and fight?"

Esofi awoke with a gasp, bolting upright in bed.

The room was bright, with sunlight streaming through the windows. It was nearly midday. Esofi glanced around and saw two unfamiliar priestesses staring at her in shock. She clutched at the blankets and drew them to her chest.

Something heavy was resting on her legs. She looked down, and Carinth lifted his head to stare at her, a little annoyed at having been woken.

"Princess—" the one in the pale-green robe began.

"What happened?" asked Esofi as Carinth climbed into her lap.

"You were poisoned," the one in the darker robe said bluntly. "But now you have recovered."

Esofi paused to collect her thoughts. The last thing she remembered was speaking to Adale. Then nothing.

Except for her vision.

No. It had not been a vision. Talcia had *not* spoken to her. It had been a dream, nothing more. Or perhaps even a hallucination, brought on by whatever she had ingested.

"Esofi?" the door opened, and Adale rushed in. "You're awake!"

"Yes, I—" But before she could say anything more, Adale was beside her, embracing her as though she was afraid Esofi might vanish on the spot.

"I don't know who did it yet, but I'm going to find out." Adale's voice shook with the effort of holding back tears. Esofi rested her head against Adale's chest while Carinth sniffed at their faces. "I promise I will. And then—"

"I know," Esofi murmured.

"We've all been so worried." Adale wiped at her eyes. "And I couldn't do anything, I couldn't help...I've just been running around uselessly."

"I'm sure that's not true," Esofi whispered.

Adale laughed, a hoarse and hollow sound. "I don't know what I'd have done if you died," she said. "Maybe I'd have died too."

"Don't say that."

They sat together in silence, Adale's hand rubbing soothing patterns into her back.

"This sort of thing doesn't happen here," Adale said quietly. "Or at least, it didn't. I don't know what to think."

"I don't either," said Esofi. "I've never felt unsafe here."

"My parents have their suspicions, but they won't tell me anything useful." Esofi could feel Adale shaking her head in disgust. "They think I'll ruin the investigation."

"Maybe we should leave," said Esofi quietly.

"Leave?" Adale repeated. "To where?"

"Ivanedi said we were welcome in the Silver Isles..."

"You still want to go there?"

"I do." Esofi glanced up at Adale. "I want to learn more about the dragons, and I want Carinth to spend more time around his own species. And...I think I'm tired of dealing with my mother."

"She said she went to the university with you. Yesterday."

Esofi looked up in surprise. "She told you that?"

"Yes. Why didn't you tell me?" There was no accusation in Adale's voice, only quiet curiosity.

"It wasn't something I planned. She found me when I was on my way to the temple and invited herself along. I'd have told you if I hadn't become ill. And I know she'll just keep following me around unless we manage to get away from her. That's why I'd like to go to the Isles."

"If that's what you want." Adale sounded uncertain though. "But you need to recover first. I won't bring you out into the wilderness until you're cleared by a healer."

"I'm fine. I feel fine." And it was true. She needed a bath and fresh clothes, and her throat felt a little raw, but there seemed to be no trace of the poison left in her. "Whoever did this didn't do a very good job."

"They're reviewing everywhere you went and everyone you spoke to yesterday," said Adale. "They even questioned Lady Catrin."

"And the baby?"

"The baby is refusing to give testimony," said Adale. "So I consider him a suspect."

Esofi laughed into Adale's chest. "It's so nice to hear you say something ridiculous."

"I can hardly take credit for that one, it was your suggestion." But Adale smiled down at her. "Are you hungry? I can have them bring us something. They've brought in the poison-tasters until they catch whoever it was, so you don't have to worry."

"Actually, I think I'd like a bath first," said Esofi. "Can you call for the water?"

The bath was drawn and heated quickly. Esofi probably could have fallen asleep in the warm water, but her thoughts were too busy to allow it. Someone had tried to kill her. She was not so naive as to think she wouldn't be a desirable target for any of Ieflaria's enemies, but she had never felt unsafe at Birsgen.

She wondered what the Silver Isles would be like. As far as she knew, no Men had set foot there in living memory. Ivanedi made it sound like a harsh and brutal land, but she expected it would be very beautiful as well, pristine and untouched.

Esofi stared down at her own body, half-floating in the water. Absurdly, her mind went to her mother's assertion that Adale would inevitably wander from her.

Of all the silly things to worry about! There was an assassin running around free, Lisette was missing, the dragons wanted her help in gaining back her magic, and her mother expected her to reestablish the Silence of the Moon.

And yet.

Esofi reached down and squeezed at some of the extra flesh around her thighs. She was more or less the same size she had been when she'd departed from Rhodia—all her old dresses fit, at least. She'd never been completely happy with her size, but she suspected that this was only because her family commented on it so frequently when she was growing up. If not for that, she probably would never think of it.

Adale was tall and thin—Ieflarians, in general, tended toward that shape without much effort. But Esofi had never been given any reason to believe Adale objected to her size.

Unless Adale was just being polite.

Esofi shook herself. No. Adale thought she was beautiful. She'd said it too many times for it to be a lie.

Besides, Esofi remembered from childhood that Gaelle sometimes criticized Esolene for being too thin. So perhaps there was no winning.

Still, Gaelle had sounded so *certain.*

Yes, Adale had cultivated a reputation for herself by the time Esofi arrived in Ieflaria, but that was her right. She hadn't been betrothed to Esofi, or anyone else at the time. She was a free woman.

Perhaps jealousy would have been the rational thing to feel, but Esofi could not begrudge Adale what she had done long before she ever learned Esofi's name. If she was honest, she was glad that at least one of them had known what they were doing on their wedding night.

"Adale?" called Esofi, hesitantly.

"Esofi?" She could hear Adale's footsteps drawing nearer to the door. "Are you all right?"

"Yes, I..." But the handle was already turning. Esofi instinctively reached for a towel, but then she stilled her hand, thinking better of it.

A gust of cool air struck her as the door opened, and she ducked down beneath the stone edge of the bath to avoid it.

"What's the matter?" asked Adale.

"Close the door! It's cold!" Esofi cried pitifully.

"All right—get, you. Get. Out. Get." Adale must have been addressing Carinth, who would try to get as close to the warm water as possible if he was allowed. The door closed, and Esofi lifted her head. "I'm sorry. What's wrong?"

"Nothing's wrong," said Esofi, feeling foolish. "I just..."

"I'll stand guard. You don't need to worry." Adale leaned back on the door, one foot flat against it, as though this was all an assassin would need to be deterred. "I don't think anyone is going to try anything again though. They have to know we're watching for them."

"It's not that," said Esofi. "It's just...when I went to the temple yesterday, with my mother...we talked about some things..."

Adale frowned. "What did she say?"

Esofi shook her head, sending water droplets flying. A few landed on Adale's skirt, darkening the fabric. "It was...I know it wasn't true. But it's stayed with me. She said I should put more care into my appearance."

"What?" Adale gave an incredulous laugh. "I don't see how you could. You spend more time getting ready in a single morning than I do in an entire week!"

"She didn't mean like that," said Esofi. "She meant..."

Esofi looked down at herself.

"What?" demanded Adale.

"She meant the way I am. Not...how I dress or how I style my hair. How much space I take up. Primarily."

"Well, I don't think that's any of her business."

"She said she thinks I'll lose your attention."

"Oooh, where is she?" Adale's fists clenched. "I don't care how much magic she has. There's too much land between us to ever have a proper war."

"Don't overreact," pleaded Esofi. "It's only her opinion. She's entitled to that."

"If her opinion is that I'd *ever* stray from you, then her opinion is wrong!" Adale began to pace the floor. "I can't believe she said that. Except, no, I can. It sounds just like the sort of horrible thing she'd do. Why would you ever believe her, even for a moment?"

"Because I've been so difficult about everything! I've been making you so unhappy. Ever since she arrived, or even before that."

"That's not true," whispered Adale. "And even if it was, I'd never, I'd *never*... How could you think I'd—"

"I'm sorry." Tears sprang to her eyes. "I knew it was nonsense, but she always knows just what to say, and I've been feeling so guilty—"

Adale moved to sit down on the edge of the bath. Esofi watched from the water as Adale pulled her own dress up over her head and dropped it carelessly on the floor behind her. Next, she removed her stockings and her undergarments.

As Adale stepped into the water, Esofi slid herself aside to make room. The bath was certainly large enough for the two of them, but Adale did not seem inclined to keep to her own space. She pulled Esofi close and kissed her.

"Forget everything she's ever said to you," Adale murmured. "I promise none of it was true. Not one word."

Despite the tenderness in her voice, Adale spoke with such conviction that Esofi could not believe she told anything other than the absolute truth.

A FEW HOURS later, Esofi and Adale curled together under a single blanket and discussed ideas for their journey. Esofi was still a little bit dreamy, resting her head against Adale's shoulder and basking in her nearness.

For a while, they talked of arranging a ship to take them to the Silver Isles, and how big it ought to be—not so small that they'd be in danger, but not so large that the dragons would mistake them for an invading force. Then the conversation turned to precisely who they'd want to bring with them on the trip, and things turned a little strange.

"I don't understand why you want her to join us," Esofi said.

"Dame Orsina would be perfect for this. Much better than having an entire battalion stumbling around after us."

"Yes, but why her?" asked Esofi. "We have Ieflarian paladins that would make perfectly acceptable guards."

"Well, her companion has magic, too," said Adale. "And I like them. I trust them."

"They've only been at Birsgen for a week or two," pointed out Esofi. She did not mean to be argumentative, but she was very confused by Adale's interest in a pair of foreigners. "For all you know, they could be completely incompetent."

"They're *not*," insisted Adale.

"How do you know?"

"Ioanna wouldn't have asked Orsina to deliver her letter if she was."

"Ioanna is eight." Esofi gripped her teacup, letting the warmth seep into her fingers. "Truthsayer or not, her opinion could probably be swayed with chocolates. But I'm surprised by your choice. I did not think you cared much for the Order of the Sun."

"Well, you're right, I don't," Adale admitted. "Her companion is the one I really want with us."

"Her companion?"

"Dame Orsina came here with another woman. Elyne. You might not have met her?"

Esofi shook her head. "I do not believe I have. What's so special about her?"

"Well…" Adale appeared to struggle with words. "It's hard to explain. I don't think you'd believe me if I told you. But her magic is very powerful. I'd feel much safer with her around."

Esofi felt a little pang of anxiety cut through her blissful haze. "You're not making any sense."

"The first time I met her was when I was trying to find Carinth," Adale seemed to be choosing her words carefully. "She was in the chapel. Then…I didn't see her again until yesterday. After you fainted, and we got the healer to you, I went to tell Captain Lehmann what had happened, but she stopped me."

Adale fell silent, clearly remembering.

"What happened next?" prompted Esofi.

"She told me I had to find Carinth. I wasn't listening to her. I was so worried about you, I could hardly think— but she did something to me. I couldn't move or speak. She told me that Gaelle had Carinth, and I had to get him back or else I might never see him again."

Esofi shifted so that she was sitting up, and the blanket fell from her shoulders. "Is this a joke?"

"I am telling it exactly as it happened. I went to Gaelle's room, and Carinth was there and it *looked* like Lexandrie was packing her things, but Gaelle denied it. So I took him and left."

Esofi wanted to speak, but words were failing her. Her lips moved soundlessly as she tried to understand what Adale was telling her.

"This morning, before you woke, I went and found Dame Orsina after the Sunrise service," Adale continued. "I confronted her about what Elyne had said and done. She did not want to answer me, but I got the truth out of her."

"And what did she say?"

"Elyne is not a woman. She is a goddess."

Esofi rubbed at her eyes. "Adale, I just survived an assassination attempt. I don't have the energy for—"

"I promise you, I'm not lying."

"Then Orsina was lying."

"Paladins don't lie."

"How much do we know about this woman?" Esofi pointed out. "Do we even know if she's really a paladin at all? She's come from a foreign land. For all we know she could be a mercenary in disguise."

"Talcia was running around here eighteen months ago dressed like a common woman and kissing maids. I don't see why this is any more difficult to believe."

Esofi pulled the blanket over her shoulders. Though there was truth to Adale's words, she was still skeptical. Surely if there was a goddess—even a minor one—wandering around the palace, she would have noticed? *Someone* should have noticed.

"She's not a powerful one," added Adale. "She's one of those little ones hardly anyone's heard of."

"And what is she doing with a paladin?"

"I don't know. It looks like they're courting." Adale paused. "Say something."

Esofi shook her head. "I don't know what to say. I don't know what to make of this."

"Orsina told me that Knight-Commander Glace knows. Ask him if you don't believe me. Or come meet her yourself," urged Adale. "Ask her to prove it. Somehow."

Esofi exhaled slowly. "If her claim turns out to be true...we could hardly command her to come with us."

"I wasn't thinking we'd command her. I was going to offer to hire Orsina on for a job. Elyne would only be with us because she was following Orsina. Nobody would suspect there's anything special about her. Which is how I think they want to keep it."

"That is strange to me. Surely she wants attention? Worshippers? Or does she have an edict for us?"

Adale shrugged. "Maybe. But maybe not. Maybe she's just here to enjoy herself. Getting swarmed by people asking for miracles would cut into that."

"I will speak to Knight-Commander Glace," said Esofi. "If what you say is true, then...I suppose it would not hurt to invite her."

Adale looked pleased.

"And where are Brandt and Svana?"

"Oh..." Adale's smile melted away, leaving only guilt behind. "I sent them off to catch that unicorn. The one they brought to you back when they were trying to..."

"You did *what*?" cried Esofi. "*Why?* I specifically promised that nobody would ever bother him again! You know I did! Why would you ever—"

"I panicked! He's the only truthsayer within Ieflaria's borders! I thought he could help us work out who poisoned you!"

Esofi groaned and covered her eyes with her hands. "Tell me you at least didn't tell them that."

"I didn't! His blessing is still a secret, at least for now."

"Maybe they won't manage to catch him." Esofi let her hands fall to her sides. "I'll have to send him an apology gift."

"Of what, the finest grass?"

"Don't make me laugh when I'm angry at you!" Esofi tried her best to glare.

"But it's my only means of defense!"

Esofi sighed. The last traces of dreamy light-headedness from the bath were finally fading away from her, and now her thoughts were beginning to turn more serious.

"Well," said Adale, "as long as we're being honest with each other...the Temple of Rikilda has offered to send you a replacement for Lisette. Another—what, Nightingale?"

Esofi pulled a pillow over her own face and groaned. "Nightshade," she said, somewhat muffled.

"And all this time I just thought she was exceptionally strange. In any case, I told them no." Adale paused. "They were very apologetic. Seemed to think Lisette had failed you."

"No!" Esofi removed the pillow. "I trust her. If she's not here, there's a good reason for it."

"Well, I hope you're right, because part of me is about ready to send her home to Rhodia."

Esofi shook her head. "I'm sure we'll have answers soon," she said. "Lisette would not be gone this long unless she had no other choice."

"YOU WANT TO go *where?*" cried Saski.

"I think it's a good idea," said Esofi.

"No! I won't allow it." Esofi had never seen Saski so distressed before. "You shouldn't even be out of bed, let alone plotting to run off and gallivant with dragons!"

"I understand your concern—"

"If you did, you wouldn't even ask me this." Saski rested a hand over her own heart, then held it out in front of her. "Look at me. I'm shaking. Did Adale put you up to this?"

"No, I just—"

"No. The answer is no. Now go back to your room before I have the guards drag you there."

Esofi's mouth fell open. "What? You can't—!"

"Esofi, you might have died yesterday!" Saski gripped her by the shoulders, and Esofi could see tears gathering in her eyes. "You can't possibly think I'd let you leave Birsgen now."

"Whoever poisoned me is most likely in Birsgen still. I might be safer elsewhere."

Saski appeared to have been stunned into silence.

"I do not mean to give offense," Esofi kept her voice low and calm. "It is only...until the one who did this is caught, I cannot help but see danger everywhere." This was not a lie, but she was unwilling to admit it was her mother's presence that truly spurred her need to leave Birsgen.

Saski did not say anything, but Esofi could feel her fingers loosening on her shoulders.

"There is nothing waiting for me in the Silver Isles that I do not know how to fight," Esofi said. "I will go secretly, so that an assassin won't be able to follow. But I can't stay here. I'll go mad."

Saski seemed to be considering her words. Then she said, "If I grant you permission to go…"

"Yes?"

"It is under the condition that you will return to Birsgen *without delay* the moment your assassin is caught."

"I will agree to that."

Saski sighed deeply. "Is there nothing I can say to convince you to remain here?"

"I am sorry," said Esofi. "I don't mean to hurt you, I just—"

"I know you don't." Saski released her shoulders and grasped her hands instead. "I appreciate how difficult these past weeks have been for you. I cannot say I blame you for wanting to leave."

IT WAS SURPRISINGLY easy to track Elyne down. It seemed that nearly everyone in the castle knew her name, despite the fact she had only just arrived. Esofi found her in one of the main sitting rooms, surrounded by several of King Dietrich and Queen Saski's most prominent painters. There was no sign of Dame Orsina.

Elyne was chattering eagerly, hands flying to emphasize her every point. The assorted artists were all watching her intently, as though she was a venerated scholar instead of a foreign girl with no title.

When they spotted Esofi standing in the doorway, they all rose to their feet—except Elyne herself, who merely appeared puzzled.

Esofi stared at her—she could not help it. But there was nothing about Elyne to suggest she might be a goddess. In fact, there was a large stain on her bodice, as though she had spilled a drink down her front recently.

"Oh!" shouted Elyne, jolting to her feet abruptly. "I'm supposed to curtsy!"

"That's quite all right," Esofi began. But Elyne was already executing a wobbling curtsy, or something resembling one. "I only wanted to—"

"Right! This! Everyone go back to what you were doing! I'm going to talk to the princess!" Elyne straightened up and walked past Esofi, out of the room. Esofi followed, a bit bemused.

"You didn't bring Carinth," said Elyne, once Esofi caught up with her. "I'm disappointed."

"I—I'm sorry. I can fetch him—"

Elyne laughed. "You're nervous. Don't be nervous. I promise I'm not intimidating. If it came to a fight, you'd probably beat me."

"Why are you here?"

"I'm stealing followers from Ridon." Elyne rubbed her hands together, as though to warm them. "Do you know, we've been travelling for *months* and Adale was the first one to realize something wasn't right with me?"

"She wants you to come to the Silver Isles with us."

"That sounds fun!" Elyne's eyes lit with excitement, like a child promised candy. "I don't have as much magic as you think I do, but I can identify any creature we encounter, no matter how obscure, and I can speak whatever language you need me to. But Orsina must come with me. I won't go anywhere without her."

"That's no trouble," Esofi promised. "All I ask is that you not tell anyone else of our plans to leave. We are hoping to do it secretly, as to not alert the one who attempted to poison me."

Elyne grew solemn. "I still don't know who did it. I told Adale the same thing. Whoever they are, I don't think they're in the castle anymore. And I really don't think it was your mother."

"My mother?" Esofi repeated.

"Of course, a lot of people still think it was..."

"My mother did *not* poison me!" The words came out far more forcefully than Esofi had intended.

"I know that!" Elyne put her hands up in the air, palms facing outward in a supplicating gesture. "But not everyone does."

"Why would they think she did it?"

"Well...mainly because they've met her, I think."

Esofi gaped at her, inelegantly.

"I'm sorry if that wasn't what you wanted to hear," said Elyne. "But I've found that telling the truth is easier than lying. In the long run."

If Elyne had been anyone else, Esofi would have ordered her out of her sight. But Elyne was a goddess. Supposedly. Even now, Esofi could not quite bring herself to believe.

"She wouldn't do that," whispered Esofi. "She is my *mother*."

"Forget I said anything, then." Elyne began edging away. Esofi supposed she could have called her back, but she did not.

Faith had always come so easily to Esofi. But Elyne's dress was stained, and it looked like she had traces of dirt on her face. Esofi knew stories of gods coming to Inthya in humble forms to test their followers, but Elyne did not give the impression that she was attempting something like that. The form she'd chosen seemed to be...*herself*, for lack of a better word.

She would have to consult with Knight-Commander Glace before things went any further.

THE ORDER OF the Sun had official headquarters in Birsgen, complete with barracks, but Knight-Commander Glace could frequently be found in the castle. He served as an advisor to their majesties, and frequently weighed in on prominent court cases or other matters of justice.

When Esofi summoned him to her room, she was not expecting an immediate response. But there was a knock at the door within half an hour, before she was even done collecting her thoughts.

"Princess!" Knight-Commander Glace sounded genuinely surprised to see Esofi upright and sitting at a table. "You have recovered—?"

"Yes."

"I am glad to hear it," he said. "And I hope you know that we are doing everything in our power to apprehend—"

"I do," said Esofi. "But I do not wish to speak of assassins with you."

"You do not?" Esofi supposed she understood his confusion. Doubtless he had already spent many hours aiding with the investigation.

"No. I actually wished to discuss a theological matter with you."

She had never seen a man look so utterly baffled before. Esofi took a breath and decided to begin.

"Today I spoke with the young woman who came with Dame Orsina from Vesolda." Esofi fiddled with one of her earrings. "I suppose you already know what I'm going to ask?"

"I have my suspicions."

"She says her name is Elyne."

Glace inclined his head. "She does say that."

The lack of a direct answer was infuriating, and so Esofi snapped, "You did not think King Dietrich and Queen Saski would want to know what you were bringing into their castle?"

"I felt it might do more harm than good," Glace replied evenly. "But I assure you, Princess, the Order is watching her carefully."

"The entire Order? Or just the paladin you have sharing a room with her?"

Glace, to his credit, did not react.

"I could inform their majesties," said Esofi. "I *should*. They've a right to know."

"If you wish to do so, I will make no attempt to stop you." Glace did not appear to be even slightly troubled by this threat. "However, I would like to point out that revealing Aelia's true nature publicly might result in—"

"Aelia?" repeated Esofi. "Is that her true name?"

"Yes. At least, it is in Ioshora. I understand she is called other things in other lands."

"I've never heard of her."

"Most haven't. She is a very minor goddess. The Order estimates she has less than thirty worshippers. If you attempt to research her, you will find her documented as the Goddess of Caprice."

"A chaos goddess?"

"Formerly. The Order of the Sun now recognizes Aelia as the Goddess of Inspiration," said Glace. "A remarkable thing, especially in such a short period of time. Usually a domain shift takes hundreds, if not thousands of years."

"I...may have raised my voice at her," said Esofi, mortification rising in her chest now that her suspicions had been truly confirmed. "Perhaps I ought to apologize."

"I don't think that will be necessary."

Esofi sighed heavily. "I don't know what to make of her. She strikes one as so...ordinary. Even with your assurance, I find myself doubting her celestial nature."

"I understand your feelings," agreed Glace. "But the Order of the Sun has discovered that minor gods do not conduct themselves in the same way as the Ten. The less powerful they are, the more like Men their behavior tends to be. She may originate from Asterium, but as of this moment, Aelia is more akin to a mortal woman than a goddess—at least in temperament."

"I'm sorry." Esofi pressed her hands to her forehead. "I just...I wasn't expecting this today."

"I do not like to see you in distress, especially after all that has happened recently." Knight-Commander Glace frowned. "If you wish it, I can order Dame Orsina back to Vesolda. Aelia will follow her."

"No." Esofi's hands fell to her sides. "That won't be necessary. But...thank you."

She couldn't really bring herself to remain angry at Glace. She disliked that he had kept this from them, but she could not deny that his intentions had been good. She would not tell Saski and Dietrich—not yet, at least. Not unless Aelia left her with no other options.

Chapter Nine

ADALE

"What are these things?" asked Esofi.

Adale looked up from her reading to see Esofi standing in the doorway between the sitting room and their bedroom, a little linen sachet in the palm of her hand. It was too small and too far away for Adale to make out any details, but she knew from experience that it would be embroidered with strange runes.

"I've seen them before, but today I'm finding them everywhere," Esofi went on. "They keep turning up in my pockets, and there was one under my pillow. Should I be worried, or just annoyed?"

A smile tugged at Adale's lips. "Annoyed, I think. They're protective charms. My mother makes them."

Adale had pulled one apart, once, when she was young. It was partially out of curiosity, but mostly because her hands had been unoccupied at the time. She'd ripped it open, hoping to find something mysterious and magical inside, since Saski's fingertips always glowed lavender when she added her magic to things. But all Adale got was some dried herbs, a scrap of fabric stained rust-red, and a few tiny, perfectly smooth stones that might have been picked up from the garden.

Adale shifted her position on the couch, disturbing both Cream and Carinth in the process. "Don't you have them in Rhodia?"

"I imagine we must. But Pemele's magic is not commonly found in the palace."

I cannot imagine why, Adale did not say because it would only hurt Esofi's feelings. Instead she said, "She must be feeling worried if she's leaving us so many."

"Do they do anything?" asked Esofi.

"Well, it's Pemele's blessing. So it's hard to tell what's magic and what's just good luck or coincidence. I've never seen one do anything notable."

Esofi slipped the little sachet into her pocket and sat down next to Adale on the couch. "What are you reading?" she asked.

"Information about the journey," said Adale. "My parents have selected a ship. Officially, they're chartering it for a mapmaking expedition, since we really don't have any decent maps of the Isles. I think it's a good cover story. Credible, but also very boring."

On maps of the continent, the Silver Isles were depicted as a cluster or five or six medium-sized islands, but it was common knowledge that there were many more than that, most too small to be depicted. Until now, there hadn't been a need for more accurate maps, for nobody had any reason to venture too deeply into the dragons' territory.

"Are they actually sending cartographers along, or is that just the story they're telling?" asked Esofi.

"No, they really are. You don't mind, do you?"

"No," said Esofi. "It sounds like something we've been needing for a while. And it will give the crew something to do during the day while we're on the island."

At Fenstell, Ivanedi had specifically mentioned that they should come to the largest island. Even with their limited knowledge of the area, there was no question of which one he meant. It was the easternmost island, vaguely crescent-shaped and three times the size of the other ones depicted on the map.

There would be no ports or docks on the islands, unless some entrepreneurial pirates had been hard at work. Adale understood they would have to find a safe place to drop anchor and then row ashore. At night, they would return to the ship. They were *not* to make camp on the island—her parents had been very clear on that point.

"Do you want to bring Daphene and Lethea with us?" asked Esofi.

"No," said Adale. "I don't think that would be wise." For while Daphene and Lethea might not object to climbing mountains and wandering through forests, the journey to the Silver Isles was meant to be a diplomatic one. Adale knew she could not trust them to behave themselves.

In fact, she probably could not even trust them to keep their departure a secret. Telling those two anything was generally the quickest way to have the news spread all over the city.

It would still be a few days before they could leave, so in the meantime Adale was staying close to Esofi. The mood in the castle was tense and anxious, and it reminded her far too much of the days after Albion's death.

Adale had tried several times to check on the status of the investigation into who had poisoned Esofi. But each time, she had been turned away at the door.

Even now, she found it difficult to believe Gaelle had not been the one responsible for it all. Who else could it have possibly been? Adale had made a list of everywhere

Esofi had been that day. Her morning and noontime meals had been taken in the palace, and the kitchen staff had been among the first to be interrogated. She'd visited with Adale's parents in the morning, and Lady Catrin after that, and in the afternoon she and Gaelle had gone to the University, followed by the Temple of Talcia. Lady Catrin was about as likely a suspect as her newborn baby, and the Temple of Talcia was more loyal to Esofi than to Adale's own parents. That only left Gaelle—or someone Adale did not know at all.

At least Esofi was making a fast recovery. The healers wanted her to stay in bed, just to be safe, but idleness was not in Esofi's nature. A few people had come to visit, only to be surprised to find Esofi up and fully dressed and seated before a stack of books, or maps, or the careful timeline of the Emperor's rise to power she was beginning to compile.

Gaelle had not been among those visitors, and neither had Lexandrie. Adale was not sure how she felt about this. On the one hand, she supposed she ought to be grateful that Gaelle wasn't around to make Esofi miserable. On the other hand, she was offended that Esofi's mother did not seem at all bothered by what had happened.

Adale was counting the days until they could leave for the Silver Isles. The plan was to leave quickly and quietly, before the break of dawn. Almost nobody would be informed of their departure, and their destination would not be public knowledge—for Esofi's own safety, her parents would claim. And while that wasn't completely untrue, both Adale and Esofi knew perfectly well that evading assassins was only secondary to evading Gaelle.

Adale's blood still boiled when she remembered Gaelle's assertation that Adale might ever be disloyal to Esofi. Did Gaelle even believe her own words? Or had it just been an attempt to hurt Esofi, to make her doubt herself and Adale?

Adale's relationship with her own parents was imperfect. They'd had their share of disagreements, especially in her adolescence, and she knew they would never completely understand one another. But never once had they attempted to *hurt* her. Nor did she believe that they would ever try. The very idea was bizarre and foreign to her. It was simply not what parents did.

And yet, that had been Esofi's entire life before coming to Ieflaria.

Gaelle did not hide her disinterest in Esofi, but it was quite the opposite with Carinth. When he climbed into her lap—which he frequently did—she became another woman entirely, the picture of a doting grandmother. Worse still, she was still showing no signs of planning to return to Rhodia.

Adale felt somewhat vindicated to know that she was not the only one who disliked Esofi's mother. The servants were not fond of her either, and it did not take much coaxing to get them to share stories of their own experiences.

Most concerning was the servant girl who *swore* that Gaelle had raised a hand, as though to strike her, when she'd delivered the wrong sort of wine. But at that moment, Lexandrie had bumped the table with enough force to knock all the glasses over, distracting Gaelle and giving the servant a chance to flee.

A small, terrible part of Adale wished Gaelle would strike someone. Of course, she didn't want any of their servants to suffer abuse, but it might be worth it to have a reason to send her home. She wondered if she ought to offer a reward to any servant brave enough to deliberately provoke violence from Gaelle.

FINALLY, THE DAY of their departure arrived.

With only Mireille and Orsina and Elyne as attendants, the trip to Valenleht was peaceful, even enjoyable. Adale did not regret sending Brandt and Svana after the unicorn, regardless of what Esofi had promised him. With those two gone and Gaelle and Lexandrie still in Birsgen, perhaps this journey would manage to be what the trip to Fenstell had not been.

Elyne, unfailingly cheerful, entertained them all with stories from lands nobody, not even Esofi, had heard of. Orsina rode outside of the carriage, but Elyne frequently opened the door to shout observations at her—much to Carinth's annoyance. After the first day, he sat in her lap with his head over her hands to prevent her from being able to reach the handle and let gusts of cold air in.

Meanwhile, Orsina worked to improve her understanding of the Ieflarian language. Adale could speak Vesoldan, but Esofi and Mireille could not. Orsina spoke haltingly, uncertain, despite Elyne's encouragement.

As for Esofi, Adale found reading her difficult. She passed the time with her embroidery and did not appear to be unhappy. She was quieter than usual, but maybe that was to be expected, given everything that had happened. Adale hoped she would open up again once they were away from Ieflaria.

Adale was making an extra effort to be attentive to Esofi's needs, especially now that they lacked any true servants. She sat as near to her as she could without encroaching on her space entirely and held her hands when she was not busy with her embroidery. Fortunately, Esofi did not seem to mind.

Valenleht was a picturesque city, though Adale had never spent much time in it due to the presence of her cousins. It had been Ieflaria's capital before Birsgen, hundreds of years ago. Now it served as Ieflaria's most important port, even though the royal court had long since moved further inland.

Unfortunately, there was no time for sight-seeing. The ship that would take them to the Silver Isles was already waiting. And while Adale knew they wouldn't leave without the princesses, she did not want to keep the crew waiting and give them a bad first impression.

When they arrived at the docks, Adale was surprised to see the ship her parents had chartered was smaller than expected, though it was certainly no tiny fishing boat. It was called the Courser, and it was a passenger ship that traversed Ieflaria's eastern and southern coasts, occasionally taking on cargo for extra profit.

Adale supposed the choice made sense, given that Esofi was insistent they not call attention to themselves. Privately, Adale might have felt safer on a military ship armed with too many cannons to count, in case the expedition went badly. But then, Esofi had been very clear that this was a diplomatic mission. She might have refused to set foot on a warship.

Or perhaps not, with Gaelle still at Birsgen.

Adale still held out hope that Gaelle would be gone by the time they returned. It seemed unlikely, but she felt they were due for a bit of good luck. There was still no sign of Lisette, and Adale wondered if they'd soon be hearing that her body had been found in a river somewhere. She had not shared this morbid thought with either Esofi or Mireille. It would not help.

Upon boarding the Courser, Esofi's mood seemed to change for the better, and rather quickly. Her smile became radiant and genuine, and she stood taller, as though the weight of her mother's presence and the would-be assassin had finally fallen from her shoulders.

The captain of the ship was retired from the Ieflarian navy after a long and colorful career hunting pirates, and Adale was certain this was why her parents had selected them. There would be no unnecessary risks taken, and the crew would not hesitate to fight if the worst did happen.

There was no shortage of entertainment for Carinth on the ship, who seemed to regard the busy sailors as his own personal performance troupe. He scampered up posts and found places to perch where he could watch them go about their work. Adale and Esofi both kept a close eye on him. A ship could be dangerous, especially for one so small. But Carinth seemed to have the sense to stay out of the way.

Nevertheless, Esofi called him back to her when it was time to go below and inspect the cabins they would be staying in.

Since this was a passenger ship first and foremost, the rooms were significantly nicer than they would have been on a naval ship. Adale and Esofi had been assigned the most spacious cabin, where there was more than enough room for all the luggage Esofi had brought.

The ship was not overly luxurious, but it was not as rough as the fortress at Fenstell had been. Adale would have no difficulty tolerating it—she had been in hunting lodges less comfortable than this. Esofi did not complain either.

It would only be a few days before they arrived at the Silver Isles. In a way, that was surprising. The Isles had always seemed so far removed from Ieflaria, even when the dragons had been actively attacking. But Adale knew the distance had never been what kept Men from its shores.

Adale left Esofi to organize their room and went back up to the deck, Carinth close behind her. She found Mireille peering over the edge of the ship's railing and into the water below.

"Did you believe Elyne's story about the giant shark?" asked Mireille.

"No," said Adale. "Do you?"

"No," said Mireille. But Adale noticed that she kept well away from the sides of the ship anyway.

They cast off within the hour, and Adale could not help but feel a surge of excitement as she watched Port Valenleht vanish on the horizon. She had not left Ieflaria in years, and now she was going somewhere that no Men had set foot in living memory.

She decided she would go back down and check on Esofi. Hopefully she'd be feeling better than ever before, now that they had truly left Birsgen behind. But as she made her way to the staircase, she noticed Elyne perched on the edge of the ship's rail like it was a chair, legs swinging free over the open water.

Adale moved toward her to ask what she was doing. Then she realized that Elyne was making very strange noises, clicking and humming and occasionally trilling. Adale peered over her shoulder and saw a few Mer swimming in the water below. They made the same sounds back at Elyne.

Realizing Adale was watching her, Elyne turned and said, "It's really meant to be spoken under the water. It sounds silly above."

Adale knew these Mer were not casual passers-by, they were an integral part of the Courser's crew, even though they could not come aboard. They would swim alongside, or ahead, watching for signs of danger. At night, or when they grew exhausted, they would sleep in underwater nets that had been fastened to the ship's side.

At first glance, Mer resembled Men, at least from the waist up. But their skin came in shades of grays and blue-greens, rather than pinks or browns, and their hair could be obsidian-black or verdant green or any color in-between. Their chests were flat and featureless, for they did not nurse their young, who hatched from strange, jellylike eggs. Their fingers were webbed together to aid in swimming, and their teeth were triangular and arranged in awful rows within their mouths. They could breathe both water and air, but their lack of legs prevented them from ever truly being part of the world above. If they even sat on the shore for too long, their silver tails would dry out.

Despite their animalistic appearances, the Mer were just as intelligent as Men and killing one was considered murder. Not that tangling with them was wise. It was difficult to get the upper hand on one of them, especially in the water—or so Adale had heard.

There were some not-so-positive stories about the Mer, mostly regarding vanished ships and missing treasure. Their reputation for extorting merchant vessels was not entirely unearned, though Adale understood this was less common than stories suggested. In modern times, Mer worked with fishermen in a mutually beneficial relationship, and some were even employed as scouts by the Ieflarian navy.

The Mer were the creation of Merla, Goddess of the Sea and Second of the Ten. Her best blessings almost always went to them. Occasionally, some would affiliate themselves with the Temple of Merla. But usually they preferred to worship her in their own way, which Adale understood involved a lot of singing and not much else.

Music was the other thing the Mer were famous for. They seemed to have an innate understanding of it, and it was said they could play any instrument placed into their hands, even if they'd never encountered it before. Some even worked as tutors, for those students who did not mind learning to sing on the rocks or dunes.

Adale had always thought this seemed inconvenient, to have to sing over the roar of the ocean, with sand flying in one's eyes, but no Mer had ever agreed to be pulled around in a hand-cart.

That evening, after dinner, the party gathered to discuss what awaited them at the Silver Isles.

"Do you think the dragons will send someone to meet us?" wondered Mireille.

"Maybe. I expect they'll see us coming. I just hope Ivanedi told them to expect us," Adale said.

"I am sure he did," said Esofi. "And if not..."

If not, Adale hoped they could get away without sinking the ship.

"The Mer say they generally stay away from the Isles," said Elyne. "I don't blame them."

"Will they be safe?" asked Adale. "Ivanedi only promised they wouldn't attack Men anymore. He didn't mention any other races..."

"Why would a dragon attack a Mer?" asked Mireille.

"To eat them?" suggested Elyne.

"Oh!" Mireille shuddered. "Esofi, you won't let that happen, will you?"

"Of course not," said Esofi. "But don't worry yourself—the Mer are not helpless either. The sea is not a place that breeds weakness. Besides, I'm sure some of them have magic of their own."

The main island came in sight on the morning of the third day, just as the sun was rising. Adale would not admit it aloud, but she was a little disappointed at the sight of it. After a lifetime of hearing tales of the Silver Isles—their danger and mystery—she had been expecting something strange and foreboding.

The island seemed nearly taller than it was wide, impossible mountains and cliffs and rough trees all reaching skyward. Adale had no idea how they would make it above the shoreline, which was little more than a thin strip of grey sand—or perhaps stone, it was too far off to tell—that went straight to verdant plant life.

That day, Esofi surprised Adale by wearing neither an Ieflarian dress, nor one of her famous Rhodian gowns. Instead, she wore blue robes and leather boots, the sort worn by mages. Adale had never seen Esofi wear such a thing, nor had she even been aware Esofi owned robes. But Esofi claimed they were more practical for the wilderness than any dress. Adale supposed she could not argue with that.

Unlike the long robes worn by priests, Esofi's were only mid-length, stopping just below her knee. Thick woolen stockings and leather boots hid the rest of her legs. The sleeves were shortened, too, rather than loose and flowing. A long-sleeved undershirt protected her arms, and she wore a pair of fur-lined gloves—though she would need to take them off if she wanted to use her magic without destroying them.

The captain reported that the Mer found a good spot to go ashore, and within the hour they were being rowed toward land. It turned out the shoreline was stones after all, and Adale stepped down upon millions upon millions of softly rounded pebbles. Carinth wasted no time and immediately began collecting the most interesting ones in his claws. Once his hands were full, he deposited them into Mireille's pocket.

"Do you think they know we're here?" asked Adale, gazing up at the distant mountains.

"I'd be surprised if they didn't," said Esofi. "I only hope they send someone down to meet us soon. I don't want to go wandering through the forests."

There seemed to be nothing to do but wait. Esofi stayed near to the rowboats, but Adale wanted to explore a bit. After promising that she wouldn't stray into the trees, she began to walk down the shore.

It wasn't like the warm, golden seasides of southern Ieflaria or Vesolda that nobles liked to escape to in the winter months, but it was pretty in a colder, rougher way. The air was cool and fresh, and she could see faint movement in the distant woods, probably little forest creatures or birds fluttering from tree to tree.

And then she came upon the horse.

It was a stallion, tall and long-legged. Standing in the shallowest part of the water, he regarded her calmly with soft, dark eyes. Oddly enough, it did not look like a feral horse. His coat was glossy and dark and seemed well cared for. If Adale had seen him at Birsgen, she would have assumed he belonged to a noble, or at least a wealthy merchant.

How might he have found its way here? Had he been on a ship that sank? Was the owner someone she knew?

Adale moved toward the stallion slowly, cautiously. She was afraid he might startle and go galloping off down the shore or, worse, into the forests. He wore no tack and no bridle that she could grab hold of.

"Hey, you," said Adale softly, reaching into her pocket on instinct to see if she had any of the sweets that Warcry liked. "Where's your master? Or are we off on an adventure?"

The horse did not shy away as she approached but allowed Adale to come nearer. As her hand came to rest on the animal's neck, it occurred to her that he smelled a little unusual. She knew a horse's scent, warm hay and musk and manure. But this animal...he smelled like the sea.

"Having you been drinking sea water? That's not good for you. We should get you home." But how in the *world* could they get him back to the Courser? He'd never fit in a rowboat.

She gazed up into the horse's face. His eyes were not brown, as she'd first assumed. They were solidly black, like pools of ink. Adale felt a frown crease her forehead and moved to pull her hand away—only to find that she could not. Her hand was bound to the horse's neck as though it had been sewn on.

"The boy climbed on the horse's back," said a very, very old memory of Adale's mother. *"And the horse began to gallop. The boy was scared and tried to jump off. But his hands and legs had become fused to the horse's back. And the horse charged into the river..."*

"I'm an idiot," Adale informed the horse. Maybe if she didn't panic, it wouldn't take off immediately. "I don't suppose you take bribes?"

The horse reared up onto its hind legs, whinnying—except the sound was harsh and distorted and wrong. Adale, still unable to free her hand, twisted to the ground, screaming wordlessly. Sharp hooves smashed back to the grey stones, and Adale barely avoided them.

Then there was a flash of silver and white. The horse screamed again, but the pain in her arm lifted and Adale felt something give under her palm. A moment later, she was clutching nothing but a pulsing mass of hideous silver goo. The horse collapsed into formless black and silver muck.

"Crown Princess!" cried Orsina, in Vesoldan. A strong hand grabbed her by the arm and pulled her free of the mess. "Are you all right?"

Adale stared up into Orsina's face, lips trembling. She could not manage any words, so she just nodded. Orsina looked back down at the melted remains of the stallion and sheathed her sword.

"Water-horse," said Orsina. "It would have drowned you."

"I should have known better," mumbled Adale.

"Adale!" screamed Esofi. Adale turned just as Esofi collided with her, arms wrapping tight around her body.

"It's all right. I'm all right," Adale reassured her, but she held Esofi close anyway. "Not a scratch on me, see?"

Esofi did not respond, but tears spilled from her eyes.

"No more wandering," said Orsina solemnly. "Dragons are not the only monsters living here. We must not forget that."

"Why would Talcia make something like *that?*" demanded Adale.

"The water-horse is not Talcia's. It's Merla's." That was Elyne, with Mireille close behind. Carinth jumped down from Mireille's shoulders and went to Adale.

"Well, Ivanedi didn't mention water-horses. Only gryphons."

"I'm sure there are many types of creatures on these islands," said Elyne. "You might be better off assuming that anything you encounter is dangerous."

Carinth was sniffing at the mess that the water-horse had left behind. Esofi leaned down and pulled him away from it as he squeaked objections.

They began the walk back to the spot where the boats were moored. Adale looked back to the trees once again, imagining what sort of creatures might be hiding there. Was everything on the Silver Isles as malevolent as the water-horse, or were there good things, too?

Carinth began making excited chirping noises, fidgeting restlessly in Esofi's arms. Adale looked at him, but he was staring up at the sky. She followed his gaze to the large, pale dragon that was approaching from the cliffs.

Elyne and Orsina both tensed, but Esofi said. "It's all right. That's Ivanedi, I am sure of it."

When the dragon came in for a landing, Adale saw Esofi's assessment was correct. The force of his wingbeats sent a wave of smaller stones flying at them, and Adale covered her eyes with her arm to protect them.

"Ivanedi!" said Esofi, stepping forward.

"You managed to find your way here," rumbled Ivanedi.

"Yes." Esofi shifted her grip on Carinth. "I'm so glad you found us."

"Have you brought many Men with you?"

"No. It is only us, and the crew of the ship that brought us here." Esofi gestured toward the Courser, drifting peacefully where she was anchored. "And a few

Mer as well. I am very pleased to see you. We've no idea how to get off this shore."

"There are paths through the trees, but they are long," said Ivanedi, turning his head to gaze toward the forests. "It is much easier to fly, if you are not afraid."

Esofi and Adale looked at each other.

"*Are* you afraid?" asked Esofi.

"I'm not if you're not," said Adale.

"I am!" cried Mireille. "There's nothing to hold on to!"

That wasn't a bad point. Ivanedi's neck was far too large for anyone to wrap their arms around, and the ridges on his back seemed like they might hurt if she sat on them wrong. The ideal solution would be some sort of saddle, but it would have to go around the base of his neck, just before his wing-joints. Not that they had the time or materials to construct such a thing.

"Maybe...we should walk," said Orsina, haltingly.

"Yes! I will walk with Orsina, and we will meet you up there," said Mireille.

"No. We are not splitting up again," Esofi said firmly.

"Mireille might be right," realized Adale. "No disrespect to Ivanedi, but...there's no surviving a fall from that height."

"There are paths our young ones use, before they learn to fly," Ivanedi explained. "You must beware of gryphons, but if you are able to best a dragon, I expect you will be safe."

"We will not go looking for trouble," promised Esofi.

"I will show you where the paths begin," said Ivanedi. "It is impossible to climb directly upward, so they double on themselves. But they will bring you to the place where many of us make our nests."

"Are there many dragons on the main island?" asked Esofi.

"Those who raise young, or wish to be among others, gather here. The ones who would rather assemble hoards and live in peace keep to the smaller islands. But once the news spreads that you have come, I expect they will make their way here to see you."

"Are they going to be angry with me?"

"Some might, but I do not think they will be foolish enough to attack you. Even the ones who still wish to see your kind destroyed respect the power you have—and your influence with our mother."

"I have no influence with her!" Esofi cried in alarm. "Do not tell them that! I only...understand...what she wishes for you. There is a difference."

From the expression on Ivanedi's face, Adale was not sure if he agreed with her assessment. But he did not contradict her. Instead, he said, "I will show you where the path up the mountainside begins. It is too narrow for me to walk myself, or I would accompany you. I will meet you where the path becomes wide enough. If you become lost, send up a beacon. But as long as you remain on the path, you should be safe."

Ivanedi directed them to a gap in the trees Adale never would have spotted on her own, for it looked just like a natural opening. But once her eyes adjusted to the dim light, she realized there was indeed a path that gently sloped upward, toward the mountains.

They could not see very far ahead because the path wrapped around the mountainside several times. But it was warmer in the forest than on the beach, for the trees buffered them from the cold ocean air.

Carinth wriggled free of Esofi's arms and began sniffing eagerly at the trail. Adale supposed he could smell traces of all the young dragons that had walked this path before him.

At first, the group was tense, all still remembering the water-horse. But as they walked on, they began to relax. If there was something dangerous in the forest, it did not show itself. It was hard to say how much time passed, for the trees were so thick they blocked the sky. Given the size of the mountain, Adale had a feeling it would be at least an hour before they made it out of the woods.

After a while, Carinth grew tired of walking, and Esofi carried him again. When she could not hold him any longer, he went to Orsina's shoulders instead. The paladin was much better suited for carrying heavy weights over long distances, and never once complained about his size.

Mireille seemed to prefer to stick close to Orsina and her sword, while Elyne occasionally stepped off the path and vanished completely, only to return right around the time when Adale began to wonder whether they ought to stop and search for her. Esofi did not speak, but she seemed content and peaceful.

After a while, Adale began to lag behind the rest of the group, stopping to examine some of the more unusual plants they passed. Very few were in bloom at this time of year, but what little she did see had bright and colorful blossoms. Adale knew that brighter colors sometimes meant danger, so she kept her hands well away from those.

Adale turned away from the plants, meaning to catch up with the others again. But deeper in the trees, a flash of color and movement caught her eye, and she paused.

The long shadows and dappled light made it difficult to pick out patterns among the long grass and tangled underbrush, and Adale stepped off the path, squinting. She was certain she could see something—a bit of white, a bit of red...

She took another step, dried leaves and old twigs cracking under her boots. Thin branches reached out to tangle in her hair and scratch at her face. But Adale barely felt this, for now she realized exactly what had caught her eye. It was a gryphon.

Adale knew from heraldry that male gryphons were magnificent, all red-gold plumage and snowy white heads, and golden fur on their hindquarters. The females were equal or even greater in size, but their feathers were all brown and gray, and their fur was dark brindle. This one was clearly a male, and he held a dead rabbit in his front claws. But nobody had ever mentioned the sheer size of them. She'd always presumed they'd be about as large a wolf.

This one was nearer to the size of a lion.

Adale held very still as she evaluated the distance between them. Could he cross it in a single leap? Would he try? She moved backward slowly, for fear that running away would trigger his predator's instinct and prompt him to lunge. But the gryphon did not move as she shuffled back, except to shift his wings a little.

When her feet touched the pathway again, Adale looked ahead to see the others were nearly out of sight. Then she turned back to the gryphon, to see if he'd changed his mind about letting her leave. It—he—regarded her with dark, intelligent eyes, and Adale found herself wondering if he spoke Ieflarian.

"Adale?" called Esofi's voice from up ahead, and Adale tore her eyes from the creature.

"I'm coming," Adale called and hurried toward them. Occasionally, she glanced back over her shoulder, but the gryphon did not follow her.

Chapter Ten

ESOFI

It was nearly midday when they finally emerged from the forest and onto the grey mountainside. Esofi was glad she'd thought to bring out her old university robes and wear sensible shoes. The walk would have been unbearable in a gown.

The forest path could probably be widened enough to allow a carriage through, but how would they get one ashore? And Esofi would feel guilty if they went to all the trouble of doing that and the horses were promptly eaten by something. Besides, creating a road would probably be the first step in destroying the Isles' natural beauty, and Esofi did not want that.

As promised, Ivanedi was waiting for them when the forest came to its end, but he was not alone. Another dragon was waiting beside him.

"This is Releth," Ivanedi said. "She has been very eager to meet you."

Releth was almost as large as Ivanedi, though a bit thinner. Despite her size, something about her gave Esofi the impression that she was much younger than him. Her scales were a deep shade of emerald green, like the forest itself, and her eyes were the palest silver—a striking combination.

Carinth leapt off Orsina's shoulders and struck the ground quite hard, but he did not seem to notice that perhaps this should have hurt. He rushed right to Releth, sniffing at her eagerly. Releth lowered her head to do the same.

Releth said something in the dragons' language. But instead of translating, Ivanedi swung his head around and looked back the way he had come. A moment later, Esofi caught sight of something else coming down the mountain path—something quite small.

It was another dragon, barely larger than Carinth, but slimmer, and its scales were a deep, striking shade of crimson. The color was not ideal for camouflage, but it was extremely pleasant to look at.

Releth spoke again. Esofi did not understand the words, but she found the meaning was quite clear—she wanted the younger one to go back. But the little one paid her no mind.

"This is Etheriet," said Ivanedi. "She is the youngest hatchling we have here. She was told to wait with the rest of the flight, but she is eager to meet Carinth."

Ethireiet pounced, bowling Carinth over. Carinth squeaked and twisted, little claws scrabbling for something to grab on to. Panic seized at Esofi for a moment before she realized they were only playing, in the same way kittens did.

"Is she your hatchling?" Esofi asked Releth.

Releth burst into deep, quaking laughter reminiscent of thunder. Despite herself, Esofi took a hasty step backward. But Releth clearly was not offended by the question, only amused. "Sister," she said, in heavily accented Ieflarian. "Half-sister. Little sister."

Adale crouched down near Carinth and Etheriet. "I didn't know dragons came in red." She put her hands for Etheriet to sniff at. Etheriet jumped free of Carinth and immediately stuck her nose in Adale's pocket.

"Hey!" cried Adale, as Etheriet withdrew with a leather glove in her mouth. "No! Don't swallow that!"

Etheriet bounded away, out of Adale's reach, but Releth reached out with a massive claw and snatched the glove away from her. Releth said something very sternly, but Etheriet seemed to care not one bit. When Adale took the glove back, there were puncture holes in the palm.

"The flight has gathered to see you," said Ivanedi. "It is not too much further now, if you are ready."

The mountainside path was steeper and wider than the one in the forest had been, and there was no barrier between the edge and a terrible fall to the trees below. Ivanedi and Releth seemed to realize this, because they kept themselves between the ledge and their visitors at all times.

By contrast, Etheriet seemed to have no concept of the danger below. Esofi was fairly certain by her size that she could not fly yet, but neither Ivanedi nor Releth did anything to deter her as she occasionally paused to peer over the edge. Fearing Carinth might decide to follow her example, Esofi picked him up and settled him across her shoulders. Fortunately, it seemed his dislike of the cold was stronger than his curiosity.

"Do most dragons live in flights, or alone?" Esofi asked as she walked. She had read accounts of both.

"It depends upon the stage of one's life," Ivanedi explained. "Usually hatchlings are born into flights, for most mothers prefer the safety in numbers. Eventually adolescents will want to strike out on their own. Some return to the flight to raise hatchlings of their own, but some never do. Other times, a lone dragon will find he has become too old to hunt for himself. Those that are not too proud to ask for help will return to the flight."

"Are there different flights on the islands, or just the one?" asked Adale.

"Only one," confirmed Ivanedi. "Though sometimes smaller ones will spring up, in colder years. We keep to this island, mostly."

The slope leveled out after a while and brought them deeper into the mountains. Trees were still relatively sparse, but other kinds of plants were obviously flourishing, whether they were long grasses or wildflowers or tangled, prickly brush.

Eventually they came to a wide clearing, surrounded on two sides by high stone. There were at least thirty dragons gathered, and Esofi's heart leapt into her throat at the sight of them. Some were very pale, like Ivanedi, while some were dark like obsidian, and others were colored in shades of green or blue. Instinct screamed at Esofi to bring up her magic and strike before she was overwhelmed, but she did not let it show on her face.

Carinth jumped down from her shoulders and went over to examine the nearest group of dragons, tail waving eagerly from side to side. They all lowered their heads to sniff at him.

"Who is in charge here?" Esofi whispered to Ivanedi.

"Younger dragons frequently defer to the authority of their elders, but we have no formal leader now that we are without an Emperor," explained Ivanedi. Esofi nodded, remembering what he had told her at Fenstell. Privately, she was still not sure how anything could be accomplished if they were without a clear leader, but she would make a good-faith effort nevertheless. The dragons had already surprised her several times. Perhaps they would manage it again.

Esofi wondered if she should address the flight. But what could she possibly say to them, after all she had done? An apology? For committing murder? Any words she came up with would be cheap and hollow in the face of the brutal realities of what had happened in Ieflaria.

But none of the dragons seemed angry. It was difficult to read their faces, of course, since they were so different from Men. But there was only curiosity in the myriad jewel-toned eyes that watched her carefully. Some were openly relaxed, sitting back on their haunches with their tails curled around their feet. A few were even flat on the ground with all four limbs tucked beneath their bodies, like cats. None of them spoke, but the gathering was not precisely quiet, either. The noise of life, of deep, heaving breaths and massive shifting limbs and claws scraping at the dry ground filled the air.

"Ivanedi says that he has magic," said Releth, nodding at Carinth.

"Yes. We only learned very recently. It was a surprise."

Soft, indistinct murmuring went through the gathering.

"Carinth," said Esofi. "Come here. I want to show them your magic."

Carinth bounded over to Esofi and sat up before her, his bright eyes curious and alert.

"Remember how you showed Grandmother?" asked Esofi, curling her fingers and calling a little spark of pink fire to her palm to demonstrate. "Can you do it again?"

Carinth looked over at Etheriet.

"You can play in just a minute, I promise," said Esofi. "Come on. Else all these dragons are going to think I'm a liar."

Carinth raised his hand, and Esofi sighed in relief. After a moment, a little flicker of azure magic sprang up in his palm. The dragons' soft murmuring turned loud, and Carinth dropped his hand and scampered behind Esofi.

"It's all right," Esofi soothed. "They're not mad at you. They're all very impressed."

Etheriet was the first to approach Carinth, sniffing at his hands like she was trying to catch a trace of the magic that had been there.

Esofi turned to address the elder dragons. "As I am sure Ivanedi has already told you I want to help you gain your magic back. If not for yourselves, then certainly for your hatchlings. This is Talcia's will as much as it is my own. But...right now, my people are still afraid of you. And...I am a little bit, as well." Was that a bad idea, to admit vulnerability? Gaelle certainly would think so. But then, the dragons were afraid of her as well. Maybe a bit of honesty would help to defuse the tension. "If we can maintain this peace between us, I should be able to take an active role in helping you regain the blessings you have lost."

One of the other dragons, not as large as Releth and Ivanedi but not nearly as small as the little ones, came forward for a closer look at Carinth.

"I hope he can begin to learn your language," said Esofi, raising her voice a little to be heard. "And I'm sure there's more he needs to know that I can't teach him."

A few other dragons, larger than Etheriet but obviously still in various stages of childhood and adolescence, gathered around Carinth. Esofi smiled. Carinth would not be an outsider among his own kind. She would bring him here often—perhaps every summer?—so he could learn to be a dragon.

When she looked around, she realized that Ivanedi had moved away from the others and was now seated in a patch of sunlight, tail wrapped around his front claws. After a glance toward Adale and the others to make sure they were all faring well, she went to him.

"I'm glad I decided to come here," she said. "I should have done it sooner."

"It is better that you waited," said Ivanedi. "They might have panicked if you'd come unannounced."

Esofi watched as Mireille knelt down and reached out, tentatively, to touch Etheriet's ridged forehead. Etheriet rose up on her hind legs and braced her front claws on Mireille's shoulders, sniffing at her face. Mireille giggled, and tried not to lose her balance.

"We had no idea you were not animals," said Esofi. "When I learned that you were capable of speech, I realized...and I have felt guilt from that moment onward. It has been the same with the unicorns and gryphons. We've assumed that they were only animals, because they have never spoken to us. Or at least, not in living memory. And...I don't understand why. It would all be so much easier if..." Tears of frustration sprang to her eyes, and Esofi forced herself to calm down.

Ivanedi watched her, inscrutable, for a long moment. "Iolar's children do not do well in isolation," he said. "You build large communities, roads that stretch across continents. You cross mountains and oceans and brave terrible dangers simply for the sake of reaching more of your own kind. And you structure yourselves in hierarchies so that you know what you are to one another. But Talcia's children are different. Your desire for connectedness is as strange to us as our solitude is to you."

"I do not mean to disrespect your ways," said Esofi. "I only...I feel such regret for the ones I have killed. And I cannot help but think, if only I'd known—"

"What would be different?" asked Ivanedi. "Would you have allowed them to destroy you simply because they were capable of speech?"

"No," said Esofi. "But I might have reasoned with them."

"There is little reasoning with those under an Emperor's compulsion."

"Does that not trouble you?"

"Why should it?"

"When your will is not your own—when you are sent to your death—when an Emperor cares more for his own spite than the lives of his subjects..."

"Is that any different from how Men live?"

Esofi was offended. "I'd never send my subjects to such pointless deaths!"

"Zethe believed wholeheartedly that destroying you was the way to win back our mother's love," said Ivanedi. "Perhaps the idea grew from a seed of spite, but it was not killing for the sake of killing. Even those who disagreed with his methods wanted the same result. He would not have gone unchallenged if that was not so."

"An Emperor can be challenged?"

"Yes, of course."

"But...how can that be when he can compel everyone to obey him?"

"It requires a strong will and an unshakable belief that the Emperor's actions cannot benefit our kind in any way. It is not an easy thing. And even if one does manage to stand against him, there is no guarantee they will win."

"Did anyone try?"

"No. Or if they did, it was not done publicly, and they did not win."

Esofi looked down at her hands. "Well...in the interest of honesty, I must tell you that not all the dragons I have killed were following the Emperor's orders. When I was very young, when I was first learning, our mother would bring us to the mountains...where there had been sightings..."

"I am well aware," said Ivanedi.

Esofi shook her head. "You know her? How?"

"I do not know her name, and I have never seen her face. But I know that a sensible dragon stays away from the Great Mother of what you call Thiyra. Every mother has told her hatchlings this, for hundreds of years. But not all listen."

"No, I suppose not," said Esofi. "There are not nearly as many in Rhodia...and they keep to the peaks, where we cannot reach them without great effort."

Ivanedi nodded. "Our young adults are frequently reckless. They believe nothing can best them. They have only seen Men from a great distance, far below, and think there is no chance a creature so small might pose a threat to their safety. And Thiyra's mountains and cliffs and caves are very attractive to our kind. There are even tales of old hoards, unguarded and untouched for generations. It can be a tempting prospect."

"I am sorry to hear that."

But Ivanedi did not seem at all troubled by this loss of young life. "Better they die in their youth, before they can pass their foolishness on to their own hatchlings."

"That sounds like something my mother would say." Esofi laughed.

"Have you brought her here with you?"

"No, I..." Esofi stopped. Ivanedi did not need to hear about her personal problems. "She did not accompany me. You don't need to worry."

Ivanedi adjusted his wings. "I acknowledge your guilt, though I do not understand it. I hope it is some consolation to know the other dragons feel the same way I do."

"I want it to stop," said Esofi. "A world cannot thrive if we're all hunting one another."

"Perhaps the world of Men cannot," Ivanedi dipped his head. "But danger is what makes our kind strong. And chaos is the nature of all things, no matter how you try to bend the world into order. How long does it take for your cities, once abandoned, to return to forests and fields? Not terribly long, I think. Order strikes me as exhausting. It is not enough to attain it. It must be constantly maintained, or it slips away."

Esofi's eyes fell upon Elyne. She was speaking animatedly to a few dragons that had gathered around her. She couldn't hear what she was saying, but the dragons seemed interested. Not far away, Orsina stood observing this, calm and collected but obviously waiting for signs of trouble.

"Talcia said to me...when I asked her if you had grown too wild for her to love...she laughed, like I was a foolish child. She said, *you play in the woods for an hour and think you know wildness.* When I think of her, I picture a woman, but maybe I should imagine her as a dragon."

"You imagine her as a Man?" asked Ivanedi.

"I know, it doesn't make much sense, does it? But all of the statues I've ever seen of her are like that. But she married Iolar, so I think she'd have to be a woman at least some of the time. Else it would get inconvenient."

"What are you two talking about?" asked Adale. Her hair was starting to come out of its braid, a side effect of allowing the younger dragons to climb on her shoulders.

"You've got a scratch on your face," worried Esofi.

"It's fine; it was an accident." Adale waved her hand, even as Esofi reached into her pocket for a handkerchief.

Soon enough, it was time to return to the ship for the night. Ivanedi said they would be welcome to stay, but they would have to sleep on the ground, or on piles of dry leaves. Nobody except Orsina found these accommodations acceptable, and Esofi had not forgotten that their majesties wanted them to sleep on the ship. So they made their way back down the mountain path—though Carinth practically had to be dragged away from all his new friends.

The walk down was much faster and easier than the walk up, and the sun was only just beginning to set when they arrived back on the beach.

There was no courier from Birsgen waiting for them when they returned to the ship, which Esofi was relieved to see. Of course, she wanted to see the assassin caught. But she knew Saski would hold her to her promise to return as soon as it was safe, so she hoped it would not be done too quickly.

Once they were back in their room, Esofi collapsed on the bed. Her feet were aching, and so were her legs. She'd barely noticed when they were on the island, but now that there was nothing to distract her, she could hardly think of anything else.

"Too bad that horse turned out to be a monster," commented Adale. "I'm not looking forward to walking up that mountain again tomorrow."

"I keep thinking of things we could do to make the island more hospitable, but then I realize I don't want to ruin it," said Esofi. "If we build a dock to bring horses, then we'll need a stable, then somewhere for the hostlers to live, and then a storehouse for all their supplies, and then before you know it, we've got a whole town."

Adale came and lay down beside Esofi. "Would that be so bad?"

"Not at first, but I know it would only be a matter of time before they start arguing with the dragons. Or the gryphons. Or whatever else lives here."

"What would they argue about?"

"I don't know, anything. Besides, who would own it? The Silver Isles isn't Ieflarian territory, but none of the races that live here have any real concept of nations. Legally speaking, it would have to—"

"Good night," said Adale, closing her eyes.

Esofi swung her arm out, striking Adale weakly in the stomach. "I'm serious!"

"Well, it sounds like the solution is to not build a dock."

"Then we'll be walking up that mountain every day until your parents call us home."

"Well, maybe not," said Adale. "Maybe we could take a rope, and a basket, and—"

"No!"

"It's either that or let Ivanedi carry us on his back." Adale paused. "Though, you rode on the Emperor's back and managed to not fall off, didn't you? And he was *trying* to drop you."

"I had two magical daggers in his wing."

"Can you make a harness out of magic? Or some kind of saddle?"

"He might find that degrading. I don't want to offend him."

"I think a gryphon would be much easier to ride," Adale speculated. "They're practically horse-shaped."

Esofi turned her face to gaze out the window. The moon was just beginning to rise over the sea. Adale wrapped one arm around Esofi's waist and pulled her close again.

"It would be nice to be able to speak with them," Esofi said. "Gryphons, I mean. If they're as intelligent as dragons...if we could foster peace between them..."

"Then they'd band together and eat us all."

"Adale!"

"I'm teasing! In any case, you're getting ahead of yourself. We've only been here a day."

"You're right," realized Esofi. "We came here to learn about the dragons, and for Carinth. It's too early for political machinations."

"Do we want peace between them?" asked Adale. "Not to be awful, but maybe it's better for us if they're enemies. They'll be too busy fighting one another to bother us."

"I don't know. Maybe. It depends on what the gryphons are like."

The door creaked open as Carinth let himself in. He'd worked out doorknobs easily, once he became tall enough to reach them. He must have been feeling lonely, because he jumped up onto the bed and settled himself between Adale and Esofi.

"We made new friends today," said Esofi, stroking his head gently. "I'm so glad. I've been worrying."

"You worry too much," said Adale. "What if things turn out all right?"

"Then I'll have to find new things to worry about."

Adale laughed and pulled her closer, making Carinth grumble in annoyance. When nobody paid him any mind, he got up and settled himself above the pillows.

THE NEXT DAY, Esofi woke before dawn and dressed quickly, such was her eagerness to return to the island. Carinth was up as soon as she was, but Adale could not be roused. Only when Esofi threatened to go without her did she drag herself out of bed.

Her legs were sore, and she could not help but think that maybe it *would* be worth it to accept a ride from Ivanedi. But that would be reckless, and she knew Saski and Dietrich were already very worried about her.

The walk up was easier, because at least this time Esofi knew approximately how long it would take. And Adale was still behaving herself, staying on the path and with the group. Mireille and Elyne were both more asleep than awake as they trudged along, but if Orsina was exhausted, she did not show it—though it seemed likely she wasn't, given the rigorous training all paladins underwent.

Once they made it to the top, Carinth was off in a moment, chasing after Etheriet and some of the older hatchlings. Esofi was content to let him socialize.

"There seem to be more of you here today," observed Adale, as Ivanedi approached them.

"They came when they heard of Carinth's magic," Ivanedi explained. "Some hope that their own hatchlings will be granted a blessing as well, if they befriend him."

"I'm not sure if I like that," Esofi frowned. As a princess, she was familiar with the sting of finding out someone she'd thought of as a friend was only seeking to further their own agenda.

"Can't blame them for trying, though," said Adale.

While Adale and Mireille went to play with the younger dragons, Esofi found a relatively clean rock to sit on and talk more with Ivanedi.

"I wanted to ask you something," said Esofi. "You speak Ieflarian so well. How did you come to learn it?"

"When I was young, a few of our elders still remembered the languages of Men. I was unusual, for I wished to learn them all, and fluently. Sometimes I would fly to your lands and secretly observe how you spoke. But as I grew older, and larger, that was no longer possible. I also owned a few books. I still have them, but they are too small for my claws to handle now. I'd surely destroy them if I tried to open them now. It is a pity. Sometimes I miss the stories within. I did not manage to memorize them all before I outgrew them."

Esofi laughed. "For all your talk about chaos, I think you might make a good Man!"

"Only for a day, or two," said Ivanedi. "Books are a useful invention, but it is little consolation when you cannot fly."

"The Emperor spoke Ieflarian nearly as well as you do," remembered Esofi. "At the time, I didn't think much of it, but now I am surprised that he would bother to learn, given his disdain for Men."

"Yes," agreed Ivanedi. "It was the one bit of wisdom I managed to impart to him."

On the other side of the clearing, Carinth and Etheriet were chasing each other in circles. Unexpectedly, Etheriet turned and pounced on Mireille, knocking the young woman off her feet and making her shriek.

Dread rose up in Esofi's stomach. "Then—you mean to say, he was a friend of yours."

"In a sense," said Ivanedi. "Do not ask me what you are thinking of asking. You carry enough guilt."

"Why shouldn't I?" whispered Esofi. She could feel tears welling up in her eyes again.

"He was warned," said Ivanedi. "Talcia spoke to him directly, and publicly, and still he would not listen. He believed he knew her heart better than she did herself! I promise you that he chose his death long before you came to Ieflaria."

"What was he to you?"

"He was my son," said Ivanedi. "His mother went to Dia Asteria when he was still a hatchling, and so I became responsible for him."

Esofi brought her hand to her mouth and bit down on her knuckle, sending dull, throbbing pain through her entire arm and up to her shoulder. But that was nothing compared to the sickening panic rising in her throat.

Adale, who had been especially attuned to her needs lately, was beside her in a moment.

"What did you say to her?" she demanded of Ivanedi, squaring up her shoulders like she thought she could take him on if it came to a fight.

"No, no, it's fine. I promise," sniffed Esofi. "I'm just— perhaps I ought to get back to the ship."

"You're bleeding," said Adale, taking Esofi's hand. Esofi's own teeth had left deep marks behind in a crescent shape. But she barely felt it over the pounding in her head and the sharp sickness in her stomach. "Elyne!"

Elyne hurried over at the sound of her name, smiling as brightly as ever—until she saw the blood on Esofi's hand.

"Can you fix it?" asked Adale.

"It won't be as good as a healer's, but I can stop the bleeding, at least." Elyne paused. "Why'd you—"

"Just fix it," Adale interrupted.

Healing magic was usually white, or palest mint-green if it came from Adalia instead of Adranus. But the magic Elyne called up was violet. Despite the look of it, it didn't hurt at all as it settled into the wound, repairing the broken skin.

"Now, be careful," admonished Elyne. "The bleeding's stopped, but your skin around that area is still weak and thin. My magic's not really meant for things like this."

"I understand," said Esofi, cradling it with her other hand. Adale hugged her around the shoulders.

"Do you really want to go back to the ship?" she asked. "I'll go with you if you like..."

"No, it's not fair to Carinth to make him leave so soon," said Esofi. "I'll be fine, I just—"

"You should fly with me," rumbled Ivanedi.

Esofi wiped her eyes on her sleeve and sniffed. "What?"

"I have things to show you," Ivanedi said. "Places that cannot be reached on foot. For the sake of your peace, I ask you to come with me."

"I'm not sure about this," said Adale. "Maybe we should..."

"No. I will go." If Ivanedi was going to take her somewhere remote so he could break her neck in private, she supposed the least she could do was give him a sporting chance. "I'm sure we won't be long."

"Esofi—"

"Where should I hold on?" Esofi asked Ivanedi, turning away from Adale to appraise the spot where his long neck joined with his back. She could probably get her legs around it, but she'd have to hold tightly to his neck.

"I promise you that no harm will come to her," Ivanedi told Adale. "Perhaps, when we return, she will even be improved."

Adale pressed her lips together and raised one eyebrow. "I'm going to want an explanation for all this once you get back."

"And you'll get one. I promise," said Esofi.

It took a few minutes to get onto Ivanedi's back safely. Her hands gripped the spines on his neck, and she hoped it would be enough to keep her in place while they flew. If not...

Well, at least the spines were blunt, and did not cut into her palms. She pulled her heavy winter cloak around herself and tried to sink deeper into it.

"Are you ready?" asked Ivanedi.

"I think so."

Without another word, Ivanedi launched himself into the air. Even knowing that it had been coming, Esofi felt a scream escape from her mouth. She risked a glance downward, at her boots dangling over empty air, impossibly far above the sparkling sea, and fought down the urge to be sick.

But she did not fall, even though the wind ripped at her as though it was trying to steal her cloak away. Was this what the couriers dealt with every single day? Perhaps they hadn't been paying them enough after all.

And Ivanedi was still rising, approaching one of the distant peaks Esofi had not thought twice about, except to briefly admire its height. She distracted herself by thinking about how tangled her hair would be once they landed. At least none of the dragons would notice, or care.

Soon enough, Ivanedi came in for a landing on a high, broad plateau.

"What is this?" asked Esofi, sliding down from his neck and looking around.

"This is the highest point in the Isles. We come here to hear our mother's voice in times of great struggle. It was here that she told Zethe to turn away from his path, before countless witnesses."

Esofi turned her face toward the edge. There was nothing there to protect her if she slipped. "What did he say in response?"

"Nothing," said Ivanedi. "Nothing, until she had gone. And he said we would proceed as planned. That once Men were gone, she would have no choice but to love us again."

Esofi walked toward the center of the plateau, trying to imagine a host of dragons gathered here, perhaps under a silver moon, listening for Talcia's guidance.

"He thought that killing every Man on Inthya would be easier than just obeying her?" asked Esofi.

"We seldom behave rationally when we are in pain," said Ivanedi. "Men and dragons alike."

Esofi moved away from the center and took a few cautious steps toward the edge, toward the ocean. The wind ruffled her hair, and she slid to her knees, not trusting herself not to trip over the edge. In the distance, she could see something tiny and pale on the water.

"I think I can see our ship," she murmured. "It's mapping the smaller islands. I didn't realize how many there really are. The maps show so few." There were certainly more than that, though—perhaps as many as fifty. Some were so tiny Esofi was not sure if they were islands or large stones that would disappear when the tides changed.

"Do you think more Men will come here?"

"I was not planning on sending any," said Esofi. "I know these islands are yours. I don't want to encroach on your lands. I'd like to come back again, when it's warmer, so Carinth can spend more time with you. But we're not planning a settlement, if that's what you're thinking of."

"The thought had crossed my mind. Men do so love to build things."

"Yes, I suppose we do. Nevertheless..."

They sat there in silence for a while, watching the sea glitter. Far below, Esofi could see birds flying over the water, carried on currents of warm air.

"May I ask you a question?" asked Ivanedi.

"Why, yes," said Esofi. "Of course. What is the matter?"

"What have you brought to our island?"

"The...the ship?" Esofi's eyes went to the Courser, below. "It's just a passenger ship, I promise there are no weapons, beyond the standard for such—"

"No," said Ivanedi. "Your attendant. The one who wears a mortal woman's body."

Esofi turned away from the beautiful view before her. "How did you know?"

"I have had my suspicions since your arrival. But when she healed you, I was certain." Ivanedi paused. "For a time I thought...I hoped...she was our mother, come back to us in a new form."

Esofi rubbed her head. "I'm sorry. I shouldn't have brought her. I didn't think."

"You are even more remarkable than I thought, to have her as your servant."

"Elyne is not my servant," said Esofi firmly. "She goes where she pleases and does what she wants. I consider myself fortunate she has consented to travel with us for a little while."

"She has made quite an impression on some of our younger ones," said Ivanedi, turning his head in the other direction, toward what Esofi assumed was the gathering place they'd left behind.

"I understand she seeks worshippers," said Esofi. "Her temperament is...not what I would expect, but she seems amicable and slow to anger. I do not know what sort of blessings she grants, but I don't think she'll do you any harm."

"I do not either," said Ivanedi. "She is very much like our mother."

"Really?" Esofi's impression of Talcia had been that she was quiet and dignified and a bit frightening. Elyne was...quite the opposite. But perhaps Ivanedi knew something Esofi did not. "What makes you say so?"

"It is difficult to explain, in your language," he said. "But she gives the impression of how our mother would have been as a hatchling. If she had ever been one."

The description made Esofi smile. "I will learn your language so you can explain it to me properly."

"You may find it difficult," he said. "Some ideas require wing-movement to be conveyed correctly. And there are words to learn that your kind have no words for."

"I expected that," said Esofi. "It is the same with the Mer." She did not speak any of the Mer languages, but she understood that they had words for concepts relating to water and weather than Men did not, and they used their tails to communicate as much as their voices. "You don't have a written alphabet, do you?"

"No," said Ivanedi. "It is not our way."

Esofi had expected that as well. Even if the dragons had been inclined to write, it would be difficult when they were so large and the rest of the world so small. "Still, I wish to learn. Both for Carinth, and to understand you better."

They lapsed into silence again.

"Do any of your kind have blessings from other gods?" asked Esofi. "Merla, or perhaps Eyvindr? I once met a unicorn with Iolar's magic."

"If they do, I have not heard of them," said Ivanedi. "Merla cares little for us, since many of us have killed her children. I do not think she would grant one of us her blessing."

"She hardly ever gives Men her blessing either. I thought that since she and Talcia have such similar natures, she might like dragons better. What about lesser gods?"

"We respect Lady Nara, for we fly in her skies. But she has no blessings to grant that we are not already hatched with, and she has not spoken to any of us in living memory. In Anora and the surrounding lands, there are creatures you call dragons. But they are very different from us. We cannot have hatchlings with them."

"Oh yes. I think I've seen illustrations." Dragons in Anora were wingless but had short legs and very long bodies, similar to serpents.

"Some mistake them for our cousins, but we have no parent in common. They were made by Ethi and Ridon working together. Our similarities are only superficial. They are very orderly and gentle, and they accumulate wisdom instead of wealth." Ivanedi paused. "Perhaps we could learn something from them. Do you remember the books I told you about?"

"The ones you collected when you were young?"

"Yes. If I brought them to you, do you think..."

"Yes!" said Esofi. "Yes, I could read them for you. If that's what you want."

"I can read well enough. It is the act of opening them and turning pages that I find difficult."

"I'd be glad to help," said Esofi. "Where do you keep them?"

Chapter Eleven

ADALE

It was irrational, since Ivanedi had been nothing but a gracious host, but watching Esofi and Ivanedi fly away was gut-wrenching. Adale knew Esofi was more than capable of defending herself if the worst should happen, but her parents would be furious if they learned about this.

Once they'd disappeared from Adale's line of sight, she turned away. Carinth was still playing with Etheriet and some of the younger dragons, and it looked like Mireille had managed to get herself included in the game as well. She seemed to have no reservations about getting on the ground and letting them climb all over her. Adale expected that her dress would be in ribbons by sunset.

Orsina, as always, watched everything from a far enough distance that she could see almost everything that was going on, stoic as any castle guard. Meanwhile Elyne sat on a rock, knees drawn up. Balanced on them was a sketchbook, and when Adale crept around to see what she was working on, she caught a glimpse of a few figure drawings of dragons before Elyne caught sight of her and quickly blocked Adale's view with her own body.

"I'm so bad at this," sighed Elyne. "Even after months of practice."

"Can't you just...you know, imagine it, and make it appear on the page?" asked Adale.

"I could, but there's no point in that. And it seems unfair, since my followers work so hard at honing their skills." Elyne closed the book and tucked it back into her bag. "Now may I ask why Esofi tried to bite her own hand off?"

"I'm not sure myself. I think Ivanedi said something that upset her."

"She can't have been that upset, if she flew off with him."

"I know she feels guilty. About all the dragons she's killed before, I mean. And I understand why, but I don't understand *why*. If that makes any sense at all. Yes, it's terrible that it had to happen, but it's not as though she went out and did it for fun. And if she hadn't, they'd have killed her instead."

"Well, I can't help with that," Elyne said. "But none of the dragons are angry with her. A little jealous, maybe. But they aren't thinking about revenge."

"That's about what I thought," sighed Adale. "And I've been telling her so! It just doesn't seem to matter."

"Maybe she just needs to feel guilty for a while, then."

Maybe Elyne was correct. But Adale felt certain Esofi should not have to feel guilty at all. It wasn't fair, and she didn't deserve it.

It was about noon when Esofi and Ivanedi returned. Esofi was smiling and holding a pile of books to her chest.

"What are all those?" asked Adale as Esofi nearly fell off Ivanedi's back and onto the ground.

"Ivanedi's been keeping books this whole time," said Esofi. "But he can't get them open, because of his claws."

"How old are they?"

"He collected them when he was young, so at least a hundred years old. I was afraid they'd be ruined. A cave isn't the sort of place for books. But they're actually in very good condition, considering."

Adale wanted to ask if he also kept treasure in his cave, but that seemed rude, and she was afraid he might get the wrong idea. She'd bring it up later, once they were back on the ship.

Carinth knew books usually meant someone was going to read him a story, and had come over as soon as Esofi touched the ground. Etheriet clearly had no idea what was going on, but she followed him over.

"Do you want to see?" asked Esofi, turning the book so that Etheriet could examine it more closely. The young dragon sniffed at the leather cover, then pulled back, nose wrinkling in clear disdain. Esofi laughed at this reaction.

"This one looks like stories of the gods," said Esofi, opening it very carefully. "But it's written in Sibari. If I hold it and turn the pages, Ivanedi can read it himself."

Adale picked up one of the other books and opened to a random page, only to find herself staring down a fully colored illustration on vellum. "Oh. This one looks... important."

"I stole it from a man who had many like it," said Ivanedi. "I do not think he missed it."

RETURNING TO THE ship at night was like going to another world—though a very pleasant one that had cooked food and hot baths. Up in the mountains, it was easy to forget about everything that waited for them back at Birsgen.

It was easy to forget Birsgen existed at all.

The ship's crew was keeping busy with their assignment. There were many more islands than anyone had realized, even though most of them were so small someone could walk around them in about an hour. Still, Esofi wanted them all documented.

Ivanedi said dragons—and other creatures—did live on the smaller isles, with the most solitary dragons making their nests farthest away from the main island. But he'd promised that no dragons would attack the ship, so long as the sailors did not approach their lairs. So far, there had been no problems.

There had been more sightings of gryphons, sometimes in the forests but usually in the skies high above, their shapes unmistakable. They did not approach and, in fact, gave no impression they had more than a cursory interest in their strange visitors. Adale hoped they'd decided Men were too large to bother trying to eat.

That night, Esofi sat before the fire, warming her hands. Carinth was settled in her lap, though occasionally he lifted his head and tried to get at her mug of spiced wine. Every time he did, she pressed one fingertip to his nose and guided it back down.

She already seemed so much happier. Whether it was her conversation with Ivanedi or just the fact that they were out of Gaelle's reach, Adale was not certain. Perhaps both.

"Come sit with us," called Esofi. Adale did not need to be asked twice, even though her aching legs would have preferred to remain on the bed.

"I remembered something today that I haven't thought about in a while," said Esofi as Adale settled next to her.

"What was it?"

"When my sisters and I were young, Mother would bring us up into the mountains every time they had a dragon sighting. It wasn't terribly often, never more than once or twice a year. Talking to Ivanedi reminded me of it."

"That sounds dangerous," commented Adale.

"I suppose it was," said Esofi, sounding surprised, as though this had never occurred to her before. "In any case, the dragons could not be allowed to stay on our land, or else they'd start taking livestock. And then when the livestock ran out, they'd carry off people."

"And that's how you learned to fight dragons?"

Esofi nodded. "It was frightening, at first. But I suppose anything can become ordinary if you do it often enough."

Adale was not sure what to say, but Esofi did not sound as though she needed consolation. She was simply recounting the past.

"At the time, I wondered why the dragons didn't learn not to bother us," added Esofi. "But when I said so, I was told there was no reason to expect sense or understanding from dragons. Now I realize they were simply young and reckless."

"Not to agree with your mother, but she was probably right about them taking livestock. It's sad it had to end in killing, but..."

"I know." Esofi sighed. "And they're so pragmatic about it! Ivanedi even said it was good we killed them before they had a chance to have foolish hatchlings."

"I shouldn't laugh at that, should I?" But a smile pulled at Adale's lips nevertheless. "But I suppose your philosophy has to be a bit cutthroat when you live in the wilderness. Or do you think Talcia means for you to change them?"

"No, I don't," said Esofi. "In fact, I suspect Talcia might agree with them. She's nearer to being a dragon than a woman, no matter how many woman-shaped statues we carve."

Adale rested a hand on Carinth's head. "Even so, I'm glad Carinth doesn't have to live like that."

"I am too." Esofi gazed down at Adale's hand. "I think...I don't regret that I was raised to be strong. But at the same time, I believe it could have been accomplished without cruelty."

"I think you'd have been strong no matter what," asserted Adale. "Just like I'd have been useless no matter what."

"Don't speak about yourself that way." Esofi's hand gripped hers. "You're always saying such terrible things about yourself. I hate to hear it."

"Iolar hates liars."

"Since when did you have a care for what Iolar hates?" Esofi bumped Adale's shoulder with hers. "In any case, you're wrong—you're certainly not useless."

"You're biased."

Esofi laughed again, a beautiful and melodious sound that Adale had heard far too little of since Gaelle's arrival. "Because I love you?"

"Yes, exactly. You understand."

"Do you think I'd rather you be exactly like me?" asked Esofi. "And instead of you making me laugh, we could just get ourselves worked up into fits of hysteria until our hearts give out from the strain?"

"Maybe not," Adale whispered, embarrassed.

"*Maybe* not." Esofi pressed her forehead to Adale's. "Maybe think on that a little longer."

AMONG THE DRAGONS, Etheriet was obviously Carinth's best friend. She waited for them at the top of the forest path every morning, though she never ventured into the trees alone. Though many dragons came to the clearing, Adale never saw one with her striking color, a rich crimson that reminded her of castle livery back home.

"We should bring her back to Birsgen with us!" suggested Mireille one day, with Etheriet hanging off her back like some sort of oversized bat. "I'll take care of her!"

"I don't think Releth would like that," said Esofi.

"Take her. I do not care," called Releth from the other side of the clearing, not lifting her head from its resting place on her front claws.

"Yes!" Mireille gathered Etheriet into her arms. "I will take you home and feed you biscuits every day until you are perfectly round."

"Is her mother in Dia Asteria?" asked Adale. From what she could see, Releth was raising the hatchling, albeit reluctantly.

"Yes," said Releth. "And we are all better for it."

Adale bit back a laugh. The dragons' brutally straightforward natures never ceased to surprise her. "You didn't like her?"

"Mairmet chose death over her hatchling. There is nothing to like."

"What happened?"

"Let's not speak of the dead," interrupted Ivanedi. "Especially when we have nothing meaningful to say."

Adale did not know that it was possible for a dragon to roll her eyes, but Releth somehow managed it.

Esofi was very serious about learning the dragons' language, training her mouth to make the strange, harsh sounds and filling pages and pages with notes to study when she returned home. Carinth sat and listened to these lessons, sometimes, though he remained as silent as ever no matter how Esofi coaxed him to try.

Adale thought the dragon's language sounded like something worth learning, but she could hardly be expected to *study* when there were miles of wilderness in every direction.

Luckily, Elyne was equally restless. And so, accompanied by a few adolescent dragons, they left to explore the area.

The eldest of their companions was named Byreth. Her scales were somewhere between brown and grey, rendering her nearly invisible when she was among the trees. Next was Zievem, who always did the exact opposite of whatever Byreth commanded. Then finally there was Mosi, who was about twice Carinth's size and followed Elyne everywhere.

Zievem and Byreth chased each other through the trees, tackling and nipping at each other. Sometimes one would claw their way midway up a tree and then spring from it, wings unfurling to catch the wind and give them more distance for a pounce. By contrast, Mosi stayed near to Adale and Elyne's heels.

None of the dragons spoke Ieflarian very well, but Elyne understood their language perfectly and translated when needed. In lieu of wings, she waved her arms up and down to convey her points. It looked more than a little silly, but Elyne insisted it was crucial. Adale wanted to ask the older two dragons questions about themselves because Mosi did not speak yet, but they were far more interested in their game.

Adale reflected on how Esofi was probably right to not want a settlement on the Isles. As nice as it would be to have a real place to stay, it wasn't worth the risk to the very fragile peace between their races.

Then Zievem lunged for Byreth, but Byreth was too fast for him, leaping aside at the last moment. Adale had just enough time to cross her arms in front of her face before Zievem collided with her.

The world spun out of control as Adale was knocked off her feet and into the air. But instead of landing on the ground, Adale tumbled down a ravine. As roots and branches flew past her face, Adale tried desperately to grab hold of something.

Then, a moment later, she hit the ground.

All was silent for a moment. Distantly, through treetops that seemed to be a mile away, she could see the sky.

"Adale?" called Elyne from somewhere far above. "Are you dead?"

Adale spat out a mouthful of dried leaves. "I don't think so," she said. She felt as though she must have a few dozen new bruises, and she was not ready to move quite yet, but none of her limbs were twisted or, worse, numb.

"Zievem says he's very sorry! And Byreth is too." Elyne paused. "Yes, you *are*—it was just as much your fault—Adale, just stay where you are! We'll be down in a moment."

Adale had landed in the middle of dense brush. She wished she'd brought a sword, instead of just her knife. It would be so satisfying to swing it like a farmer's scythe and clear all the branches away.

Cautiously, Adale got back to her feet and pushed her way through the brush. After a few minutes, she came to an open patch of dirt where she could sit and catch her breath while she waited for Elyne and the dragons to find her. As she sat, she examined the new cuts on her arms and wondered if Elyne could heal them well enough that Esofi might never find out about this.

Movement caught her eye, and Adale looked around, hoping Elyne had found her already. But it wasn't Elyne or another dragon. It was actually something quite small, only just bigger than a housecat.

A fox? she wondered, catching a little flash of red. Then the thing came nearer, and Adale realized it was a very, very small gryphon.

From what she knew of their coloration, the one in front of her was male, but it was not quite fully grown yet. Bright red feathers were still coming in among the dull colors of childhood.

"Oh," said Adale. "Hello. Are you lost too?"

If the gryphon understood her words, he did nothing to show it. Adale knew the gryphons were intelligent. But maybe this one was not old enough to speak yet. Or maybe he just didn't speak her language? If he'd lived his entire life on the Isles, he'd have no reason to.

"Adale?"

Elyne's voice brought her back to reality. Adale turned but could still no sign of her. "I'm over here," she called, trying her best to keep her voice soft so the gryphon would not startle. "I found a baby gryphon."

"Be careful! The parents are probably not far away."

The gryphon did not hiss at Adale or fluff up his feathers in a warning. But when she reached her hand out in his direction, he got to his feet and shuffled further away, toward the dark trees.

"All right, fine," said Adale. "I'll be right here if you change your mind."

The young gryphon chirred, a surprisingly loud sound considering his size. Adale raised her eyebrows, wondering what this meant. Then something rippled in the trees behind him and an adult gryphon, this one female, stepped out of the trees. Her long talons dug into the dirt, and she stared at Adale with dark, hungry eyes.

"Elyne...?" called Adale, but it came out pitifully weak.

Then the mother gryphon screamed and lunged for her. Adale scrambled backward, only barely missing those awful talons as they struck the ground. Half-stumbling, she darted behind the nearest tree, heart racing, knowing it would only delay the gryphons for a moment. "ELYNE?" she yelled.

The gryphon rounded the tree, and Adale had just enough time to marvel at the size of her beak before a blast of violet light struck her in the face. She screeched in displeasure, and Adale felt the sound deep in her bones.

Not far away stood Elyne, her hands bright with magic. But instead of fleeing, the gryphon appeared to square her shoulders and opened her beak.

This time it was not just sound that emerged from her mouth. A wave of sparkling magic, mahogany-red in color, caught Elyne directly in the chest.

"Elyne!" cried Adale. But Elyne only took a few steps backward to right herself. Then she opened her mouth and screamed at the gryphon. The sound was simultaneously hoarse and shrill, the sound dipping and rising like a wordless song. The gryphon's dark eyes narrowed, and she screamed back, only for Elyne to cut her off with a shriek of her own.

The gryphon cried out again, but now she sounded plaintive, almost pitiful. Elyne replied with another shriek, and the gryphon turned around and spread her wings wide. Within a moment, she had vanished into the woods, her offspring hurrying after her.

"What did you say to her?" marveled Adale.

"Told her I knew her mother." Elyne massaged her throat with her fingers and coughed. "I'm going to feel that tomorrow. Are you all right?"

"Yes, I think so," said Adale. "I've—I've never seen *anything* like that before. Is it normal for gryphons to shout magic?"

"Yes. It's much easier than trying to use those bird talons." Elyne held up her hands and curled her fingers awkwardly to demonstrate. "In any case, don't take it personally. They were only hungry."

"Oh yes, that's fine, then," Adale rolled her eyes. "How long is it going to take us to get back?"

Zievem and Byreth came shuffling through the trees with what appeared to be expressions of guilt on their face. But Adale held her arms out wide to show that she was unharmed. Still, there was no more play-fighting that day until they returned to the flight.

Elyne could heal the worst of the cuts, but there was no way Esofi would miss the damage to her hair and clothes, nor the bruise forming on the side of her face.

When they finally made it back to Esofi and the rest of the flight, Adale braced herself for Esofi's horrified reaction. But Esofi wasn't sitting on the stones, talking with some of the elder dragons. Instead, she was standing in the middle of the clearing, speaking to a uniformed courier.

"Is everything all right?" asked Adale, hurrying up. "Esofi, what's happened?"

"Everything is fine! We've had a letter from your parents."

"They caught the assassin?"

"No, it's not about that. It's my mother. They say...she has left Birsgen. She is returning to Rhodia."

Adale's mouth fell open in shock. "What?"

"I know, I can hardly believe it myself." Esofi shook her head, though she was still smiling. "But look, it has their seal."

"Well..." Adale was not sure what to say. Certainly she was delighted—but this all seemed *wrong*. Too easy. She took the letter from Esofi, her eyes falling to her parents' signatures at the bottom, followed by their seal, and then a lattice drawn in ink so that no forgeries could be added on as a post-script. "Are they asking us to come home?"

"They said we can if we want, but that wasn't the agreement." Esofi reached forward and picked a leaf out of Adale's hair. "What happened to you?"

"I fell down a hill," said Adale. "But it wasn't my fault."

AS THE DAYS passed, Adale found herself thinking less and less of home. She knew Esofi still worried about Lisette, and Adale herself was still suspicious of Gaelle's apparent concession, but things were going well. There had been no hostility from any dragons in the flight, and they'd even had a few visitors from the smaller islands, lone dragons who preferred silence and solitude over the noise and chaos of a flight. Some wanted to see Esofi and comment on how they expected her to be taller, but most were interested in Carinth and his magic.

Because of this, Carinth was becoming very adept at summoning the blue light to his hands. He never tried to throw it, or shape it, and Esofi said that was probably a good thing, at his age.

Every night, back on the ship, Esofi told Adale a little more about her family. Not all the stories were concerning, like being taken up to the mountains to fight dragons at an extremely young age. Some were merely annoying, like Esofi being instructed not to accept requests for dances since she was already engaged.

One particular night, Esofi was in the middle of describing how Gaelle had insisted the entire court come outside to observe a lunar eclipse in the middle of a terrible snowstorm—and the fight that had ensued when King Alain's mother, Esofi's paternal grandmother, announced to the entire gathering that Gaelle was a religious fanatic and she was going back to bed. This might have passed, for Grandmother Adrienne was *very* old and sometimes forgot where she was, but then her son had followed her inside.

"They didn't speak for months," Esofi confided. "At the time, I wondered if they ever would again."

Adale could not imagine her parents going so long without speaking to each other. "Didn't the Temple of Pemele try to help?" she asked.

"I'm not sure. I was quite young at the time, and it wasn't the sort of thing children were told about. I just remember how there were always servants running between them to relay messages, even when they were in the same room."

"Can you imagine what they'd do if we went that long without speaking to each other?" asked Adale. "Archpriestess Tofa would be climbing in through our window. No, wait, she wouldn't need to. My parents would let her in through the front door."

Esofi giggled. "With her bag full of all those *things*!"

"That is her solution to everything, isn't it?" agreed Adale.

"If we did fight that badly, I think I'd rather have a priestess of Pemele as a mediator," said Esofi. "No disrespect to Dayluue, but...there are some problems that passion alone cannot fix."

"I don't think I could go months without speaking to you," said Adale. "I'm not sure I'm capable of staying angry that long."

"I wrote to Albion, when it first happened," said Esofi. "I remember, I wanted so much for us to promise we'd never fight like that. But I never sent the letter, I threw it in the fire."

"Why?" asked Adale.

"I'm not sure," Esofi admitted. "Maybe, in a way, I thought it would be bad luck. Tempting fate, I suppose. Who knows? I was young."

There was a knock at the door, and Adale frowned, irritated at the interruption. Esofi looked confused as well, for it was quite late in the evening.

"Yes?" called Esofi.

"It's me," came Orsina's voice from the other side of the door. "I apologize for disturbing you, but Ivanedi has come to the ship."

"What?" began Esofi, but Adale was already on her feet and pulling the door open. Orsina stood there, still fully dressed in her armor.

"I'm sorry for the intrusion," Orsina began.

"No, no, it's fine," said Esofi, pulling a heavy dressing-gown on over her nightgown. "Ivanedi is here?"

"Yes. He gave the crew a terrible fright. He wishes to speak to you."

Esofi all but ran past Orsina, and Adale followed her up. When they arrived above, much of the crew was gathered toward one side of the ship, all staring down into the water. Adale and Esofi pushed their way through the group to peer over the edge.

Adale had not thought a dragon would be capable of swimming, but Ivanedi managed it. His long neck kept his head well above water, but his body was submerged, and his feet were churning endlessly to keep him afloat.

"Ivanedi?" asked Esofi. "What's wrong?"

"I apologize for alarming you, but I have just received strange news," Ivanedi said. "It seems that another ship has been visiting the minor isles, in secret."

"Pirates?" asked Adale. But what did the dragons have that pirates might be interested in? Unless they were hoping to find hoards of gold and jewels, like in ancient legends.

"No," said Ivanedi. "No. I am told it was...a delegation. Not unlike your own. They have come on behalf of the nation of Rhodia."

"Oh no," said Adale.

Esofi covered her eyes. "I should have known...I was a fool to think she'd just *leave.*"

"But how did she know we were here?" Adale asked. "We left in secret."

"She may not have followed you," said Ivanedi. "Queen Gaelle of Rhodia has been claiming that, through her, Talcia will grant us our magic once more. But she will only do so if we agree to a formal alliance with her country."

Esofi sputtered. "She—*what?*"

"Tell them all she's lying!" Adale cried. "She got lucky with Carinth, maybe, and she might be good at teaching children how to fight. But she doesn't have the power to *give* anyone their magic!"

"What could she be thinking?" whispered Esofi. "She must know they'll turn on her once they realize she's lied. Or does she truly believe her own words?"

"Is it possible she's telling the truth?" asked Ivanedi.

"No!" Adale cried.

"Wait," said Esofi. "Maybe."

"Esofi!"

Esofi shook her head, an expression of determination on her face. "Like it or not, Talcia may have spoken to my mother. It's unlikely, but not impossible."

Adale turned back to Ivanedi. "Has she done anything to prove her claims yet?"

"No. As a result, there is no consensus on a course of action."

Esofi chewed her lower lip. "Well...perhaps we ought to just leave her to it. If she's telling the truth, we have no right to stop her. And if she's not, she'll have to deal with the consequences of her actions sooner or later."

"You think she'll leave the rest of the world alone if she's got her own army of dragons?" demanded Adale. "You think she'll just go home and sit in her palace drinking tea for the rest of her life?"

Esofi stared at Adale.

"We've got to stop her," said Adale. "Or she'll make Emperor Ionnes look like a child playing with toy soldiers."

"What do you propose we do, then?"

"We need to prove she's lying," asserted Adale. "I refuse to believe Talcia spoke to her, unless it was to tell her to stop making everyone miserable. She's the opposite of everything Talcia wants the dragons to be. She's jealous and angry and *cruel*. Saying she knows how to get the dragons' magic back makes no sense, given everything we know about why they lost it to begin with."

Secretly, Adale did not feel as confident as her words sounded. She had no idea how they might go about proving Gaelle was a liar. But there was no way she was telling the truth. Yes, Talcia had granted Brandt and Svana magic, but that was different. This was...beyond all reason.

"Did you wish to confront her?" asked Ivanedi. "If you did, we expect she will come to us tomorrow, to deliver her claims to the flight."

"Do we want to confront her?" Adale looked at Esofi. But for once, Esofi just stared back at her helplessly. "All right, we'll come back to that one later. Ivanedi, what else can you tell us?"

"I have not seen her for myself, yet. My understanding is that she has been visiting the outermost islands. The dragons who saw her ship mistook her at first for the map-makers here, and so they did not attack. When she began making her claims, news spread throughout the outer isles. It only reached us within the hour."

"Is anyone supporting her?"

"Not outright. Not yet. But I know some are very eager, and it will not take much more persuading for them to follow her."

"What exactly is she asking for, with her alliance?" asked Adale.

"She had not made any specific requests, but it sounds as though she might be seeking aid against the

Elves. We would not be opposed to this. We remember our mother's warnings, even as Men do not."

"Does she really need help with the Elves?" asked Adale. "I had the impression Thiyra had an entire force for dealing with that."

"I could not say."

"Right. I'm putting a stop to this before it has a chance to get started," said Adale. "Esofi, you stay here with Carinth. I'm going to go see exactly what she's claiming."

"Now?"

Adale deflated. It would be dark soon and too cold to be wandering around in the mountains. "No. Tomorrow morning, the moment the sun comes up."

Esofi was not weak, and she did not need protecting. But in the dwindling light, she seemed so soft and fragile, like a rabbit or some other gentle prey animal.

If Esofi could fight the Emperor for Ieflaria, then Adale could certainly fight Gaelle for Esofi. Adale didn't have magic, but she knew how to talk to people, and she thought dragons counted as people. It was the least she could do, she decided. And then nobody would ever be able to say she did not deserve Esofi, not even Adale herself.

ESOFI BARELY SLEPT at all that night, and so Adale did not either.

But this turned out to work to her advantage, because Esofi was sound asleep at sunrise when Adale got up.

Carinth wanted to go with Adale, rising eagerly once he realized she was up. The confusion in his little face when he realized that she was leaving without him was painful to look at.

"You look after Mera," whispered Adale. "I've got some work to do."

Perhaps he understood her after all, because he turned and jumped back up on the bed and laid down beside Esofi, golden eyes glimmering. Adale shut the door behind her as quietly as she could manage and hurried abovedeck, where Elyne and Orsina were waiting. Today, Mireille would remain with Esofi.

Heavy grey clouds hung in the sky, obscuring the weak sunlight. When they arrived on the familiar beach, Adale was beginning to feel soft, stinging raindrops on her skin.

She had been hoping Ivanedi would meet them on the beach to give them more information, but nobody was there when they came ashore. She looked up at the mountain and wondered if Gaelle was already there, spreading her lies.

"Do we have a plan of action?" asked Orsina.

"Yes," said Adale. "We're going to stop Gaelle."

"I was hoping perhaps there was more to it than that."

"I don't want a fight with her," Adale said. "If I can just talk to her in front of the dragons—ask her some questions—I'm hoping they'll realize she's lying."

"And what if she attacks you?" Orsina asked bluntly.

"Orsina's right," said Elyne. "You don't have any magic, and Gaelle has...more magic than anyone really needs."

"You've seen her use it?" asked Adale.

"No, but I can see it on her." Elyne waved her hands in front of her eyes. "She has as much as Esofi does."

"Not more?"

"I don't think so. At least...that's how it looks to me."

"Then they'd be evenly matched in a fight?"

"I'd imagine so." Elyne paused. "Do you want to go back for her?"

"No," said Adale. Ever since Gaelle's arrival, Esofi had made it sound as though her mother was significantly more powerful than she was, that fighting her directly was little more than suicide. But... what if that wasn't true after all? What if Esofi was a match for her?

But it didn't matter because Esofi wouldn't have to fight Gaelle because Adale was going to do it for her.

"If I knife her and leave her body in a ditch, will you tell Esofi that we didn't encounter her?" asked Adale.

"Yes," said Elyne.

"No," said Orsina.

"I was hoping Ivanedi would come," said Adale, tilting her head to gaze up at the sky. "I didn't feel like walking today."

"Let me try something," Elyne said. "Stand back."

Adale and Orsina both took a few shuffling steps away. Adale glanced at Orsina in confusion, but she didn't seem to know what was going on either.

"Don't move," said Elyne, backing away as well. "I don't want to crush you."

But before Adale could ask any questions, Elyne *leapt*, spinning in midair like a dancer. And as she spun, her form began to twist and change. When she landed, it was not Elyne that stood before them, but a dragon with violet scales.

"Did it work?" asked Elyne.

"You tell me!" laughed Adale, a little giddy. "That was incredible! Do me next."

"Find me a few thousand more worshippers, and I might be able to manage it for an hour."

"You're quite small," observed Orsina, who apparently did not find this as exciting as Adale did.

"I have sixty-two worshippers! This is the best I can do!"

It was true that Elyne was not as large as Ivanedi or Releth, but she was not as small as the adolescent dragons. She would be large enough to carry Adale and Orsina, as long as they were careful.

"You're not going to, you know, change back in midair, are you?" asked Adale. "If you run out of magic—"

"Holding a shape doesn't cost power," Elyne explained. "Changing from one to another does. If I ran out of magic now, I'd be stuck like this until I got some more prayers or went back to Asterium."

That was certainly reassuring, though it raised the question of why Elyne was going around as an ordinary woman when she could look like anything on Inthya.

"I was unaware that dragons could be purple," Orsina observed stoically.

"Which of us has existed since the moment of creation?" retorted Elyne. Then she leaned down and bumped her head against Orsina's, nearly knocking the paladin into the sea.

"Let's focus," said Adale, thoroughly unaccustomed to being the voice of reason. "Elyne, do you need to practice flying before you take us up?"

"Mmm...maybe. Yes. Maybe."

"Yes," said Orsina firmly.

Elyne spread her wings and shot off into the sky, kicking up a wave of stones that pelted at Adale and Orsina like hail. They watched as she circled the shoreline, veering this way and that as she became accustomed to her new body.

When Elyne began to drift out toward the open sea, Orsina cupped her hands around her mouth and shouted, "All right! You have it! Come back!"

Elyne turned back without argument, which surprised Adale. Her landing was significantly more graceful than her take-off, though Adale still covered her eyes to protect against flying pebbles.

"It's wonderful!" said Elyne. "I should do this more often. Here, sit at the base of my neck, right before the wing-joint. I'll have us up there in minutes."

It would have been easier with some sort of saddle, but Orsina and Adale managed to get themselves onto Elyne's back. Orsina went in front, and Adale sat just behind her.

"We're not too heavy, are we?" worried Adale.

"It's not the most comfortable thing in the world, but I'll manage," Elyne said. "Try to hold still. If you feel yourself slipping, just start crying and screaming and hitting me."

Adale opened her mouth to reply, but words were ripped away from her as Elyne leapt into the sky without warning. She clutched at Orsina's waist, staring downward as the world fell away from them, unable to rip her eyes away from the shrinking shoreline. Pins fell from her hair, freeing her braid from its coronet.

The forest that took over an hour to pass through on foot passed them by in a matter of moments. Higher and higher they soared, Elyne's powerful amethyst wings pushing the world down and away. Adale had never attempted to compose poetry before, but in that moment, she began to consider the possibility.

All too soon, it was over. They reached the clearing, and Elyne came in for a landing. At the sight of an unfamiliar dragon in what may or may not have been an unnatural color, many of the other dragons began to come nearer, both confused and welcoming.

"You have come," said Ivanedi, pushing his way to the front. "I had thought you might not."

"I'm sorting this out now, before it gets away from us," announced Adale, stumbling down from her place on Elyne's neck. "Where's Gaelle? Is she here?"

"Not yet," said Ivanedi. "But she will be. And she is bringing others with her, dragons she has already won to her side."

"Who are these dragons, exactly?"

"Her loudest supporter is Drethet. He is a young adult, respected for his strength and power. Many of the others are similar—dragons who choose to live on the outer isles tend to be young adults, no longer hatchlings requiring care, but not old enough to be concerned with eggs of their own. It is not always the case, but they are the majority."

"Listen to me!" said Adale, turning to face the other dragons. "I know the woman who is coming to speak to you. She claims she speaks for Talcia, but she's lying. She is an angry and jealous and violent woman. If you follow her, you'll be right back to where you were when you followed Zethe."

"She says she gave your hatchling magic," said one of the other dragons.

"She is lying," said Adale, even as a traitorous voice within her whispered that *she didn't know that for sure.* "Carinth was hatched with magic. If you listen to her, she'll send you off to kill her enemies and Talcia will never speak to you again."

"She is coming!" said another one of the dragons, though Adale was not certain which. She pushed her way through the gathering—no easy feat—ducking wings and claws and tails until she emerged from the front of the group and found herself facing Queen Gaelle.

Esofi's mother was not alone. Four mages, all in blue robes, accompanied her, stationed around her like bodyguards. And behind them were even more dragons, unfamiliar ones, whom Adale had never seen at the clearing before. The foremost one was pale brown, with bright green eyes, and he looked to Gaelle constantly as though waiting for an order.

"You." Gaelle's eyes narrowed as she took in Adale's presence. "I was wondering if you'd have the nerve to confront me. Where is Esofi?"

"Wouldn't you like to know?" asked Adale, unwilling to admit she was still on the ship. Besides, it might work to her advantage if Gaelle thought Esofi was hiding somewhere nearby, lying in wait and ready to strike.

"I don't really care," said Gaelle. "Though I'm not surprised she doesn't have the nerve to face me herself. I've nothing to say to you. You may go." And she flicked her wrist as though dismissing a servant.

"I'm not going anywhere," said Adale. "These dragons are Ieflaria's allies, and I won't allow you to deceive them into following you."

"I'm not deceiving anyone," said Gaelle. "I am the Great Mother of the Silence of the Moon. What woman on Inthya knows Talcia's will better than I?"

"You say you can get the dragons their magic back, so why don't you prove it?" said Adale. She pointed to Ivanedi. "Make Talcia give him magic."

"He has done nothing to deserve it," said Gaelle with a sneer.

"You can't expect all these dragons to just take your word on it. They're too smart for that." The size of the gathering did not precisely support this statement, but a little flattery never went amiss, did it? "Prove that you're not just out to use them to fight your enemies."

Some of the dragons were now murmuring in what sounded like agreement to Adale's ears—though she was not sure if this was because they honestly wanted proof, or if they were just all hoping they'd be the one selected to receive a Blessing.

"Very well," said Gaelle. She looked around the gathering and then crouched down, placing her hands on her own knees. After a moment, Etheriet pushed her way forward, clambering across the stones to meet Gaelle.

Orsina inhaled sharply, and Adale saw that there was panic in the paladin's face.

"What's the matter?" Adale whispered.

"Etheriet already has—"

Gaelle spoke softly to Etheriet, too softly for Adale to hear. But Etheriet listened attentively, her little ears flicking. When Gaelle put her hand out, in the same way she had done to Carinth at Fenstell, Etheriet copied her.

And a little flicker of carnelian-colored magic sparked to life at Etheriet's claws.

It felt as though the world was spinning around her, even as she stood rooted in place. Adale fought down the bile rising in her throat as the dragons around her all murmured in shock and wonder.

Gaelle lifted her head, smiling a smug smile that Adale's cousins would have been proud of.

"Is that enough for you?" she asked.

"Etheriet has always had magic," said Elyne. "You didn't grant it to her!"

"Who are you to say that? You'd have made that claim no matter who I helped."

Elyne's form began to shift again, but this time she was getting smaller—transforming back into a woman. This time, the cries of amazement were shouts and snarls.

But it wasn't Elyne—not exactly. This woman was taller, and paler, with long hair that shimmered with impossible colors as the light hit it, and her eyes were bright purple. This was not Elyne. This was *Aelia*, former chaos goddess.

"Is it her?" asked one of the dragons. "Is it our mother?"

Even Gaelle seemed taken aback, hesitant. Only because of Adale's familiarity with Rhodian dresses could she tell that Gaelle was adjusting her feet, preparing to back away.

It was wrong, but Adale could not help but hope Elyne would go along with it, pretend to be Talcia for the sake of finishing this quickly. She wouldn't even have to lie directly, just...not correct them.

"Etheriet has had magic her entire life," said Elyne. "Short as that may have been. You've a talent for bringing it out in little ones, but do not mistake that for the ability to grant blessings."

Gaelle's eyes were calculating. "You are not Talcia," she said. "What are you? A demon, maybe? Or just an impersonator? Are you upset that I've ruined your plans to steal her worshippers for yourself?"

"No," said Elyne.

"Yes," said Gaelle. "You're a very little goddess begging for prayers, aren't you? One of these days you might just flicker out of existence. Just the sort of pathetic thing I'd expect to associate with my daughter."

"You truly believe what you're claiming, don't you?" marveled Elyne. "I thought you were just desperate for power, but I was wrong. You really think she wants you to do this."

"If my worthless daughter was granted a dragon egg, then it follows that my reward will be far greater," said Gaelle. "No one in history has glorified Talcia more than I!"

"Dragons aren't rewards!" cried Adale. "And if you want Talcia to reward you, you might try not being a complete *bitch!*"

In a movement as fast as a snake striking, Gaelle lashed out with a whip of blood-colored magic.

Orsina leapt in front of Adale, and a golden shield blossomed from the palm of her hand, intercepting Gaelle's magic. It withstood the first blow, but shattered on the second—something Adale had not even realized was possible.

"Go!" Orsina yelled to Adale. Then another blast of magic struck her in the chest, knocking her back. If not for her armor, Adale was sure the damage would have been awful. As it was, Orsina struggled to regain her footing.

Gaelle raised both arms up toward the sky. Adale had no idea what she was doing, but it looked like it wasn't going to be good for her. Elyne shoved Adale back, out of the way, and she hit the ground. Adale lifted her head just in time to see Elyne's entire body engulfed in magical fire. When it cleared, there was nothing remaining in the place where she had stood.

Adale started to push herself upward, resolving to at least die on her feet instead of in the dirt. But one of Ivanedi's enormous claws rested gently on Gaelle's shoulder, and she turned.

"What are you doing?" he asked in a very soft voice.

"Is it not obvious?"

"Not unless you have fallen to madness," said Ivanedi. He nodded to the charred spot where Elyne had once stood. "What do you have to say for yourself?"

"What—that? That was nothing," said Gaelle.

"That was our mother's sister," said Ivanedi.

A hand grabbed the back of Adale's coat and hauled her to her feet. It was Orsina, her face scratched and hair tangled but otherwise no worse for the wear.

"Elyne, she..." began Adale.

"She'll be fine. This happens all the time," said Orsina.

Gaelle's mouth moved soundlessly, as though she was struggling to interpret Ivanedi's words. Finally she sputtered, "What nonsense—that was a chaos goddess!"

"And is our mother not foremost amongst chaos goddesses?"

"Of course not!" Gaelle looked around at the other dragons, clearly expecting them to come to her defense. "Why—why would—"

"I did not come here expecting to hear a theological disagreement," commented Orsina. "Particularly not this one."

"I would like an answer for this," said Ivanedi.

"Are you mocking me? There is nothing to answer for!" Gaelle cried in obvious frustration.

"Will you address her claims that Etheriet was born with magic?"

"She was lying. Is that not obvious?"

The dragons were murmuring again, but this time it didn't sound like the majority were in her favor.

"Are you dragons or not?" cried Gaelle. "What do you care for a weak shadow of a goddess when I can offer you true power?"

"It was not so long ago that we followed one who promised us the same thing," said Ivanedi.

"I don't particularly care whether you believe me or not," said Gaelle. "Those who come with me to Rhodia will be rewarded."

"Drethet has supported you since your arrival on our islands," said Ivanedi, nodding to the pale brown dragon, who narrowed his eyes suspiciously. "Grant him magic, and I will give you my support."

Gaelle laughed, but the sound was brittle. "What makes you think I want your support?"

"Etheriet is young. It is not impossible to believe that Talcia saw her innocence and granted her magic when she was hatched, as a gesture of goodwill after Zethe's death," said Ivanedi. "But we all know that Drethet is not blessed. If you can give him magic, none will be able to oppose you. My entire flight will follow you. Regardless of what you have done here today."

"And when I grant him magic, you'll think up another reason why it shouldn't count," retorted Gaelle. "And then you'll expect me to grant magic to another. And another. Do you think I am a fool?"

"If you can't do it, just say so," said Adale.

"You shut up!" snarled Gaelle. "No mortal is more favored by Talcia than I!"

"Maybe once. Maybe when you were young. But Esofi's got just as much magic as you do, and she's the one who was given Carinth. I don't think you're anyone's favorite anymore." Adale tried not to sound too giddy.

Gaelle looked at Drethet and his ears lifted eagerly, in the exact same way that Carinth's did when he saw someone eating something. He believed in her wholeheartedly, Adale realized, and her heart sank in her chest. He was going to be so hurt, so disappointed...

Unless Gaelle managed to succeed.

She couldn't. It was impossible.

And yet...Adale could not unthink that thought.

"Give me your claw," Gaelle said to Drethet.

Drethet's hand was massive compared to Gaelle, almost comically so. He curled his digits in the same way Etheriet had, and Adale held her breath. Gaelle stood there frowning at him, at his palm.

Waiting.

The silence went on, and on, and on.

"Try harder," Gaelle growled at Drethet.

"I am—"

"Idiot!" Gaelle dropped both hands to her side. "You are unworthy."

"But..." It was strange to hear such a magnificent creature sound so plaintive. "I...I did try."

"Evidently not!"

Adale exhaled loudly, unable to hold her breath for any longer. "I think it's time for us to leave."

"Then go!" cried Gaelle. "Go back to chasing after serving-maids and drinking yourself into a stupor!"

"Don't you realize you've lost?" asked Adale. "You've not been chosen by Talcia for anything."

"That's impossible," said Gaelle with such perfect certainty that for a moment, despite everything, Adale believed her.

Elyne was right, she realized. Gaelle really did believe what she was saying. Adale was not sure if this was better or worse than her just being an outright liar. In a strange way, it made Adale hate her just a little bit less. It was actually rather sad.

"You," said Gaelle, pointing to another dragon. "Perhaps you are worthy. Come forward."

When the next dragon stepped forward, Adale realized it was Byreth, the adolescent dragon who had been partially responsible for her encounter with the gryphons. Unlike Drethet, she looked uncertain, even worried. Adale tried to give her a comforting smile.

This time, Gaelle only tried for a few minutes before snarling at Byreth that she was unworthy. The moment Gaelle released her claw, Byreth turned and ran behind another, much larger dragon who glared at Gaelle like she was thinking of flicking her off the mountaintop.

The discontented murmuring was starting up again, and Adale could see real panic in Gaelle's face now. One of the dragons stepped away from the gathering and launched himself into the sky, apparently deciding he'd had enough excitement for the day. After him, a few others followed suit.

"Let's go," Adale said to Orsina. "Esofi's probably worrying."

"You do not wish to stay?"

"No." Adale turned and began to walk toward the path that would take them back to the ocean. "There is nothing more to see."

Chapter Twelve

ESOFI

"It should have been me," said Esofi. "I should have been the one to face her."

She regretted the words as soon as she spoke them—they sounded so terribly ungrateful. But Adale just laughed.

"You don't have to do everything yourself, you know," said Adale, pulling her close for an embrace. "Besides, I like knowing I'm not completely useless."

Adale had come to her immediately upon arriving back at the Courser, smiling broadly and claiming that the matter was settled. Esofi sat, Carinth in her lap, and listened as Adale explained what had transpired on the mountain. Orsina stood silently, only nodding occasionally for confirmation when Adale looked in her direction.

"I know. I know. I just..." Esofi wasn't sure how to describe what she was feeling. It was an oddly hollow sensation, as though something was missing. "And Elyne will be well?"

"When her body is killed, her consciousness returns to her plane in Asterium." Orsina gestured vaguely upward. "She just needs time to...pull herself together... before she can reform on Inthya."

"How much time?" asked Esofi, thinking of childhood stories that always ended with chaos gods being banished to Asterium for decades or even centuries.

"She was not locked into her body, so it should not be too long. It depends on how much magic she has in reserve and how recently she last received prayers."

"It seems too easy," sighed Esofi. "I...I can't help but worry she won't give up so quickly."

"You think she'll try the gryphons instead?" asked Adale.

"Perhaps." Esofi stroked Carinth's head absently. "She's not used to losing."

"The gryphons already have magic," Orsina reminded them. "She has nothing to entice them with."

"Yes! That's right!" Adale's face lit in a smile. "We don't have anything to worry about."

Esofi forced a smile for Adale's sake, but a knock at the door saved her from having to come up with a reply. Mireille leapt to her feet and answered it.

One of the Courser's crew was standing there, and panic rose in Esofi's throat. But he was smiling neutrally, obviously untroubled. She forced herself to be calm, to breathe.

"A courier has arrived for Princess Esofi," he reported.

"*Now* what?" asked Adale.

"I'll be there in a moment," said Esofi, setting Carinth down on the ground and brushing at her skirt.

The courier waiting for them above was a rare male one, and he bowed deeply as the princesses approached. In his hand, he held a letter sealed in crimson ink. "I've a message for Princess Esofi," he said.

Esofi took the letter from the courier and broke the seal.

"It's from your parents," she reported. "...now ask you to return to Ieflaria...as agreed as a condition of your departure...upon the arrest of the assassin that attempted to poison..."

"They caught them?" Adale tried to grab the letter from Esofi's hands, but Esofi held it tightly. "Who was it?"

"It does not say." Esofi turned over the page over to make sure she had not missed something, but the reverse side was blank.

"Well, that's infuriating," said Adale. She looked over at the courier. "Do you know who's been arrested? There's got to be some gossip, they can't keep something like this a secret for long."

"I do not know her name," said the courier, "but a priestess from the Temple of Talcia has been arrested."

"What?" Esofi shook her head. "That can't be right."

"Which priestess?" asked Adale.

"I do not know, Crown Princess."

"There must have been some kind of mistake. I know every one of those women personally," said Esofi.

"I will agree that it doesn't seem right," Adale said slowly. "But...you did go to the temple the day it happened?"

"You can't believe this is true!" cried Esofi.

"I'm not saying I do. Just that...it's not completely impossible."

"Of course it is! Perhaps you'd like to accuse the cat next. This is clearly just a trick to get me to come home." Esofi glared at the courier, even though she knew he was not responsible for the deception. "You may tell their Majesties that I will honor my agreement and return to Birsgen when the true assassin is caught, and not a moment sooner. And you may also tell them I will not hear such slander against the Temple of Talcia."

"If...that is what you wish, Princess," said the courier, looking to Adale for confirmation.

"Are you sure about this, Esofi?"

"Yes!"

Adale sighed. "All right, but I'm not taking the blame for this one. You be sure to tell their majesties that Princess Esofi was the one who refused to come home, not me."

"WHY AREN'T YOU happy?" Esofi whispered to her reflection.

Turn and fight.

But the fight was over. Gaelle was disgraced. She would not terrorize the world with an army of dragons. There was nothing left for her in Ieflaria or on the Isles. There was nothing left for her to do but return home.

Turn and fight.

She should have felt relief, light and joyful. But dread churned in her stomach. This was not the end. Gaelle did not lose, she was incapable of it. This was only a temporary setback, and when she returned, she would be even angrier...

They should have left her to her lies. The dragons would have worked it out for themselves eventually. Besides, Gaelle was only going to use them to fight elves, not people...

Probably.

It was barely midday, but Esofi found herself crawling into bed and pulling the covers over her face. Very nearly accustomed to the soft but constant rocking of the ship, she drifted in and out of awareness for a time, thinking of the priestesses at Birsgen and wondering which of them might have been arrested.

Maybe Asta? She was loud and sometimes brash. No doubt there was *someone* in Birsgen who wanted her out of the way—one of the other temples, perhaps. The more she thought about it, the more likely it seemed. A simple investigation would reveal the truth of the matter. She would compose a formal letter to their majesties...once her energy returned to her.

Esofi was mentally composing what she would say when the door opened.

"Esofi?" called Adale, cautiously.

Esofi made a soft noise to let Adale know that she was awake.

"Elyne is back," reported Adale. "She tried to manifest on the ship, but she missed, and they had to pull her out of the ocean."

"I should go thank her," said Esofi, not moving.

"She died protecting me, technically. I think she gets a medal." Adale came and sat beside her. "Are you going to be all right?"

"I don't even know why I'm not," admitted Esofi. "I wish I could just stop thinking."

Adale pressed her hand to Esofi's back, running it up and down her spine. "I don't blame you," she said. "And...I'm sorry."

"For what?" Esofi rolled over and rubbed some sleep from her eyes.

"Just..." Adale struggled for words. "Everything."

"None of this was your fault."

"Yes, but I'm still sorry."

"You were right, you know," said Esofi. "I could face the Emperor, but I couldn't face her. Isn't that ridiculous?"

"Well...I think not wanting to fight one's mother is not a terribly uncommon thing."

Esofi laughed, and for a moment, she felt like herself again. Adale leaned over to kiss her neck.

"Were you going to get up, or should I take my boots off?" asked Adale.

"Oh, I have no idea." Esofi shook her head. "I should get up."

"Only if you want to. There's nothing that needs to be done." Adale paused. "My parents are going to be upset."

"Well, serves them right."

"And I'm sure they'll find some way to turn it around so it's my fault instead of yours." But Adale was smiling. Being in trouble with her parents was such a common occurrence it did not really bother her. "But do you really think they arrested a priestess just to trick you into coming home?"

It sounded ridiculous when she put it that way. "No, I just...it has to be a mistake."

"I hope you're right," said Adale. "Not that I want this to go on any longer. I just know how badly it would hurt you if it turns out to be true."

"It can't be. It makes no sense." Esofi shook her head. "Never mind. I'm done thinking about it until they uncover the real culprit."

"I wonder what the dragons are doing now." When Esofi did not respond, Adale added, "We can go visit them tomorrow. Carinth was very upset he didn't get to see Etheriet today, and she was disappointed when she saw I hadn't brought him."

"It must be difficult to have nobody her own age on the island," mused Esofi. "We'll go tomorrow. I need to make sure Gaelle is truly gone regardless."

WHEN THEY ARRIVED on the beach the next morning, a dragon was waiting for them. But it wasn't Ivanedi. It was Releth. She paced back and forth across the stones, tail sweeping from side to side anxiously, as she waited for the rowboat to meet the land.

"Releth?" called Esofi, as soon as they were near enough to be heard over the roar of the ocean.

"Etheriet is gone. I cannot find her," Releth's claws clicked on the stones. "Have you seen her?"

"No, we're sorry," said Adale. "When did you see her last?"

"Yesterday. Last night. I could not find her when I woke. I thought perhaps she had gone to your ship, to see Carinth..."

"Maybe she tried to. Would she have strayed off the path?" asked Adale.

"No," said Esofi. Her voice felt strange, like it was coming from somewhere far away. "Gaelle took her."

"What?" asked Adale.

"Gaelle took Etheriet." When had she stopped calling her Mother? Esofi was not sure. Perhaps it did not matter. "She couldn't have Carinth, so she decided to take Etheriet instead."

"I will kill her," Releth said flatly. "I will sink her ship and—"

"No!" cried Esofi. "She'll kill you!"

"Better than leaving Etheriet in her hands!"

"I'll get her back!" Esofi cried. "I swear I will! But it's my fault she has no mother. I can't be responsible for her having no sister, either."

"What are you talking about?" Adale asked.

"I'm not a fool! I know why Ivanedi did not wish to speak of Mairmet!" Esofi looked from Adale to Releth. "Am I wrong?"

"You would take the blame for the setting of the sun!" cried Releth. "Do you even feel true guilt, or do you just believe that you are the only one among us capable of making her own decisions? Not even Zethe would have compelled Mairmet to fly into danger when she was caring for a hatchling. Her hatred of Men was greater than her love for her daughter."

Esofi's mouth moved, but no sound came out.

"Releth, we'll get Etheriet back for you," Adale said. "I swear. But if you come with us, you'll give us away. Even if she doesn't kill you, she'll see you coming from miles away."

Releth huffed in annoyance but sat down on her hind legs, wings drooping. "If you fail, I will go after her myself."

"If we fail, we'll probably be dead, so nobody will be around to stop you," said Adale.

Esofi wanted to chastise Adale for saying such a thing, but part of her knew she was right. Gaelle wasn't going to let them walk away again, not after what had happened yesterday. The realization was awful, but also...strangely freeing, in a way she could not articulate.

"She's almost certainly on her way back to Rhodia," murmured Esofi.

"If that's the case, she's probably planning to stop in Valenleht for supplies before they attempt to cross the Summer Strait," said Adale. "Or maybe a smaller port town, if she's afraid we'll follow her."

"Did any other dragons go with her?" asked Esofi.

"No," said Releth. "Not after what happened yesterday."

"We'll go now," said Esofi. "There's no time to waste. If we tell the authorities to delay her in Valenleht—I only hope the courier can outfly her."

"I can get myself to Valenleht," volunteered Elyne. "Or at least, near enough. I can deliver a letter to the harbormaster, or whoever else you'd like."

"Are you certain? What if you...miss again?"

"The ship was *moving*," said Elyne hotly.

"It's worth a try," said Adale. "Should we send her to some of the other towns as well? In case Gaelle decides to be sneaky about it?"

"Not too many, every jump takes magic," cautioned Elyne. "If I run out, I won't be able to get back to you."

"Are we certain she will take the same route home?" asked Orsina. "Might she attempt the Winter Strait?"

"No, not so near to midwinter—" Esofi began, but then she stopped. "Gods, I hope not."

The Winter Strait was dangerous at any time of year, but not more so than in the colder months, when massive mountains of glittering ice could tear through wooden hulls like paper. The Summer Strait was a warzone, and it was still preferable to the Winter. Would Gaelle attempt it, for the sake of shaking any pursuers?

"If she does go north, where would she stop for supplies?" asked Elyne.

"I don't know, probably..." Adale looked at Esofi, realization in her face.

"...Fenstell," Esofi completed. Fenstell, home to a small battalion of mages who were more loyal to Rhodia than Ieflaria. Why would Gaelle risk bringing Etheriet anywhere else? "That's where she's going. I know it."

Adale shook her head. "She's risking her life, travelling through the north at this time of year."

"I think she'd do it, though," said Esofi. "We need to move, quickly."

"You will bring her back?" asked Releth.

"Yes. I swear." Esofi met her eyes steadily. "My mother has no business raising children. No matter what their species."

THE COURSER PLOWED through the water at what the captain swore was her highest speed, but Esofi felt as though they were crawling. She paced from stern to stem until Adale came and made her get out of the sailors' way.

They'd composed letters for Elyne to deliver to Fenstell's harbormaster, as well as Commander Gero, asking them to delay Gaelle's departure by any means necessary. Esofi had advised that an indirect approach would be best. If Gaelle was told outright that her ship was being held, she would become dangerous and unpredictable. But if Fenstell could come up with plausible reasons for a delay, Gaelle wouldn't suspect Esofi was coming after her.

At least, not immediately. Gaelle wasn't stupid. She would catch on eventually. But Esofi was hopeful the Courser wasn't more than a day behind her. And despite the presence of the encampment, Fenstell was still a small town. It would take time to gather all the supplies the Rhodians would need for the journey home.

Upon receiving the letters, Elyne vanished right in front of Esofi's eyes, as though she had never been on the ship at all. Esofi tried not to think about her landing in the ocean again, and the letters being ruined.

Orsina, meanwhile, found a spot near the front railing and stood there, her eyes fixed on the distant horizon. Esofi hadn't spoken to her much—she was a very quiet young woman, as paladins tended to be. But Esofi was grateful for her help and that she had gone to face Gaelle without question.

Esofi approached her quietly, still formulating what she wanted to say. She was not sure if she should thank her for her help or apologize for all the trouble. But when Orsina turned around, she was smiling peacefully.

Esofi had several questions about how Orsina and Elyne's relationship worked, but she did not want to be rude. Besides, maybe it was none of her business. They both seemed happy, and that was the most important thing.

"I am grateful to you for accompanying Adale to confront my mother," Esofi said. "I know this is not what you came to Ieflaria to do."

"I am glad to be of use," said Orsina. "Besides, it has been an interesting experience. I never thought I'd see a single dragon up close, let alone an entire colony of them."

"Are you worried for Elyne?" asked Esofi.

"Oh, no. There's nothing that can really hurt her. At least, not for long. Still...I hate it when we have to be apart. I like to keep an eye on her."

Elyne would not return to the ship—it was moving too quickly for that to be feasible. She would meet them in Fenstell, hopefully at the docks, if all went well.

"You should get some rest," came Adale's voice from behind her. Esofi turned around to face her.

Adale was right. There was no way her confrontation with Gaelle would not end in a duel. She needed to be at full energy. But Esofi could not possibly imagine sleeping now.

If there was ever a time for divine intervention, Esofi supposed now would be it. But that was not what the gods were for.

Still, why did Talcia not whisper in her mother's ear to turn away from her path? Or perhaps she had, and

Gaelle simply ignored it. From Adale and Orsina's report, it seemed Gaelle had confused her own ambitions with the voice of Talcia. Perhaps even Talcia had decided the time for talking was past.

They came in sight of Fenstell just before midday. Esofi had hardly eaten anything since waking, and what little she had managed had been at Adale's near-constant urging.

Esofi had only brought a single Rhodian gown with her to the Isles, a comparatively simple gown in grey-blue silk and decorated with palest pink ribbon. She had not really expected to want or need it.

But Esofi had learned to fight in gowns, impractical as they might seem to observers. When she dressed herself that morning, she only hesitated for a moment before she selected it from her wardrobe. Nobody commented on her choice as she emerged onto the upper deck that morning.

Fenstell was a quiet village, and life was going on as usual despite the presence of the encampment of the cliffs. A few fishing boats were already out in deeper waters, but in the harbor, Esofi could see a very large ship flying the blue and white Rhodian flag.

"Do you think she's aboard or up at the camp with the mages?" asked Adale.

"I suppose we're going to find out," said Esofi.

THERE WAS A single mage on guard beside the footbridge leading up to Gaelle's ship, but Esofi knew there would be many, many more on board. Esofi turned to the others.

"Wait here until I call for you," said Esofi. "I don't want to have to worry about hurting one of you by accident."

"What?" cried Adale in dismay.

"I'll call down to you the moment it's clear," said Esofi, keeping her voice measured. "But if there's as many mages up there as I suspect, you will only be in my way."

Adale was obviously planning to argue, but Esofi decided not to give her the opportunity. She strode forward rapidly in the direction of the mage.

"Wait—" began the mage as Esofi approached. But before she could say another word, Esofi stuck her in the chest with rose-pink light, sending her tumbling into the harbor. Esofi dashed up the pier without checking to see if she was all right.

The upper deck of Gaelle's ship was unremarkable and peaceful. But Esofi's Rhodian dress earned her only a few extra seconds before the nearest mage cried out in surprise.

But Esofi was ready for them all. Powered by righteous fury, as a paladin might say.

"Where is she?" yelled Esofi, as the mage slammed into a pile of crates. She was not certain if she was asking for Gaelle or Etheriet. Perhaps it didn't really matter. But nobody answered her.

Esofi slipped her feet out of her shoes. Moving very carefully, she pressed the heel of her left foot to the toe of her right and pulled her foot out of her stocking. To anyone watching, it would appear as though she was merely shifting in place. She set her now-bare foot down on top of her other stocking and pulled her left leg free as well. The wooden planks were icy cold under her feet, and she shifted to her toes instinctively.

"Esofi!"

Esofi risked looking around in time to see Lexandrie emerging from the lower decks. Her face was pale and incredulous.

"What are you doing here?" hissed Lexandrie.

"Where is Etheriet?"

"You need to leave," said Lexandrie. "Please. You'll only make everything worse."

"I've barely started," Esofi snapped. "Get out of my way. Or did you want to fight, too?"

"You're not the one who has to live with her!" cried Lexandrie. "Just let her have this, so she can feel like she won!"

"This is kidnapping, Lexandrie," said Esofi.

"It's just a dragon!" Lexandrie glanced back over her shoulder. "I don't understand why you even care."

"Get out of my way!"

"Yes, please do," said a new voice from the darkened staircase. A moment later, Lexandrie stumbled forward as though she had been pushed and Gaelle stepped into the light.

"Well, this is a surprise," she said. "I was under the impression you wanted me to leave."

"Where is Etheriet?"

"Who?"

"The dragon. Where is she?"

"I don't know what you're talking about. Did you really come all the way here just to rant nonsense at me?"

"It's kidnapping," said Esofi. "You have to realize that. She's not an animal, she's an intelligent creature, and she belongs with her family."

"Are you finished?" asked Gaelle.

"I am not leaving until you give her to me."

"Then I hope you enjoy the trip to Rhodia."

"If this ship attempts to leave the harbor, I will have it sunk."

Gaelle laughed, short and sharp, like the strike of a dagger. "How delightful. I might be intimidated, if I believed you for even a moment. Now, please leave. I don't want to spend the next three months stuck on a ship with you."

"I'm not going," repeated Esofi. "But I will duel you for her."

This time, Gaelle's laugh was deeper, longer. "Go, go, just go," she said, waving her hand in that dismissive way that she always did. "Unless you mean for me to die of laughter."

Esofi gathered her magic at her hands again, and Gaelle's lips quirked in a half-smile.

"I will not ask again," said Esofi.

"What in the world have these Ieflarians been telling you?" asked Gaelle. "I can only imagine. They believe you're some manner of hero because you slew an inordinately angry dragon, because they're too ignorant to realize what a mundane achievement that is. And it seems you've started to listen too closely to their praise. They've made you think you're powerful. That you're *special*. But they don't know the first thing about Talcia's blessings, do they? They are farmers and goatherds and woodcutters. They don't know anything at all about magic. You may have fooled your people into believing there's anything remarkable about you. You may have even fooled yourself. But I am not so easily manipulated. I see you for what you truly are."

Esofi's strike was lightning-fast, but Gaelle had a shield up before the magic could touch her. It smashed against the crimson barrier and dissipated.

"This is your last chance," said Gaelle. "Leave, before I destroy all your delusions and leave you with nothing."

"I can't allow you to take Etheriet."

"Why? Are you jealous?" Gaelle's smile was ugly. "You liked being the only woman on Inthya with a dragon for a son, didn't you?"

"No—" began Esofi, but the rest of her words were lost when Gaelle lashed out at her with both hands blazing. Esofi backed away rapidly, but Gaelle did not stop, barreling forward while blood-colored magic swirled around her like a storm.

"It's so obvious!" cried Gaelle, smashing against Esofi's hastily constructed shield. It shuddered under the barrage but held up. "You are jealous, aren't you? You can't stand that Talcia loves me more than you! You can't stand that she's given me more! Everything you've done has been to spite me!"

"None of that is true!"

"Do you know what your greatest failing is?" asked Gaelle, pulling her magic back to her hands, where it gathered like two bloody beacons.

"Cake, I believe," said Esofi, fighting to keep her voice from quavering. "As you have told me many times before."

"Hah. Yes, that is a close second, isn't it? But your real problem, Esofi, is that you assume that I'm as stupid as these Ieflarians you surround yourself with."

"I'm not taking Etheriet because I'm jealous of you," said Esofi. "I'm taking her because she *is not yours*. And even if you did have any right to her, you're a dreadful mother and she deserves far better."

Gaelle struck without warning, blasting magic at Esofi with both hands. This time, Esofi was the one to raise a shield, though she was rather expecting it to shatter under the force of Gaelle's magic. Yet, miraculously, it held. Esofi hoped that she did not look as surprised as she felt.

Back in Rhodia, Esofi had watched Gaelle duel other members of the Silence, those rare few strong enough to stand against her for more than a few minutes. One might have guessed that they allowed Gaelle to win out of fear or respect, but there was nothing Gaelle hated more than deliberate failure. And it seemed she was always able to tell when someone was not fighting with every drop of their magic. It was part of what made her such an effective teacher.

Esofi had never dueled Gaelle herself—she had never felt compelled to try, nor had Gaelle ever called upon her to do so. The only one of her sisters who ever had was Eliosa, who held her own admirably but eventually lost like all the rest.

Esofi struck again, but this time Gaelle did not shield herself. Instead, she reached out and *caught* Esofi's magic with her hands, keeping the pink light suspended within her own red. Then she drew her arms back and sent it back at Esofi.

Esofi gasped. She would not have thought such a thing was possible. But then, she had always known there were things Gaelle had never taught her children, knowledge she saved only for herself.

Esofi could not deflect her own magic. It slammed into her, reabsorbing into the core of Esofi's self at full force. Esofi was knocked off her feet and onto the cold wooden planks of the ship's deck.

Gaelle strode nearer, but Esofi stayed where she had landed. Now was her chance to take Gaelle by surprise. She wouldn't get another one. She adjusted her feet in preparation.

Confusion flickered across Gaelle's face. "Why aren't you wearing sh—"

Esofi called her magic to her feet and *kicked*.

It was a skill she had learned she possessed as a very young child. But it was not proper to fight with one's feet and so Esofi had neglected it until they'd all forgotten she could do it at all.

Including Gaelle, it seemed, for she had just enough time to see the shock on her face before her mother went staggering backward, only just barely avoiding a fall. Esofi sprang back to her feet and kicked again, gripping her skirt in one hand to keep it out of her way.

Esofi knew she had to end this quickly. If Gaelle managed to reorient herself, she would have the advantage. They might have been evenly matched in terms of power—and that was a bizarre thing to realize after she'd spent so many years assuming otherwise—but Gaelle still had the upper hand when it came to experience.

Esofi moved as lightly as she could manage, recalling the way she'd experimented during her first visit to Fenstell, the day Adale had wandered into the training room and found Esofi standing there with no stockings and no explanations. When she built up momentum, it was easy to keep moving, to keep kicking. The muscles in her upper legs had gone largely unused over the years, and she knew she would feel them aching once the thrill of the fight died away. But for Etheriet, and for herself, she would endure it.

Perhaps Esofi had known from the start that this was the only way it could end. She'd refused to admit it to herself, but in retrospect, it was obvious. Gaelle did not respect logic or reason or laws. She only respected power

Gaelle lashed out with her magic again, directionless and brutal. But fighting with her feet meant Esofi's hands were free to call up a shield without sacrificing a means of attack.

Gaelle was an experienced duelist, but Esofi had a feeling she'd never faced an opponent that could attack and defend simultaneously.

Gaelle caught Esofi's magic again, but Esofi was already in motion when she sent it back at her, dodging it easily and avoiding its impact. After a moment, it dissolved into empty air. Esofi spun and kicked outward again, her magic flying toward Gaelle.

This time, when Esofi's magic struck her, Gaelle did not keep her balance. She fell backward, her head slamming against the ship's railing. Esofi raised another shield, readying herself for another attack.

But Gaelle did not move. Her head was rested against the ship's wooden siding, and her eyes were closed. Esofi hesitated a moment longer before she dismissed her magic. She did nothing to stop the other mages from hurrying to her side. For better or for worse, it would take far more than a blow to the head to kill Gaelle.

Esofi swallowed and went back to the footbridge that connected the ship and the pier. But it was not just Adale and Orsina that stood there waiting. At some point during the fight, they'd been joined by soldiers from Fenstell. Commander Gero stood at the front.

"May we come up now, Princess?" he called.

Esofi nodded vigorously. "If anyone gives you trouble, arrest them. I'm going to search for the hatchling."

Esofi turned away and went down the steps leading to the lower levels, and the personal cabins. Nobody did anything to stop her.

It wasn't difficult to find her mother's room. As was common in Rhodian ships, the best and largest cabin was near the front. The door was locked, but Esofi called her magic to her hands and blasted the handle and locking mechanism to the ground.

The room was not very different from the one Esofi herself had stayed in during her journey from Rhodia to Ieflaria. And sitting on Gaelle's bed, curled up like a cat, was a tiny red dragon. Esofi gasped and rushed forward.

Etheriet lifted her head and chirped eagerly, wings fluttering, as she jumped into Esofi's arms.

"There you are," Esofi murmured. "Let's get you home."

ESOFI WANTED TO bring Etheriet back to the Isles immediately, but holding a foreign queen at port was a complicated matter. While she would have liked nothing more than to let Gaelle leave and never see her again, she knew she could not trust her to actually return to Rhodia. So she had written to their majesties, asking for an escort so they could be sure of Gaelle's departure.

As Esofi had predicted, Gaelle's last act of defiance was to order Fenstell's mages home. She could not leave the ship, and so had sent Lexandrie in her place. None of the mages had dared disobeyed, and Esofi could not blame them. She'd expected nothing less.

But strangely, she didn't think she minded. From the time she had spent in the Isles, she truly believed that there were no more coordinated attacks coming, at least not during her lifetime. Perhaps they could even hire some of the friendlier dragons to guard against their own kind, at least until they had more Ieflarians trained as battlemages.

If Etheriet was feeling homesick, she did nothing to show it. She and Carinth chased each other all around Fenstell while Mireille chased after *them*, trying to make sure they didn't get themselves in any trouble.

King Dietrich and Queen Saski arrived in Fenstell four days after Esofi's final confrontation with Gaelle. Nobody had been expecting them, least of all Adale and Esofi, and so when they entered the citadel and knocked on Adale and Esofi's bedroom door without warning, Esofi thought for a moment that she was dreaming.

But then Saski immediately launched into a rant about the condition of her heart and the years Esofi had taken off her life, and Esofi knew this was reality. In contrast to his wife, Dietrich merely stood there giving Esofi the same solemn stare she had only ever seen him give Adale.

Esofi waited patiently for Saski to be finished. Then she said, "Who is the priestess that has been arrested? I wish for her to be released."

"Released!" cried Saski.

"Esofi," Dietrich said calmly. "I know this is difficult to accept, but she has already confessed."

"Then it was a false confession!"

Dietrich and Saski exchanged looks.

"Priestess Eydis is being held in the castle dungeons," began Dietrich. "She—"

"Eydis?" cried Esofi in horror. "Have you all gone mad!? I know Eydis, she would never—she is the very *last* person in Birsgen who would—I cannot believe this. I must go to her immediately."

"Esofi, you must listen to us," said Saski. "We suspected the Temple of Talcia the moment that you fell ill. I know you hold the priestesses in high esteem, but many of them are wary of the Silence of the Moon. When your mother arrived, speaking openly of reinstating it...Eydis panicked. She has sworn that you were not her intended target, that the poison was meant for Gaelle, to frighten her into leaving Ieflaria before a Silence could be established. Nevertheless...she will stand trial for what she has done, and I expect she will be expelled from the temple as well."

If not for Adale's steadying hand on her shoulder, Esofi might have crumpled to the ground. She managed to choke out, "Have the twins brought the unicorn? Adale sent them—he can confirm—"

"Yes," said Dietrich, looking displeased. "He confirmed Eydis' story. In return for his aid, the twins promised him a title. And so now I must invent one unless the Order of the Sun manages to recruit him."

"Did any of the other priestesses know about what Eydis did?" asked Adale. Esofi looked at her in alarm, nausea rising up in her stomach. She trusted the temple so implicitly she had not even considered the possibility.

"No," said Dietrich. "Our...new truthsayer...confirmed that Eydis acted alone, though one of the acolytes confessed that she suspected Eydis was to blame when news of your illness reached them."

"But she did not speak out?"

"I do not blame her for that," said Esofi quietly. The acolytes were very young. To accuse a priestess of attempted murder was more than she would ever expect from them.

"There is something else," said Dietrich. "Your waiting lady...Lady Lisette...she returned to Birsgen just before our departure. The healers wished for her to remain there and await your return, but—"

"The healers?" repeated Esofi. "What has happened to her?"

"She is waiting to speak with you."

Adale and Esofi looked at each other. "Where is she?" asked Esofi. "I'll go to her immediately."

"In a moment," said Dietrich. "I understand you're keeping your mother's ship in the harbor?"

"Only until she can be escorted far enough from Ieflaria that she won't bother turning around to steal another hatchling," said Esofi. "I'm sorry. I hope you weren't planning to purchase white marble from Rhodia at any point in the next twenty years. I don't think you'll get a very fair price."

LISETTE WAS DRESSED in a simple black gown and her hair was unstyled when Adale and Esofi found her waiting in one of the citadel's only sitting rooms. When Lisette turned away from the window, Esofi saw that her face was bruised, one of her eyes so black it looked like it might have been painted. Esofi could also see signs of a recently healed split lip. Most notable, though, was the sling on her arm.

"Princess." Lisette gave the shortest, sharpest curtsy in the world. "I apologize for my delay."

"No, no, it's all right," Esofi soothed. "What happened?"

"I managed to locate the missing courier after I left your camp," said Lisette. "She was deep in the forests, quite a distance from the main road. She told me she had been blasted from the sky by a mage wielding Talcia's magic."

"*What?*" cried Adale, but Lisette went on.

"An ordinary woman might not have been so badly injured, but those with Nara's blessing are fragile. It was my intention to bring her back to Birsgen immediately, but Queen Gaelle charged a few of her employees with making sure she was truly dead. Thus our delay."

"No, no, that...that is understandable." Esofi swallowed. "I am very sorry. I am shocked she would do such a thing." But really, was she? After everything she had seen Gaelle do over the last few weeks? "Nara is the Eleventh in Thiyra. When the temple finds out..."

For they would, sooner or later. Couriers crossed entire continents, carrying gossip as well as letters.

"She attacked a courier just so we wouldn't be warned she was coming to Fenstell?" asked Adale.

"I imagine she wanted us to be taken by surprise. Especially since she was hoping to leave with Carinth." Esofi rubbed at her eyes. "Lisette—I'm sorry."

"Two Nightshades and several Rhodian mages are dead. I do not believe I can ever realistically expect to return to Rhodia now." Lisette paused. "Fortunately, I do not think that will be any great loss."

"Are you allowed to kill other Nightshades?" worried Adale. "They won't throw you out for it, will you?"

"Of course not," said Lisette. "We'd hardly be of any use to anyone if that were the case."

"Don't worry," Esofi said. "Ieflaria is our home now—yours and mine and Mireille's. We've no reason to ever go back to Rhodia. I'll always be glad to have you in my service."

IT TOOK NEARLY an entire day of begging, arguing, and promises to Dietrich and Saski, but Adale and Esofi boarded the Courser the next day at sunrise. From Fenstell, it was not far to the Isles, where they knew Releth was waiting anxiously.

Winter would be upon them soon, so they could not stay too long. Even if the temperature were not unbearable, Esofi did not want to miss her second midwinter in Ieflaria. Already she was looking forward to the celebration. Maybe they should invite a few dragons to come visit, to foster a bit more goodwill between their races.

Esofi leaned forward onto the railing, turning her face in the direction of the distant Isles. Already, she could see the first of them, small as it was. Behind her, over the roaring of the wind and the sea, she could hear Mireille's laughter as Carinth and Etheriet tried to both fit onto her shoulders at once.

"What are you thinking about?" asked Adale. Esofi turned to see her wife standing there behind her.

"Everything," said Esofi. Adale wrapped an arm around her waist. Normally Esofi would object to this public display of affection, but today she could not bring herself to care very much.

"What would make you feel better?" asked Adale. "We could break into the dungeons and set Eydis free."

"No," said Esofi. Now that the shock had died away, outrage and grief were beginning to gather in its stead. She had trusted Eydis, trusted her completely. Esofi had done so much for the temple, to restore both Talcia's worship and the use of her magic. But not even that had been enough to assuage her fears of a Silence in Birsgen.

Why hadn't it been enough?

"Do you think they'll execute her?" asked Esofi.

Adale exhaled loudly. "Not if you *really* don't want them to."

"I...I don't know what I want. But I don't want her to die." Eydis was young, and she had done something exceptionally stupid. Esofi was hurt and angry, but she did not hate Eydis. Killing her felt like something Gaelle would do.

"You know it'll be ages before it goes to a trial," said Adale. "You've got time to propose a different punishment. If that's what you want."

"I'll have to review some old cases. Search for precedents..."

Adale pulled her as closely as she could manage. "It can only get better now," she whispered. "There's nothing left to be afraid of."

For now, thought Esofi, but she did not say it. Yes, there would always be new problems to deal with—some petty, some very much not. But knowing she would not have to face them alone was...comforting.

"I expect the priestesses of Dayluue will be bothering us again once we get home," Esofi said.

"I'll bribe them."

Esofi laughed. "To say you're infertile?"

"Yes. Or, no. Maybe I can hire two women who look like us to go in our place."

"That sounds like more trouble than it's worth."

"No! It's the best idea I've ever had."

"You really don't mind?" asked Esofi. "If we never end up having a child?"

"Well, it's too late for that, because we already do," said Adale. "I don't care what anyone says. Carinth is our son, even if he is a dragon. But I meant it when I said I'll never love something that doesn't exist more than I'll ever love you."

Esofi brushed a stray curl out of her face. "I still don't know what I want," she said. "But...I'm a little bit less worried about being as terrible a mother as Gaelle was."

"I don't think you could be as bad as her even if you tried!" Adale laughed. "Besides, even if you're too strict, I'll make up for it by being too lenient. Between the two of us, it will come out perfectly balanced."

"I am not certain that's how it works."

"It might be. You don't know."

"No, I suppose I don't."

Adale laughed. "I was expecting more of an argument than that!"

"There's nothing to argue about," said Esofi. "You're right."

Esofi turned away from the ocean to survey the upper deck. Instead of two small dragons on Mireille's shoulders, there were now three. The third one was purple. Orsina hurried over to remove that one, speaking solemnly in Vesoldan even as Elyne wriggled uncooperatively in her hands.

"What did we decide to do for Elyne?" asked Esofi. "Are we giving her a medal?"

"For making the ultimate sacrifice, however temporary? I think it would be a nice gesture. Unless you wanted to build her a temple."

"Do you think she'd want one?"

"No," said Adale. "I don't think she's that sort of goddess."

Esofi considered this. Adale was probably right. "We'll think of something. But later." It was impossible to come up with any good ideas when everything was so happy and peaceful, when Adale's arm encircled her waist.

There was still work to be done, but the worst of it was over. And if Esofi could face Gaelle and not only live to tell about it, but emerge victorious, perhaps she had no reason to be afraid of whatever the future held.

About the Author

Effie is definitely a human being with all her own skin, and not a robot. She writes science fiction and fantasy novels and lives with her cat in the greater Philadelphia area.

Email: effiecalvin@gmail.com

Twitter: @EffieCalvin

Website: www.effiecalvin.com

Other books by this author

Tales of Inthya Series

The Queen of Ieflaria

Daughter of the Sun

Also Available from NineStar Press

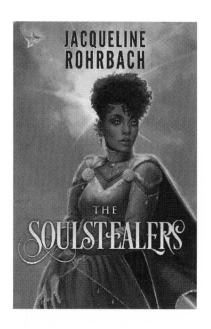

Connect with NineStar Press

www.ninestarpress.com

www.facebook.com/ninestarpress

www.facebook.com/groups/NineStarNiche

www.twitter.com/ninestarpress

www.tumblr.com/blog/ninestarpress